MIA'S JOURNEY

DIANE BYINGTON

---

1.   http://StreetlightGraphics.com

For all the dreamers who will eventually save the world.

Chapter 1: The Heebie-Jeebies

Running around the soft, yielding track at the Johnson Space Center—five laps, fifteen, thirty—gives me time to ponder, and what comes to mind this day is not the danger of going to space. Although there is always some risk, no astronaut has died on a mission since the Columbia disaster in 2003, and NASA has made enormous strides in safety measures since then. No, if I die in space, it'll be quick, so there's no use fretting about it.

Instead, I daydream about how it will feel to be without gravity, without sound, without a tether to the world I've always known—it will be glorious, exhilarating, free. Most of all, I think about that old poem by John Gillespie Magee, "High Flight," in which he describes his test pilot experience. The first two lines and the last two are my favorites, and I recite them to myself:

"Oh! I have slipped the surly bonds of Earth
And danced the skies on laughter-silvered wings;"
and
"The high untrespassed sanctity of space,
Put out my hand, and touched the face of God."

Those lines never fail to send a chill throughout my body. I'm so eager to slip the surly bonds of Earth that I wonder how I can wait for three weeks until my launch. And even though I don't understand what it means to touch the face of God, I intend to find out. Just the concept of "space"—high, untrespassed, magnificent—has always felt sacred to me.

My family members and nonastronaut friends shake their heads at my eagerness to spend six months floating around on the International Space Station, a small, fragile tin can where every aspect of my physiological and mental life will be scrutinized, and I can only see my husband, Ramón, through a video monitor. But the other astronauts—including Ramón—understand exactly what that poem means to me. Even though we don't talk about it, I suspect it means the same to them.

I run until my legs give out and the regular afternoon storm breaks my concentration. Almost nine miles today. My friend Alice, one of the two astronauts who will accompany me to the ISS, meets me afterward, and we lift weights and chatter about last-minute details until it's time to go home.

For the past few weeks, as the awareness of my approaching launch bears down on us, Ramón and I have been making love every night. Only one more week remains before I enter into two weeks of quarantine. Tonight, our lovemaking is especially tender. Not that sex with him hasn't always been wonderful, but now, aware of the approaching drought, we both rise to even greater heights. Before my breathing returns to normal, Ramón whispers, "Give me a few minutes, and we'll do it again."

I laugh and nuzzle his shoulder. "We've got plenty of time, silly." We've been married for four years and together for two years before that, so we're not new to each other. I'll miss him terribly while I'm gone, of course, and I'm happy to share the physical intimacy while we have the chance. Still, enough is enough for one night.

I roll over and turn off the lamp, curling up into my sleeping position. "Tomorrow morning, maybe?"

"Well, okay." His words are slurred with encroaching sleep. "But I have to get up early. Five o'clock work for you?"

I groan. "Seriously? No, I'd rather do it now." I roll toward him and throw my leg over his hip. I'm calling his bluff, but truthfully, either way is fine with me. On the one hand, it's late, and I'm tired and sated. On the other, Ramón is a wonderful lover.

I run my hands down his back and feel him shiver. I love his short, muscular body that attests to growing up on a farm as well as the hours he spends in the gym, his easy smile that curls higher on the right side than the left, his quick intellect. His combination of strength and sweetness won me over when we first met at a NASA luncheon six years ago. Before that, I'd been too busy to focus on relationships, but as soon as I saw him, I was hooked.

"Okay, okay," he says, feigning grumpiness. "I get off around seven tomorrow evening. Dinner and a special alone time? Skip the movie?"

"Deal."

I roll back over, and he pulls me to his chest. "I love you, *corazón*."

"Love you too."

His even breathing tells me he's asleep almost immediately.

I'm sleepy, too, but my mind doesn't want to shut down. Ramón has been to the ISS three times and was even its commander for four months, so for him, going to space is all in a day's work. But this will be my first trip. Every time I remember the launch, my body tingles with the anticipated rush of seeing the Earth from space. I've waited forty-one years for this experience, and I'm convinced that nothing, not even making love with my hunky husband, will ever be better than that.

As I wait for sleep to claim me, I twirl my wedding ring on my finger and run through the launch sequence. The three of us—Alice, Dirk, and I—will cram into the Dragon spacecraft. When the technicians are satisfied that everything is fine, they'll leave us alone and close the hatch. *Liftoff!* The noise, ah, the noise, and the overwhelming level of vibration that Ramón says will be a surprise no matter how many simulations I've done. And the feeling of being pushed backward into my seat so hard that I'll fear my bones will break. They won't, but I suspect I'll wonder about it. The three stages of separation, and then blissful, utter silence! We'll stare at each other in wonder and laugh out loud.

After we transfer to the space station, I'll be treated to the experience of a lifetime. The Earth will whiz by, two hundred forty miles away, moving at over seventeen thousand miles per hour. My heartbeat speeds up every time I think about it.

Every ninety-two minutes, there is a complete orbit, meaning a time of light, a time of dark, and another spectacular sunrise. When I finally see that sunrise, I'm certain I'll feel whole, complete.

Now I'm too excited to sleep. I get up and pour myself a glass of white wine. Taking it out to the patio, I stare up at the late summer sky. Stars twinkle dimly through Houston's humidity. Soon, I'll see them so much more clearly.

Then the fear hits me like a punch to the gut. Radiation is much stronger in space than on Earth. And there's no freaking air to breathe if something goes wrong. I take a deep breath and admit what I never ever tell anyone: I'm scared. Deep-to-the-bone scared.

But I won't let fear stop me. Something I read in a self-help book by Jack Canfield comes to mind: "Everything you want is on the other side of fear."

Yes. What I want is to prove my fears baseless. I can do this; I'm sure of it. Seasoned astronauts speak of getting the heebie-jeebies before a launch, and this must be them. Still, something feels off, almost as though my airplane has gone into a stall and the controls aren't responding to my touch.

Shake it off, I mutter to myself. I've never been superstitious, and I won't start now. I remind myself that our crew is the best, and together, we can deal with any crisis. But the ISS is so very far away from everything and everyone I love.

Sheesh. Stop.

Quickly, I finish my wine and slip back into bed beside the slumbering Ramón. There are still a few hours before I have to wake up and start the day. I'm scheduled to give a speech to some high school STEM students about space travel at nine in the morning, and I need to prepare before I go. After that, I'll work in the plant lab for the rest of the day, getting ready for the launch. Oh, and I need to call Mom sometime. She left a message saying she's worried about me.

I'll be fine.

Chapter 2: No. It Can't Happen to Me

Awareness trickles in slowly. The first thing I notice is the sledge-hammer pounding into my forehead, over and over. I've never had such a terrible headache. And some god-awful noises—loud bangs and chirps—make me want to scream. Something is horribly wrong. Eventually, I force my eyes open. My right leg, covered in a white sheet, is held in the air by a rope and pulley. Traction. What the hell?

Ramón grabs my hand. "Oh, corazón, I'm so happy you're awake."

The last thing I remember is making love to him and going to bed. I don't understand where we are or why he's happy I'm awake. This clearly isn't our bedroom, and I've never had a headache in a dream before. When Ramón sees my confused expression, he says, "You were in an accident this morning on the way to make your speech."

What speech? I can't remember a speech. Nothing makes sense.

"A car hit you while you were walking toward the high school where you were supposed to give a talk. You're in the hospital with a broken leg and a brain injury. But you'll be fine after a while."

My launch. Three weeks away. I can't have a broken leg. "A while. How long is that?"

He knows what I'm asking, but he bites his lip and looks away. When he turns back, there are tears in his eyes. "I'd rather cut off my arm than tell you this, but the doctors say it will take several months for your leg to heal. Sweetie, you won't be going on this mission.

NASA has already assigned a replacement." He leans over to kiss my cheek.

I've trained for two years for this trip, so I can't miss my launch. I lick my lips. "How long... how long have I been out of it?"

"You had the accident this morning, and it's only nine in the evening now." He clears his throat. "We're waiting for the surgeon to take you into the operating room to fix your leg. It should be soon."

All I can process is that I'll miss my launch. Nothing else matters.

After a while, my slowed brain comprehends that the bangs and chirps have something to do with me. God, I wish they'd stop. My head feels like it's exploding with every beat of my heart, and my leg hurts like an elephant sat on it.

Eventually, I croak out one word: "Jeb?"

"I called him. He'll be in to see you tomorrow. He wants you to know that, even though you'll miss this launch, he'll put you on the roster as soon as you heal. You shouldn't worry about that."

Not worry? I'm confused, not worried. And tired, so tired.

"What happened, again?"

I drift off as he's telling me.

A doctor stops by to see me early the next morning. Apparently, the surgery to piece my leg back together went well, but I'm exhausted from lack of sleep. Nurses woke me every half hour during the night to take my vitals and make sure my pupils were the same size. I'm dozing when I hear the doctor talking to Ramón, who spent the night in a recliner beside my bed.

"She had a hard night, I gather," says the doctor.

"Yeah. Lots of nightmares. She woke up screaming several times."

Eventually, I remember a dream: my space capsule exploded while I was in the darkness of space. I was dying, and it scared me out of my mind.

I shiver and open my eyes.

"Oh, there she is." The doctor checks my eyes again and asks me a few questions. "What's your name?"

That's easy. "Mia Gray."

"How many fingers am I holding up?"

"Three."

"Very good. What month and year is it?"

That one takes a little time. "Uh, September 2018?"

"Okay, what's one hundred minus seven?"

No way will my mind do subtraction, even such an easy one. I go completely blank. "I... I don't know." When I shake my head, the headache returns, so I cry instead.

Ramón grabs my hand as I blubber. "It's okay, corazón."

The doctor leans over me. "It'll come back to you, I promise. You did well on the others, so you'll be fine before long. In fact, your MRI looks good enough to send you home. I'm thinking about tomorrow. That work for you?"

I nod.

Visitors and phone calls keep me busy all morning. Dirk and Alice, the astronauts who are going up on my former mission, come to visit. They're appropriately sad that I won't be joining them, and they promise to stay in touch. I hold it together while they're in the room but cry for a long time after they leave.

My mom calls to tell me she knew something was wrong yesterday morning. She'd called me several times, and when I didn't answer, she almost jumped on a plane. She's thrilled I'm alive.

The day goes on like that. I doze between visitors. Finally, Ramón tells people I can't see anyone else today, and I sleep again.

In the afternoon, he shakes me awake. "Mia, there's someone who needs to speak with you."

I open my eyes, surprised at his serious tone. Standing over me is a young Black man whom I don't think I've seen before. He smiles when my eyes settle on him.

"Sorry to bother you, Dr. Gray. I'm Detective Dartt, of the Houston Police Department. I'm in charge of your case. Are you able to answer a few questions?"

"I think so. I have some questions of my own."

When Ramón raises the head of the hospital bed, the room spins, and I grab on to the sides for stability. I blink a few times until Detective Dartt comes into focus.

He pulls a chair close to my bed. "Do you know what happened to you yesterday?"

"I got hit by a car, I guess."

"What do you remember?"

My mind is a blank between going to bed Monday evening and waking up in the hospital last night. I start to shake. "Nothing at all."

He takes a breath. "I'd hoped some memory would have returned by now. It's not uncommon to have gaps for a while, but ideally, it'll return soon. Here's what we know. You were on your way to Clear Brook High School to give a talk, is that right?"

Ramón nods, so I do too.

"From what we can make out, you parallel parked near the school and walked to the corner. As you crossed the street, an SUV that was speeding down that street hit you. The driver is a young substitute teacher who was late to work. I'm sorry to tell you this, but she says you walked right out in front of her vehicle, and she couldn't stop in time. There weren't any other witnesses, so we're trying to figure out what really happened."

I take that in. "I... I can't remember it, so I don't know what to tell you. Walking in front of a speeding car is definitely not something I would normally do." I think for a moment. "Was I looking at my phone?"

"No, ma'am. It was in your purse. Could something have distracted you?"

"All I know is I was going to give a talk, but I've done that dozens of times. I shouldn't have been distracted by it."

He's quiet for a moment. "Uh, have you been upset about something in your life lately? Despondent, maybe?"

I glance at Ramón, and he's frowning. Turning back to the detective, I squint and try to understand what he's saying. Suddenly, I get it. "You think I did it deliberately? No way. I can't believe you would even suggest that. The driver must have not been paying attention. Was there a traffic light?"

"No. But there was a crosswalk, and you were in it. She definitely should have stopped."

He asks me more questions, but I'm too exhausted to follow the conversation anymore. My eyes close. Ramón tells the detective to come back another time.

"No problem. Feel better. I'll talk with you soon." And he leaves.

When I've rested some, I tell Ramón, "I was in the crosswalk. She should have stopped."

"That's right, sweetie. You weren't at fault. That driver is trying to sow doubt about what happened. It'll get sorted out; I promise. Now, you just focus on getting better."

Chapter 3: The Official Verdict

Three weeks later

I watch the launch from my couch, tears streaming down my face. Everything goes flawlessly, except that I'm here and not there.

Depression closes in like a plastic bag over my head. Since the accident, I've felt like I'm suffocating half the time. I get around the house in a wheelchair, with my broken leg sticking out in front. Ramón waits on me hand and foot. I'm like my dad, who suffers from ALS. That realization gives me the creeps. Also, I have a hard time forming my words, just as he does, and I need help to do most things. I can feed myself, fortunately, but Ramón does the cooking, cleaning, and the shopping. Like my mom.

Within the depression is an all-consuming rage. It's directed at Ramón more often than I wish, like the morning when my poached egg was too hard. I knew he was doing his best, but I couldn't help it—I yelled at him. If I could have made my own damn egg, I would have. Afterward, I apologized profusely, and he brushed it off. The man is a saint. Still, I'm happiest when he's at work and I can be depressed without having to act cheerful for his sake.

Detective Dartt came by last week to see if any memories had popped up. No matter how hard I try, I'm unable to conjure up a thing. He informed me the investigation was over. The police decided that, since I was in the crosswalk, the car should have stopped for me. But because there were so few skid marks, they think I walked out in front of it when it was too close to miss me. Ashley was speeding, so she's been charged with that. Otherwise, it seems to have been an accident.

He wished me well and left me to rage alone.

How I hate calling what happened to me an "accident"! I bristle every time someone says that word. It sounds like a minor thing—*accident*—rather than something utterly life changing. The problem is that I don't have a substitute word. I could call it "the wreck," but that isn't much better. "Wreck" implies two vehicles crashing, and that wasn't what happened. I was "run down," and that is my favorite term, but other people cringe when I say it. For now, I'm stuck with "accident," especially since that's the official verdict.

NASA has assigned me a social worker to help me access my memories, but so far, zilch. Karin says it's understandable that I'm angry at the driver for hitting me and at Ramón for being healthy when I'm not, but at some point, I'll need to let it go. Maybe my anger is stopping the memories from returning. Shit happens, she says, and I should move forward with the cards life has dealt me. I won't be in a wheelchair forever. When my leg heals, I can begin retraining for my job. Jeb will assign me to another mission, and this time will only be a distant, terrible memory.

Denial, anger, bargaining, depression, and acceptance—these are the stages of loss Karin has taught me. I seem to rotate among the first four stages all day, every day. I can't even imagine getting to the acceptance stage.

What I really want to know is why I didn't jump out of the way of that speeding car. My reflexes are good, or at least, they were. I don't know what happened, and it drives me crazy. I might be able to move forward if I could just figure out why I didn't see it.

What bothers me the most is the nagging question of whether I deliberately walked out in front of that car. The last thing I remember from the night before the accident was being terrified of going into space. Could I have been so scared that I sabotaged myself to get out of going on the mission? During the daytime, I'm sure I wouldn't—couldn't possibly—*didn't* do that. But the question whispers in my mind several times every night, and each time, I push it away as I lie awake, wondering.

Chapter 4: The First Simulation

A year later

The airman at the gate salutes as I drive into the Johnson Space Center. I'm a civilian, so she doesn't have to do that, but the gesture bolsters my confidence. I smile and wave then drive to the Virtual Reality Lab, where I park and take some deep breaths before walking into the building. Today is the one-year anniversary of the day my life turned to shit, but I won't let that grim reminder divert me from working as hard as I can.

I don't want to be distracted by my colleagues' pity or answer questions about my health, not until I've successfully completed at least one simulation. Fortunately, I don't see anyone I know as I make my way to the lab. Mike, my trainer, greets me.

"Hi, Mia. Ready to nail it today?" he asks, a twinkle in his eyes.

I flash him my most confident smile. "You bet. Make it as hard as you can."

I'll be testing on the SAFER sim. The SAFER is essentially a backpack with thrusters that astronauts wear during a space walk so they can safely return to the ISS if their tethers break. An untethered astronaut needs to make it back to the space station within five to ten minutes, before the thrusters run out of fuel.

Last year, I'd thought the test ridiculously easy, and I always made it back to the station in less than two minutes. However, despite eight tries in the past month, I still haven't succeeded. The first six times, the incessant tumbling when I became untethered made me so nauseated that I had to stop immediately. My seventh attempt, last week, went better. My stomach came under control relatively easily. Unfortunately, I wasn't able to force my terrified fingers in their thick gloves to flip the switch that would turn on the SAFER. My eighth try had been the same.

Today, I feel strong and focused, more like my old self. I'm ready to get this sim over with and move on to the more difficult ones I must complete before being assigned to a new mission.

Before I left home this morning, Ramón gave me a long hug. "This time, you'll make it. I can feel it. You'll be back to full training before you know it."

Hugs like that aren't common these days, and I nearly choked up. Instead, I said, "Thanks, honey. I appreciate it." I did my best to swagger out the front door and walk to my car without limping.

Smiling at the memory of his arms around me, I settle into the chair and don the virtual reality equipment. When Mike starts the program, I find myself outside the International Space Station with the task of replacing a battery. It seems so real that I immediately forget it's a simulation. Beyond the ISS is the sight I love more than anything: the Earth, enormous and blue and mostly cloudless on this day. I allow myself only a brief glance before focusing all my attention on the task before me.

When that's accomplished, I brace for what I know is coming. Sure enough, the tether holding me to the station breaks, and I tumble away from the truss. Head over heels, over and over, the Earth moving in and out of my vision.

I take a few beats to get oriented and calm my stomach and then look around for the space station. There it is, off to the left, moving farther away by the second. I force myself to keep breathing and turn on the thrusters. That completed, I straighten out and give myself a quick push toward the station.

When I'm closer, I realize I need to turn a little to the right to get to the air lock. Unfortunately, in my eagerness, I turn too far and find myself spinning. My eyes won't focus, and I'm afraid I might vomit. I panic and overcorrect to the left. Now I'm going to miss the station altogether and spin out into space until I run out of air. *Shit, shit, shit!*

My mind shuts down, and I wail, "*Nooooo.*"

Mike stops the session. "Too bad," he says, lifting off my headset. "You almost made it this time."

I wipe the sweat from my face and try not to sound as shaky as I feel. "Yeah. I know. Can I try again?"

He removes the rest of my gear. "Sorry. I've got another session in ten minutes. But you've made significant progress. Next time, you'll do it, I bet."

Something in his tone gets to me. "But I'm the worst one you've ever worked with, right?"

He shrugs. "Everybody's got to start somewhere. You're just dealing with problems the others don't have."

I thank him and trudge out of the lab, holding back tears. It's humiliating to have to work so hard to regain skills I never even used to appreciate. I start to fall down a rabbit hole toward depression, but I pull myself back. I know how hard it is to climb out of that hole, and I won't go there today.

Hard work and determination have always been my middle names. I *will* get back to my old self, or I'll die trying.

That's better.

My phone rings as I leave the building, holding on to the brick wall for stability and blinking against the afternoon sun. The secretary to my boss, Chief Astronaut Jeb Whittaker, is on the line. Can I come to Jeb's office in an hour?

"Sure. I'll be there." Good thing he's given me an hour, because by then, I'll be fine. I breathe a sigh of relief when I reach my car. Inside, I tilt back the seat and bask in the cold flow of air-conditioning. The internal spinning gradually diminishes, but my mind won't slow down. I wonder what Jeb wants. I hope this meeting is to assign me to another mission. That will require at least two years of training, so I should be a hundred percent well before launch.

Forty minutes after I arrive, I'm still sitting outside Jeb's closed door. He usually comes out to greet me as soon as I answer one of his summonses. I stand up and pace back and forth, trying to hold my annoyance in check.

I'd interpreted the summons as a positive sign. Now, I'm not so sure.

Finally, the door opens, and Jeb emerges. With his crew cut and pressed khaki uniform, he is the consummate military commander. Striding to me with his hand out, he smiles. "Sorry, Mia. Didn't mean to keep you waiting. Come on in."

We shake hands, and I forget all my angst. I should have known better than to doubt him. Today is an auspicious day to receive a new assignment.

Inside the office, Brianna Peterson, the head of human resources for the astronaut corps, greets me with a fake smile. *What's she doing here?* The astronauts joke that Brianna only comes out of her dragon's lair when there's bad news to impart.

My mind begins to spin in a downward trajectory. Apparently, this will not be the conversation I'd hoped for A headache forms above my right eye.

Jeb sits behind his desk and motions for me to take the empty seat beside Brianna.

I perch on the edge of the chair and tell myself to relax, breathe deeply, and wait for whatever is going to happen. Whatever it is, I know I can handle it. I've handled worse.

"How you feeling?" Jeb speaks in a rushed, awkward way.

"Much better." Throwing him my relaxed, confident smile, I continue. "I'm working in the plant lab three hours a day and racing through the sims. I'll be up to speed soon."

Brianna clears her throat. "That's not what we've heard."

"Huh. What have you heard?" *Bitch.*

Brianna drums her fake nails on the desk. "We've spoken to several people. Their comments are confidential, but they were all consistent. They don't think you're doing as well as you think you are."

I struggle to guess what Brianna is up to, but the headache slows my thinking. "All right," I say, drawing out the words with my rarely used Southern accent in order to buy some time. "What are you saying?"

Jeb and Brianna exchange a look, and Jeb takes over. "As you know, post-concussion syndrome is the official diagnosis of your current cognitive condition. And your right leg was fractured in four places. I hate to tell you this, Mia, but I've concluded that you're not physically or mentally fit to go to space."

Whoa. The person he describes sounds terrible, but that isn't me. At least, not all of me. When I speak, I try to sound as detached as he did. "Not yet, maybe, but I'm getting better every day. Diagnoses are just labels, and labels only tell part of the story. Why, specifically, do you think I'm unfit?"

Jeb looks down at the papers on his desk for half a minute before lifting his gaze back to mine. "Your leg still isn't strong, despite all the physical therapy. But that isn't the major problem. Your mental reflexes aren't what they used to be. And your judgments aren't consistently good. Your emotions are sometimes so intense and volatile... I'm afraid you might not respond appropriately in an emergency."

Oh shit. My world turns dark for a second. I take a breath and touch my wedding ring while I try to stay upright until my vision clears. When it does, I keep my face impassive and wait, because Jeb doesn't seem finished.

He stares out the window for a moment before continuing. "Although improvement is certainly possible, it's unlikely you will experience any appreciable recovery in the next few months and possibly not even for years." He hesitates. "If ever."

He frowns, as though in pain, and speaks softly. "I'm sorry, but I'm grounding you permanently. We can't take the risk of sending you to space."

My headache ratchets up to jackhammer strength, and I have a hard time processing his words. Grounded? Forever? *No way*. After a moment, my mind starts working again, although my eyes sting with unshed tears.

I look down at my hands, clenched in my lap, and try to regain control of my reactions. This might be my only chance to convince him to change his mind. I consciously relax my fists, take a deep breath, and glance up. Jeb and Brianna are both staring at me, compassion in their eyes.

Jeb isn't known for changing directions once he's decided something, but I have to try. "Two months ago, in this very office, you told me you'd give it another six months before you reevaluated me. It's why I've been working so hard. Why are you rushing the decision now?"

Suddenly, his mouth presses into a straight line, and when he responds, his tone is brusque. "I've got to think about our overall mission rather than one person. A new astronaut class is about to graduate, and they're superb. I need your slot for a newcomer." He gives me a hard look. "We've put a lot of money into training you, but do you honestly think you'll ever be able to measure up to the recruits? I don't, and it's my decision to make. I don't need another four months to decide."

I inhale so fast it starts a coughing fit. When I'm under control, I say, "I've measured up in the past, and I'll do it again. Everyone agrees I'm getting better. I know you've put a lot of money into training me, so please give me a little longer to prove I can do it."

Jeb says nothing, just stares at me with that hard face.

In a singsong voice, Brianna jumps in. "Even though you can't fly anymore, you have many options. I have a few suggestions. For example, the plant lab will probably keep you on part-time or even full-time, depending on how your recovery goes. And I'm sure many universities would clamor to hire you to teach agronomy."

I shake my head in frustration. Tears threaten to spill over, but I force them away. I will *not* cry, not in front of my boss and the dragon.

Brianna continues talking, sounding like she's discussing the weather instead of someone's life. *My* life.

Ignoring her, I consider Jeb's comment about my emotional reactions. There is a smidgeon of truth in what he said but only a smidgeon. For a few months after the accident, I did get angry more quickly than before. But surely, that wasn't unusual, given my injuries. I've been more even-tempered for the past few months. And at first, I cried a lot. That's gotten better too. Sometimes, I get depressed, true, but not at a clinical level. Anybody in my position would be depressed.

Someone must have talked to him and exaggerated the story. The only health care provider I've spoken to about my difficulties is Karin, my psychotherapist, and she promised not to tell anyone. I trust her, so it must have been someone else.

Ramón. Unfortunately, he was the target of a few of my temper tantrums in the first months of my healing journey. Each time, I apologized profusely as soon as I calmed down, and he seemed to be okay. Nothing bad has happened between us in several months. Why would he sabotage me?

Suddenly, the memory of his long hug comes back to me. The unusual hug. And his unusual support. They might have resulted from his guilty conscience.

I interrupt Brianna's monologue. "I'd like to go back to what Jeb said. Who told you about my emotional responses? Was it Ramón?"

Jeb bites his lip and glances away. "You know I can't tell you that. I'm sorry."

I stand. Bracing my hands on his desk, I lean over until my nose is inches from his. I have to stand on my tiptoes to do it because five feet two doesn't get me far. But I'm used to making myself seem taller. I locate my strongest voice and say, "Was. It. Ramón?"

He looks pained. In his gentlest voice, he says, "I'm sorry, Mia, but I can't tell you that."

I slump back into my chair. Jeb didn't deny that Ramón was the rat. This was his way of answering my question while maintaining deniability.

The son of a bitch. Ramón, more than Jeb. My boss is merely doing his job, no matter how misguided he is. Ramón is another story entirely.

Brianna places her hand on my shoulder. "You had a brain injury, Mia. Emotional reactions are part of the condition. It's no denunciation of you."

I shrug away from the offending hand and glare at Brianna. "Suppose I don't want to take any of your 'suggestions.' What then?"

Brianna gives me the fake smile that drives me crazy. "The average age of retirement for astronauts is forty-eight. You're only forty-two, but because of your injuries, we think we can arrange for you to retire early and qualify for a small pension. If you don't want that, the other option is to give you an unpaid leave of absence for a year. Next year, if you insist, we can revisit the situation. But keep in mind that we won't be revisiting you going to space, ever. We might get you a job in research or public relations. No guarantees, though."

Suddenly, I'm exhausted. I can't do this anymore. I nod and stand up. "That one." I stalk out of the office, holding my head high.

Son of a bitch.

Why would Ramón do this to me? I have no fucking idea.

I sit in my car for a long time, reeling from the impact of the conversation. Raw, brutal pain overwhelms me. I feel like a bear caught in a trap, knowing my world has ended yet screaming and pulling to get loose.

Eventually, my mind starts to work, and I'm able to push the emotions away for now. I have choices to make about my immediate future. At some point, I'll confront Ramón and find out why he did it but not yet. I can't take any more stress right now.

The one thing I know for sure is that I have to get far away for a while and clear my head, and then I'll decide what to do.

Chapter 5: Ready to Ride

The first thing I need to do is pack my stuff and leave the house without seeing Ramón. If I face him now, I'm not sure I can be responsible for my actions. I drive home and see that he's not here. But he'll race home as soon as he hears what happened. I don't have long.

I pull out my suitcase and throw handfuls of clothes and books inside and am walking through the living room with the suitcase in one hand and my purse and computer bag in the other. Then the front door opens. *Damn.* Ramón stands in the doorway, giving me his assessing look—the one that draws back a little and frowns, showing his worry about me.

I used to cherish the looks he gave me. Back then, his soft brown eyes did "love" extremely well. Not anymore. Now I see through his sweet surface into the slimy saboteur inside.

I had hoped not to do this now, but I won't back away. I set down my suitcase and prepare for battle. "You told them I wasn't fit to go into space. It was you." I purse my lips to keep from saying more—or to keep from crying out in despair. Jeb would probably have grounded me even without Ramón's input, but that doesn't excuse my husband's disloyalty.

He holds up his hands in a gesture for quiet. "Corazón, calm down. They already knew about the mental confusion from your medical tests. They just asked me to confirm. I didn't—"

"Well, you're rid of me now. You don't need to put up with any more of my 'mental confusion.' I'll be in touch after I decide what to do." I pick up my suitcase and walk toward the door. He has to move out of my way or get mowed down.

He moves. When I'm even with him, he grabs my shoulders. "Why don't we sit and talk about this like reasonable human beings?"

I want to smack him for insinuating I'm not being reasonable, but I keep walking down the front steps and toward my car.

He follows.

In a stern voice, he says, "You're overreacting, you know. It's something you do all the time since the accident. But it'll be okay. We'll—"

"*We* won't do anything."

I throw my suitcase and computer in the trunk and slide behind the wheel. I start the engine and give Ramón one more baleful glance.

"I don't think you're safe to drive," he says in a low, angry voice. "At least let me take you wherever you want to go."

"I don't know where I'm going," I snap. "But I can most certainly drive myself. I'll be in touch when I'm not so angry and hurt."

I peel out of the driveway and stop a block away to get my shaking hands under control. *Well, that wasn't so bad.*

I'd lied to Ramón when I said I didn't know where I was going. I've known from the moment I decided to leave—to my mom's house in Florida. I need to be with someone who loves me unconditionally. Until this morning, I'd thought there were two people. Now I know there's only one.

After a few moments, I've calmed down and am ready to roll. But first, I need to visit the lab and say goodbye to my plants and to my lab assistant, Toni.

The lab is my home away from home. I've worked there for seven years, even before applying to become an astronaut. And for the past year, it has been my refuge from all the things I can't do. Plants calm me like nothing else, and my brain works reasonably well when I'm with them. Also, Ramón isn't around to tell me I look tired or ask if I need to go home and rest.

I'm determined to take one experiment with me, if for no other reason than to spite NASA for grounding me. They're mine—all I have left of my shattered life.

I park in my assigned spot and march into the building, assessing the situation. I've filled the lab with my experiments, all having to do with growing plants in space. Which one should I take? Some are in such big containers there's no way I can carry them. Others need specialized lights and feeding regimens. *Hmm.* This is hard.

As I glance around the room, the reality of my situation sinks in. I've just told my boss I wanted a leave of absence and informed my husband I was leaving town. Were those the overreactions and poor judgments Jeb and Brianna talked about? Maybe, but I'm not wrong to be leaving. I really need to get out of town and process everything before deciding on my next step.

If Jeb had given me more time, everything would have been fine. Overreactions and poor judgments aren't the biggest part of me. I can sense my real self—the capable, thoughtful, calm self—inside, waiting to get out.

My eyes light on the only experiment I can feasibly take: my lettuce plants growing in simulated Martian regolith. They're doing well, mostly because of the earthworms I've introduced into the medium. The combination of pig slurry and earthworms that break up the dust and rock have made the difference between dead plants and live ones. Because of my experiments, it might be possible to grow food in habitation in Martian soil. I'll take that container, a box of worms, and some slurry and continue my research in Florida. When I succeed, Jeb will understand that I've healed, and he'll be eager to take me back.

It's the best I can do, given the situation.

Toni, my assistant, walks into the lab as I struggle to carry the container out the door. The younger woman independently managed our research during the first six months after my accident, when I spent most of my time lying in bed, staring blankly at the ceiling. Now that I'm back a few hours every day, she and I work together closely.

She gives me a curious look. "What are you doing? How can I help?"

I snort. "You shouldn't get involved in this. NASA won't be happy, and I don't care. Why don't you go get a cup of coffee?"

"Uh, are you taking this experiment somewhere?"

"Yeah. I'm sure you'll hear about it soon." I smile, although the smile feels more like a grimace. "Thanks for everything, Toni. Take care of things for me, will you?"

Toni gives me a questioning look, but I don't respond.

Finally, she nods and holds the door open. She'll probably be on the phone to Jeb or Ramón as soon as I leave. *So be it.*

I carry the box out to my car and gently place it on the back seat. On my second trip, I carry out a box of worms, a container of fertilizer, a watering can, and a can of pig slurry. Finally, I pick up my research notebook and turn to wish my other plants well. Toni will care for them properly. But without my input, NASA's approach to growing plants on Mars might change.

Damn.

Blinking furiously, I walk out for possibly the last time. Toni stands in the doorway, looking sad and shaking her head. We hug.

"I'll keep in touch," I say.

"I'll wait for your call. Take care."

And that is that. I'm ready to ride.

Chapter 6: Unmoored

Before long, my car and I are heading east on I-10. Traffic on the interstate gradually lightens, and soon, I'm able to drive without white-knuckling it.

After two hours of driving, my eyes keep trying to close. So far, I've been able to force them to stay open, but the shock of the confrontations with my boss and husband is creeping up on me. No matter how hard I try to ignore the signs of exhaustion and cognitive overwhelm, I know my mind and body are shutting down.

I must find a safe place where I can close my eyes for an hour, or I might crash my beloved Tesla. That would not be good. The Mercury 7 astronauts were given Corvettes, but I had to buy my own vehicle. The Tesla, which I purchased when I became an astronaut, is my prized possession.

I need to stop, soon.

Within five miles, a rest area appears. *Hallelujah!* I turn off the highway and slide into the parking spot farthest from the restroom. I don't want anybody denting my baby while I sleep.

Some people have kids, but I've always been too career oriented to figure out how I could work them into my schedule. Instead, I have plants. And this car. I love its advanced engineering and acceleration, the smell of the leather interior, and the way the driver's seat snuggles me when it's tilted back all the way. I'm eager to allow that seat to lull me into a blissful rest.

I set my phone to play one of the many relaxation exercises I've stored on it. *Calm down. Breathe. Allow your mind to go quiet. Close your eyes. Imagine yourself on a beach.* No, that image won't do. My heartbeat speeds up, remembering the sight of my brother's drowned body lying on the white sand. His skin looked like rubber. I shudder and switch to another program. *Imagine yourself on a mountaintop, with a stream gurgling in the background.* Yes, that works.

My muscles relax a little as the speaker drones on, but my thoughts keep jumping around, always returning to Ramón. Before the accident, he and I were equals, fellow astronauts who loved each other with a fierce devotion. Since then, I've changed, but so has he. Aside from the obvious sabotage, he's become a scolding parent who constantly tells me what to do.

The things that bug me the most are subtle, but they work on my self-confidence. Such as "Have you done your physical therapy today?" I *always* do my physical therapy. Every day. And I've told him so, more than once, but he keeps asking.

Another example: when I search for my car keys, he'll find them and ask, "Are you sure you're up to going to the grocery store? I've got the list, and I'll stop on my way home from work." I haven't been grocery shopping since the accident. He beats me to it, every time, and acts like he's doing me a favor. I *miss* shopping, but he won't listen. And I miss that woman—my old self—who did whatever she wanted, regardless of what he said. What happened to her? I intend to find out.

When the relaxation exercise ends, I realize I've been so mired in my resentments that I've missed it. I open my eyes but see only scrubby plants and cars. My stomach growls, and I remember I haven't eaten since breakfast. Maybe I'll feel better after some food.

I start the car and drive on. The next exit sign lists several restaurants, so I turn off the highway and find the darkest, quietest-looking one in the area. Inside, I slide into a booth away from the window so the outside glare won't bother my eyes. They're sensitive to light, and driving asks a lot of them. A bowl of chicken noodle soup and a piece of toast sound great. Oh yes, and a glass of wine.

The food comes right away. Twenty minutes later, I feel much better. The soup has calmed my upset stomach, and the wine soothed my nerves. I pay the bill but continue sitting in the booth, staring vacantly at a television screen in the corner that shows a women's talk show but without sound. I might have once been a guest on that show, but the details are sketchy in my memory.

Slowly, my eyelids close. My head jerks. The wine wasn't such a good idea after all. Crap, now I'm too tired to drive. If I don't do something quickly, I might fall asleep in this booth. I can see the headlines in tomorrow's paper: *Drunken Astronaut Spends the Night in Jail.* That would not strengthen my case with Jeb.

Turning to glance out the window, I notice a large sign for a chain motel across the parking lot. Has that been there the whole time, or was it built while I was having lunch? *Ha.* I walk out of the restaurant and into the motel lobby.

"A room, please. A single will be fine."

The woman at the desk looks at me suspiciously. I'm not so famous that she would likely recognize me, so I might be slurring my words. People tell me I sound like I'm drunk when I'm doing it, but the problem is an overly tired brain that doesn't communicate with my mouth well enough. Even though other people can hear me slur, I usually can't. I give her a small smile, and the woman shrugs.

"How many nights?"

"Just tonight." I pay for the room then move my car into the assigned spot. I can't summon the energy to care right now if someone dings it. After opening the door to the room, I stand in the doorway and flash to the last room where I stayed with Ramón. He'd surprised me with a trip to our favorite resort in Kauai for our anniversary last month. It was a fancy all-inclusive with suites right on the beach. This room is nothing like that. Stale, generic, possibly dirty. But it will do.

I drop my suitcase, turn down the bedspread, and collapse onto the faded blue sheets. Two hours later, I awake with a piercing headache. My right leg throbs from hours of pressing down on the accelerator, and the room spins when I try to focus on the ceiling fan, even though I'm pretty sure it isn't really moving.

Damn, damn, damn. I'd hoped to drive on after a brief nap, but clearly, that won't happen. I rummage in my purse for a pain pill, swallow it, and fall back into bed.

The next time I wake is in the middle of the night. I watch the motel's sign blink on and off through the window, but I'm too tired to get up and close the blinds. This time, I don't go right back to sleep. The emotions I pushed away earlier return in a fury, leaving me feeling completely unmoored from the life I've known. My career is gone and possibly my marriage, and the strength and vitality I count upon have disappeared. I bang on the pillow and kick my feet until the tantrum wears itself out.

No matter what Jeb says, I won't give up on my goal of getting to space. I'll do something so fantastic that Jeb will take me back, and Ramón will apologize. I don't know yet what it will be, but I'll find it.

I ignore the voice in the back of my mind that wonders what will become of me if my plan doesn't work.

Chapter 7: Unresurrected in Louisiana

No matter how late I go to bed or how poorly I sleep, every day at six o'clock, my eyes ping open, and I'm awake, ready to start the day. This morning, I notice that my leg has stopped hurting, and my headache has almost disappeared. *Great!* I'm ready to drive on.

As usual, my mind turns to Ramón. My entire being continues to radiate fury at his betrayal. Soon, Ashley joins him as an object of my anger. Ashley is the woman who hit me a year ago and ruined my life. I don't know what she looks like, but I know she's young, white, and ditzy. She pled guilty to reckless driving and lost her license for a year, but that's all. I picture her back at work, a little remorseful but living with it. Whereas I've been told I might never go back. *Damn her, anyway.*

Okay, breathe. Move on.

I turn on my cell phone to find a dozen texts from Ramón and also a voicemail from my mom. I immediately call her back.

Her voice is as clear and melodious as a sunny day by a lake. "Where are you, honey?"

"Somewhere in Texas, I think. I'm headed home, though. I..."

"Ramón told me what happened. I'm so sorry. I'll be glad to see you, but can you drive that far by yourself? Maybe I should come and get you."

Even though yesterday was one of the worst days of my life, I'm not so bad that I need my mom to drive to the rescue. "I'm not sure how long it'll take, but I'll get there. I won't do anything dangerous."

"All right. I trust your judgment. But would you call Ramón and let him know you're okay?"

"No way. I'm not ready to talk to him. Did he tell you what he did?" I can hear the pain in my voice.

"He answered the investigator's questions truthfully. He's a good man, and he loves you. It put him in quite a bind." Her tone changes. "Honey, even you know you aren't back to your old self. Don't you?"

I'm not sure how to answer. "I'm not *completely* back to my old self yet. That's true. But I'm getting better. There was no reason to ground me permanently."

Mom sighs. "Yes, you're much better than you were. Come home and rest and let me take care of you. We'll talk some more. But please, call Ramón."

"If you want him to know how I'm doing, you call him. I won't do it."

"All right. Call me tonight and let me know how the day went, all right? By the way, you're slurring your words again."

Am I? *Shit.* I sound fine to myself. But I'm still dangerously tired. That much, I can tell.

After we hang up, I take a shower. That simple act wears me out. I walk over to the restaurant and eat breakfast, convinced I'll feel better after eggs and coffee. But I don't. *Just a brief nap, and then I'll leave.*

I wake again at one p.m., hours past checkout time. My head aches. After I swallow another pain pill, I call the motel office to extend my stay and fall back to sleep.

I'm outside the ISS, dressed in my space suit, working on something. When I pull myself around an arm of the space station, I almost bump into another astronaut.

We face each other, both holding on to the ladder, our legs floating out behind us. This isn't the Chinese astronaut who came outside with me. No, it's someone else. A man, I think. He looks vaguely familiar, but

I can't place him. He's definitely not from this mission. His eyes gaze at me intently through his visor. They are trying to tell me something, but I don't understand. For whatever reason, helplessness and fear paralyze me.

I jerk awake and sit up in bed, heart beating in my throat, sweat pouring between my breasts, and consumed by terror. Who was that man? And why was he out there, staring at me? And why did seeing him terrify me so much? I've had this dream maybe a dozen times, and each time, it's exactly the same. It never progresses beyond the two of us staring at each other and then me waking up, drenched in sweat and fear, my throat raw from the strain of holding back a scream.

Daylight floods through a gap in the blinds. Still afternoon, then. I spot a coffee maker on the dresser and, with shaking hands, make a cup. Sipping the bitter brew, I call Karin. I resisted going to our sessions at first, but now I rely on the older woman's years of experience in treating brain-injury survivors.

Her secretary puts through my call. "Mia," says Karin. "I'm so glad to hear from you. How are you? Where are you?"

Everyone is asking me the same thing. Good grief, what am I, a lost child? "I'm not sure about either of those questions. But I had the spaceman dream again, just now."

Karin inhales sharply. "Oh, I'm sorry. Are your feet on the floor?"

This is her way of distracting me from my fear, I suppose. "I'm doing it now." I stand on the thin carpet and feel its coolness on my bare soles. After a moment, the terror subsides. Soon, I'm breathing normally.

"I'm better now. Thanks." I sit on the room's only chair.

"Good," she says. "Was the dream the same as before?"

"Yeah."

"We've talked about this. The spaceman might be someone you used to know or someone you need to know. Or maybe an unacknowledged part of yourself is trying to send you a message. If you can, next time try to speak to him, ask him what he wants."

I shudder. "I don't know if I can do that. He scares me too much."

"I know. You couldn't do it today. But one day, you will. Be patient. It'll happen." After a pause, she asks, "So, where are you?"

"In a motel room somewhere east of Houston. I got too tired to drive anymore last night."

"Look around and see if you find anything that tells you where you are."

A phone book is in a drawer. "Lake Charles, Louisiana. Why does it matter?"

"It just helps me to know where you are. Do you remember why you went there?"

"Yeah. Sure. I left Ramón. The son of a bitch sided with Jeb against me, and now I'm grounded. I'm on my way to Florida, to stay with my mom for a while." I hesitate. "Did you side with Jeb against me too?"

"No, I did not. An investigator contacted me and asked me about your progress or lack of it. I cited confidentiality laws, and he went away. Mia, we've discussed this. Whatever we say in our sessions will remain between us. My notes are sparse—just enough to remind me of what happened that day. Even with a court order, they wouldn't get enough from me to decide about your future."

I'd thought so, but it's nice to hear Karin say it.

After a moment, she continues. "Ramón called me yesterday and told me what happened. It must have been a devastating blow for you, coming out of the blue like it did. You were so hoping to go to space."

I nod, holding back tears as I knead my toes in the carpet. "Yeah. But I'll appeal the decision. I'll get my own doctors, and they'll say I'm fine. Will you be one of them?" I hold my breath and wait.

I hear Karin take a sip of the iced tea she keeps by her side when she's working. Finally, she answers. "That's a longer conversation than we should have on the phone. Let's talk about it when you get back. When will that be?"

"I don't know. I'm playing it by ear. You always say I need not to be so rigid. So here I am, in Bumfuck, Louisiana, not being rigid."

Karin laughs. "Well, fine. We can have phone meetings. Better yet, Skype would allow us to see each other while we talk. I'm glad you called, Mia. I was worried about you. Be careful driving. It's a long way to Florida, and you're still recovering. Oh, just a second." She covers the mouthpiece and has a muffled conversation with someone. "I need to go. My next client is here. I'll transfer you to Linda, and she'll set up a couple of appointments. Take care, okay?"

"Thanks, Karin."

After I schedule two Skype appointments, I feel better. Karin will support my appeal, I'm sure. I'll get my job back and make it to space, one way or the other.

Suddenly, a thought cuts through my self-absorption. *My plants!* I need to water them. *Oh, shit, shit, shit.* How could I have left them untended for so long?

My lettuce plants have become thin brown sticks that droop over the soil in what is clearly a death signature. The heat and lack of water for a day and a half got to them. No matter what I do now, there will be no resurrection for these plants.

I could kick myself for my thoughtlessness. These were my babies, and I left them to roast in a hot car while I slept, blissfully unaware of the damage I was doing. Good thing I've never had children. God only knows what my inattention would do to them.

An unwanted thought springs up: What if Jeb and the others are right, and I'm not physically or mentally fit for space? The possibility penetrates my consciousness for a few seconds before I push it away. All will be well. Maybe it won't be tomorrow, but I *will* go up in space one day.

I'll start over with plants when I get to Florida. Lettuce is easy to grow.

Even though it's late in the day, I decide to drive for a while. I feel Florida calling me, a wayward daughter, back to its bosom. *Home.* Inside the motel room, I pack my few things and leave the room key on the bureau.

Considerably chastened, I drive east. I'm glad I only took one experiment from the lab. The others will surely receive better care than these poor little plants did. I wasn't irresponsible before the accident, but it appears I am now. And it's all Ashley's fault.

Ashley.

I want to throw up at the sound of her name. After training for years in dangerous situations, a giant SUV named Explorer, driven by *Ashley,* ruined my life. I grind my teeth and tighten my hands on the steering wheel until my fingers are numb.

Okay, STOP. Think of something else.

I can't stop thinking about the accident, even though I still don't remember a thing about it. Karin says I'm experiencing "thought loops," in which my mind goes around and around a topic, like a cow chewing its cud, only I never swallow. Apparently, thought loops aren't unusual after a trauma, but they are a useless sap of my time and energy. The only way out is to think of something pleasant. *Okay. What is pleasant about my life now?* I can't think of a single thing.

Thinking about space has always been a pleasant experience. But today, even that fails me. My thoughts turn to Jeb. I'll appeal his decision, of course, but I'll need to hire a lawyer. I received a small insurance settlement from the accident, so I'll use that. I try to figure out how many hours I can afford of my attorney's time before I'm flat broke, since I'm now unemployed and without a salary. And, possibly, without a husband.

Shit. Another loop.

Frustrated, I flick on Sirius Radio and zone out with the Spa station as the miles speed by.

Chapter 8: Walking on Eggshells

Three days later, in the middle of a blistering afternoon, I drive into my hometown of Valencia, Florida. I like to tell people it's located in the exact center of the state, from both north to south and east to west. That isn't quite accurate, but it's close. Many people don't realize that a different Florida exists inland from the two coasts—one that is hotter, slower, older, and more conservative.

At the city limits, I spot a sign that reads, "Home of astronaut Mia Gray." An official picture of me in my space suit has been affixed to the bottom. My heart sinks. I'd forgotten about that sign. The city council will probably take it down when they discover what happened.

I drive to my mom's business, which is almost as familiar as the house I grew up in. The freestanding sign, "Pat's Nursery and Garden Center," is leaning precariously. It's also covered with mildew and badly needs to be pressure-washed. Only three cars sit in the parking lot, probably because fewer people plant gardens in the fall than in the spring.

I get out of the car and stretch while looking around. A teenaged boy waits on a customer. That must be my nephew, Jacob. Another boy waters the bedding plants, but I don't recognize him. The place looks ragged around the edges, as though it hasn't gotten nearly enough love recently. Mom might still be grieving Dad's death, or maybe something else is amiss.

I walk into the building and knock at the office door.

"Come in," says a voice I love.

Grinning, I open the door and see Mom sitting at her desk, reading glasses perched on her nose. Her hair has gone completely white in the six months since I last saw her. Or has it been that way for a while and I didn't notice? I can't be sure. When she smiles at me, I'm struck by all the wrinkles in her lovely face.

"You're here." Mom holds on to the desk and pushes herself to standing. A wince replaces her smile for a second. I reach out to steady her, but she regains her balance.

We hug for a long time. The scent of her earthy shampoo and a slight whiff of her perfume take me back to childhood, when I felt surrounded by her love. Wiping away tears of joy, I study her.

Until Mom's hair went white, it was the same dark brown as mine. We even wear it the same way: short and straight to the chin, except I have bangs and Mom doesn't. We're both short and wiry, but Mom has shrunk a couple of inches.

I work out the numbers. She was twenty-eight when I was born, which makes her seventy. *Oh, gosh.* Why is she even working at her age? I'll bring up that subject later.

"Oh, honey, I'm thrilled to see you. How are you?"

I consider the question as I pick up a pile of magazines from the office's other chair and place them on the floor. I plop down and watch her ease back into her desk chair.

"Tired, I guess. It was a long trip, but I made it fine." I pause. "How are you? You look a little tired yourself."

Mom laughs. "Oh, just a few aches and pains. Nothing to worry about."

Silence falls. I've worked so hard to get here that I'm not sure where to begin now that I've arrived. "Uh, Mom—"

"Let's go home and get you some food and a shower. Jacob can take care of the place for a couple of hours." She stands and gathers her things. "I'll tell him I'm leaving. By the way, I figured you'd be coming in this afternoon, so I invited Ava to join us for dinner. How about the Chinese buffet?"

"Sure, that's fine." I'd hoped to have some time alone with Mom before facing Ava. I love my sister, of course, but she can be difficult. Still, I don't want to start out causing problems.

Mom locks the office door and calls for Jacob, who's unloading bags of fertilizer. The last time I saw him, at my dad's funeral six months before, he was two or three inches shorter. He's sprouted up, and my mom has shrunk. *Weird.*

We hug, and Jacob agrees to watch the place until it closes at six. "I bet we won't get more than a couple people."

"Thanks, honey," says Mom. "You're a gem."

We walk to our vehicles. I'd parked next to Mom's old Toyota pickup, and I watch as she gingerly pulls herself into the cab. Something is definitely wrong.

We drive to the family home, three miles away. It isn't huge by current standards, but it has three bedrooms, two baths, and a screened porch. Ava and I shared a bedroom until our brother, Ben, drowned when I was twelve and Ava ten. After a couple of months, I moved into Ben's room. It was creepy at first. I'd halfway expected him to pop out of the closet and yell at me for being in his room, but I gradually adjusted. Now, when I set my suitcase by the bed, I notice that my high school posters of various space missions are still tacked to the walls, their edges yellowed and curled. The room needs a major remodel.

I sit at the kitchen table as Mom arranges glasses of sweetened iced tea, a container of chocolate chip cookies, and watermelon balls. "I hope that's enough. Ava's going to meet us at the restaurant at six. Is that okay?"

"Sure. I'm not very hungry, though." Because Mom taught me never to arrive anyplace hungry, I'd stopped for lunch an hour before.

I eat a few bites as I look around. It's great to sit in the old kitchen where nothing ever changes.

Except... something has changed. Gradually, I realize that all the paraphernalia from Dad's long illness has vanished. No hospital bed in the living room, no wheelchair, no potty chair. Even though I attended his funeral, it's strange that he's not propped up in the chair and struggling to breathe. The room smells fresh instead of like stale urine, and it's a welcome relief. I have such mixed feelings about his death. He always acted like he was disappointed in me, no matter what I accomplished, so I'm happy to not have to face him with my news. On the other hand, I miss the sweet man he was before Ben died. Also, the last five years of his life as he went downhill were tragic. No one should have to die like that.

I don't feel up to talking about Dad now, so we chat about my trip, which went smoothly after that first night. I took breaks when I got tired and slept well every night without nightmares. Eventually, Mom clears her throat, and I have an idea what's coming.

"Honey, I know you've just arrived, and you're welcome here for as long as you want. I'll be happy for the company. But... do you have an idea how long it'll be?"

It's a fair question, but I have no idea how to answer it. "Uh, I'm not sure. Maybe forever?" I chuckle a little, like I'm joking, but I watch Mom carefully to see how that goes over.

She purses her lips and slowly nods. "It's that bad between you and Ramón?"

I shrug. "I need a break from him and from my life, and then I'll see. Do you mind if I stay here until I decide? Realistically, maybe a month or two?"

"You can stay forever if you want. It's lonely without your dad." She looks out the window and blinks a few times. "But Ramón is a good man. He loves you. And I don't think you should chuck out your life so quickly. But that's just my opinion. I know you'll do the right thing. Let me know what you're thinking as you go along, okay?"

"Yes. Of course."

Ava is late, as usual. When she finally arrives, she gives me a brief hug. "Let's get our food, and then we can talk, okay?"

Strangers would not take us for sisters. Whereas Mom and I look much alike, Ava resembles our dad. She's half a foot taller, with shoulder-length blond hair and blue eyes. We were close as kids, but for years now, we only talk on the phone once or twice a year. Ava called once after I got out of the hospital and then never again. Not that I called her.

After we fill our plates at the buffet and sit down, Ava says, "Honestly, I don't know why people come in right before closing time and then meander around the store. When I tell them it's time to close, they walk out without buying a thing. I swear, I don't know why I bother."

Ava owns the only independent bookstore in Valencia, and she has struggled for years to keep it afloat. Fortunately, her husband, Jeff, works as a large-equipment operator, so his salary saves them in hard times.

"How are things going?" I ask, mostly to be polite.

"All right," she replies, giving me a quizzical look. "What about you? I hear you've left Ramón."

"Yeah." Everybody in my family loves my husband. Heck, everybody everywhere loves him, especially his public persona. He's an astronaut superstar. He comes from a large family of farmers and artists in New Mexico, and he's the type who never meets a stranger. I'm the one people struggle to like, even in my family. I'm always so sharp-edged, so driven, I make people uncomfortable. It's been worse since the accident, because nobody knows what to say to me.

Ramón. I didn't leave him just because of what he told the investigators, although that was the trigger. No, it's more than that. He hovers and controls, and I get angry and retreat. It's not a healthy dynamic, but neither of us seems able to change. I don't want to get into it with Ava, though, especially not tonight.

"Too bad," she says. "What about your brain injury? And your leg?"

I hate when people call it a brain injury. That term sounds like my brain is beyond repair, which it isn't. Yes, I injured my brain, but I still hate to think of it that way. I prefer the term "head injury" or, better yet, "concussion."

The egg roll I just bit into sticks in my throat, and I take a drink of water. "Still healing. I'm about ready to start running, though, and I might be eligible for the next mission."

I can't help lying to her. Ava, with her perfect family, and the friends she's had since high school, and her attitude about space exploration being a waste of time when there are so many problems here on earth. Well, truthfully, there's more between us than that. When I graduated from high school, I received a partial scholarship to the University of Florida and never looked back. Ava wasn't so fortunate. She didn't get a scholarship, and the family's finances wouldn't stretch enough for both of us to attend university. She attended community college and quit after two years to get married. I still carry guilt for becoming a star at Ava's expense.

I wonder if everyone feels like they're walking on eggshells when they return to their hometowns and confront the family dynamics they can easily ignore when they're away. *Probably.*

"Hey, let's get seconds," says Ava. "Mom, you want us to bring you something?"

"A little egg custard would be nice."

"Sure." At the buffet, Ava turns to me, frowning. "I'm glad you're here. Do you see what's happening to her?"

"God, she looks so much older. Is that because of Dad?"

She scrunches up her face. "It's a lot of things. That, plus she needs to get a knee and a hip replaced. She's in constant pain, but she can't stop working. She's trying to sell the nursery, but nobody wants to buy it in its current shape."

"Can't she just close it and sell the land? It's got to be worth something."

"You honestly don't know? They mortgaged the land when Dad got sick. Now she owes more than it's worth unless she gets a lot for the business. That's why I'm glad you're here. We're doing our best to keep the business going. I do the books, and Jacob helps after school. Jeff's over there every Saturday doing the heavy work. But we're worn out. You need to take over the place and get it running so she can sell it."

I hate when someone tells me what I need to do, but I let it go for the moment. "What about retirement income?"

Ava grunts. "Just Social Security, and it's not enough to live on. Dad's pension from the church was tiny, and Mom didn't save much over the years. Their savings didn't last long when he got sick. You honestly didn't know all this?"

"I honestly didn't."

"Well, you know it now. And you need to stay and take care of this mess instead of playing around in space."

I mimic my sister's tone. "And you need to stop dumping on me when I've just arrived." I take a breath. "Look, I'll do my best while I'm here, but I'm an astronaut, not a nursery owner. I can provide some money, but I won't be around long enough to rescue the business." Despite what I told Mom about staying forever, I know it won't happen. I want—need—to get to space, and nothing else matters.

Ava huffs and stomps back to the booth, where Mom waits for her dessert. Tacitly, Ava and I agree to a truce.

While we enjoy a last cup of jasmine tea, an obese white man in his thirties, arms covered with tattoos, approaches our booth. A boy of around five or six hangs on to his leg. The man looks at me and says, "Excuse me, but are you Mia Gray, the astronaut?"

I nod and smile as graciously as I can. This kind of thing happens occasionally. It's likely to happen more often in Valencia since at least a quarter of the population drives past my picture every day.

"My boy would like your autograph, if you don't mind. He's a big fan."

The child looks scared to death. There's no way that boy has a clue who I am. But I understand. The dad was embarrassed to approach me, so he palmed it off on the kid.

"Sure." Astronauts are encouraged to carry photographs of ourselves for just such occasions. I pull one from my purse, along with a pen. Smiling at the child, I ask his name.

He hides behind his father's legs. "Billy," the father says.

I sign the photo: "To Billy. Reach for the stars. Best, Mia Gray." I hand it to the father. "Here you go. Have a nice evening."

He mumbles his thanks, and the two of them shuffle back to their table.

"Let's get out of here," I say, "before anybody else gets wind that I'm back."

Chapter 9: Rest Won't Get Me to Space

The next morning, I'm halfway convinced another Explorer hit me during the night. Everything aches, and I'm completely exhausted. I roll over and go back to sleep. At ten o'clock, I wake again, feeling a little better. In the kitchen, I see a note from my mom telling me to rest for as long as I can. She'll come home at lunch, and we can talk. *Sweet.*

After a cup of coffee and a piece of toast, I feel good enough to wander out to the screened porch. Even though it's early October, the air is still and stifling. Autumn probably won't arrive until mid-November, when the temperature will drop by a few degrees. But I enjoy the heat, especially compared to the air-conditioned house, so I sit in a chair and relax.

Yesterday, when I arrived, I placed my container with its dead lettuce leaves on the porch beside Mom's flowers. It looks pitiful beside the bright geraniums. I'll do something about that soon but not today.

When I try to plan my day, absolutely nothing comes to me. I'd hoped to magically transform into my old, competent self once I got home, but it hasn't happened. Instead, I spend two hours staring out at the backyard, watching butterflies flicker around a bush and a group of white ibis pick at bugs in the grass. Several times, I try to get up and at least take a shower and get dressed, but I'm glued to the chair.

Mom finds me just where I'd landed hours earlier. "It's so great to see you here," she says. "Can I get you some lunch? I have tuna salad."

"No thanks. I'm sorry I'm no help, but I just can't seem to move." I'm embarrassed to admit that, but it's true.

"You take as long as you need to heal. I'm glad I can take care of you a little. Ramón did everything for you when I visited, and there wasn't really room for me to do anything."

"Yeah. I know. That's what it's like for me too."

"He means well. He's like a mother hen, that man."

We chuckle and fall silent.

She disappears into the kitchen and returns with a sandwich and a glass of iced tea. Iced tea, the signature drink of the South, I think. And then I giggle because I've finally had a thought.

Silently, Mom eats, and I stare outside. Finally, I shake myself from my stupor and ask, "How's business today?"

"We did fairly well this morning. Several people bought mulch. A couple of contractors are putting in new landscaping. That kind of thing. But the big box store up the street has gobbled up most of our customers. We can't sell at their prices, and people don't understand the difference in quality between us and them."

"Mom, why didn't you tell me about the problems you're having? Ava told me last night."

She bites her lip. "I didn't want to bother you, honey. You've got your own problems, and they're worse than mine. Things will work out. They always do."

It's so like her to make light of her situation. But I can't turn away from her as I turned away from my job situation and my marriage. Mom needs me, and I refuse to make running away from my problems a way of life.

"What are you going to do?" I ask.

"I don't know. Pray for a miracle, I guess." She tries to smile, but her expression is bleak.

I form my words carefully. "While I'm here, I'll be happy to work at the nursery. But all those things I said yesterday about staying forever? They were just in the relief of being home. I've got to go back to Houston if I'm going to get to space, and that's all I want right now: one time in space before I retire." I pause, staring out at the yard. This next part is delicate. "I've got some money left from the insurance settlement. Would fifteen thousand fix up the business enough that you can sell it?"

If it isn't enough, I can sell the Tesla. Thinking of that brings a lump to my throat. But my mom needs the money more than I do. Maybe my lawyer will take my appeal for a percentage of my salary, assuming I'm hired back.

Mom grunts. "That money is for your rehabilitation, and you never know how much you'll need. But I could take maybe five thousand. That would make a big difference, and maybe then I can get a buyer. Besides, I'm backed up a little with the bank." She pauses. "Come to think of it, if you could loan me eight thousand, that would really help. I'll pay you back when I sell the business."

"Sure. I'll write a check today. Just let me know when you need more. I'll help you all I can."

She laughs. "And here I was, trying to help you. You make it hard, you know."

"Have you been talking to Ramón? That's what he always says." I clear my throat. "Don't change the subject. You're limping. What's that about?"

"Oh, I'm just getting old. Aches and pains. After I sell the business, I might get a couple of joints replaced. But I'm all right. Don't worry."

I shake my head and laugh. "You won't allow yourself to be helped either. We're a pair, aren't we? Now I know where I got it."

"Your dad was the same way. Don't blame it only on me."

The silence draws out as I consider how to phrase my next question. Finally, I ask, "How are you doing with your grief?"

Before he got sick, Dad was the pastor of a local nondenominational church, and to his congregation, he was a wonderful, caring man who was always there for them. But it seemed like he parked his niceness at the curb when he got home. He'd rarely spoken a kind word to the rest of us in the years after Ben's death. Ava and I had often wondered why Mom stayed with him. We certainly wouldn't have. So bringing up the subject is tricky.

Mom sniffs. "I don't know. The house is so quiet now. I've been thinking of getting a dog or something. But I'm too tired in the evenings to walk it. Frank wasn't easy, but we were married for forty-six years. That's a long time."

I don't know what to say. In fact, I suddenly realize that this talk has taken more out of me than I can spare. "Sorry to be abrupt, but I need to take a nap. I'll write your check first, though. How about if I make supper tonight?"

Mom brightens. "Sure, honey. You remember where the Publix is, don't you? I'll make a list of things I need, if you don't mind. Fix whatever you want. Anything I don't have to cook is my favorite meal." She laughs and heads out to the kitchen while I shuffle into my bedroom.

After a long nap, I pull myself out of bed and go to the grocery store. It's my first time grocery shopping since the accident, and I'm proud of myself. I'm also grateful that I don't see anyone I know, and nobody recognizes me. I pick up a roasted chicken and boil some corn on the cob. That plus a salad is all I can pull together. As soon as supper is over, I tumble back into bed.

The next morning, I feel much better. After pulling on running clothes, I decide to head downtown and see how far I get. Valencia Lake is one and a half miles away, and I'll try to run the entire way. Before the accident, I ran half-marathons and even one full marathon, but this will be my first time running in a year. I don't give a shit that my doctor hasn't given permission for me to run. I'm on my own now.

After only a few blocks, my knee aches, my ankle screams, and my breathing is so ragged that I stop and lean over to catch my breath. *Damnation.* I hobble back to the house, feeling like warmed-over dog shit.

Mom is eating oatmeal when I drag myself in. "Oh, sweetie, how can I help?"

"I'm okay." In the bathroom, I swallow three anti-inflammatories then pick up a prescription bottle and stare at the pain pills inside. Only four left. I'll soon have to get the prescription refilled. *No.* I'm done with taking pain pills. I'll overcome the pain on my own and stop depending on outside help. After throwing the bottle into the trash, I limp out to the kitchen.

"Well, that was a disaster," I say as I sit on a barstool. "God, I'm hopeless."

Mom phrases her words carefully, as though she understands that sympathy might not be the best response just now. "I guess you have to work up to running. But you'll make it. Don't give up." She pauses. "If you're feeling better, maybe you could help me at the nursery for a few days. A shipment of seedlings needs to be potted today. Would that be possible?"

The nursery again. The nursery has always been the center of Mom's world, even more than her kids, I think as resentment surfaces. I push it down. "Sure. I'll head over when the ibuprofen kicks in."

The phone rings and keeps ringing. First, it's the Rotary Club asking me to come and speak. Then the Kiwanis Club. Then the Women's Club. *Shit.* The man at the restaurant must have told everyone he knows that I'm in town. I put them all off as nicely as I can, claiming to be on vacation. After that, I let the voicemails pile up.

I don't even answer when Darla, my best friend from high school, calls. As happy as I am to hear from her, I'll call her back when I can sound cheerful.

Instead, I Skype with Karin. It's my first Skype appointment, and it works well. She encourages me to rest as much as possible. Her advice is coming from a place of concern, but rest won't get me into space. I've tried it, and it doesn't work.

I'll run again tomorrow. Until then, I have seedlings to pot.

Chapter 10: You Don't Like Hip-Hop. How about Classical?

My next day's attempt at running ends the same way as the first. Back at the house, I dig the bottle of pain pills from the trash and swallow a pill. Mind over matter isn't working so far.

I've just opened the NASA news on my tablet when Mom clears her throat. "Honey, it's Wednesday. I usually go to church in the evening for the prayer service. Do you want to go? It would mean a lot to me to show you off."

I haven't been to church since I started college, other than for Ava's wedding. Dad always berated me for my decision, but I've never wavered in my resolve. I couldn't stand watching him act like a paragon of virtue when he was so different at home.

Now that he's gone, so is my excuse.

I sigh. How to explain? "I know you don't understand, but my church is in space. Even though I haven't been there yet, seeing videos of the blue Earth rotating makes me feel closer to God than sitting inside a church. Being outdoors is the same. I'm sorry to disappoint you, but I won't be going with you."

I brace for an argument. She looks sad, but she nods. "I don't understand, but I accept. I usually go over to the cemetery after the service. Would you at least do that with me?"

I'm beaten, and I know it. "All right. Shall I meet you there at seven thirty? Please don't tell people I'm coming, though."

"Fine." She smiles and grabs her purse as she heads for the door. "See you at the nursery whenever you get there."

I wonder if I should give church another try now that my dad won't be there. Maybe God will let me go to space if I return to church and pray diligently.

Nah. One doesn't bargain with God. I'll have to find another way.

At the nursery, I help however I can. Today, that involves ringing up customers, recommending cures for unhealthy plants, and guiding people to the best choices for their individual situations. The work is second nature to me, especially with my Ph.D. in plant biology. On this day, however, nothing goes well. I can't think of the simplest words or add numbers in my head, and even operating the store's basic computer system is nearly beyond me.

One woman about my mom's age carries a few pots of herbs to the register. I try to ring her up, but I can't for the life of me remember the correct code. I have to search for it in the book beside the register, despite having put it in four times already today.

As I look it up, the woman says, "Well, hello, Mia. I'm Francie Wheeler. My husband and I go to church with your mom. I haven't seen you in a long time. How are you doing?"

"Oh, hi, Mrs. Wheeler." I try not to lose my place as I run my eyes down the codes. "I'm fine."

"It's amazing how much you look like your father. His passing was quite a loss for the community."

"Yes, ma'am." I force my mouth into a small smile when what I want to do is groan. How could I have thought it would be fun to be back in Valencia? Nobody in the entire rest of the world tells me I look like my dad. They didn't know him, and that's the point. Even though it isn't true that I look like him, such comments are frequent in Valencia.

I find the correct code and ring up the sale, but my head feels like it might explode. I'm too burned out to ring up any more customers right now, so I retreat to the greenhouse to repot plants. Finally, something I can manage. I shut down my mind and allow my hands to take over as I pull root-bound perennials out of their pots, knock off the dirt, spread out the roots, and replant them into larger pots. The act is a meditation for me. My breaths become deeper, and my nervous system relaxes.

To keep myself company, I turn on my phone to play some music. What comes up is a hip-hop album I'd used to keep from falling asleep while driving across the country. I lay the phone on the bench and turn up the volume, dancing a little as I work.

After a while, I realize that every plant I pick up is slightly tilted away from me. That's odd. The stems aren't loose in their pots. Normally, plants straighten up and quickly grow toward the sky, even if they'd been leaning when they were originally potted.

Looking around, I see that every plant in the greenhouse is leaning away from me, just a little. And then I get it. Maybe they aren't so much leaning away from *me* but from the music, which is next to me. I laugh out loud, enjoying the sound. I'm not sure when I last laughed with such abandon. At least a year, I suppose.

"All right," I tell the plants. "You don't like hip-hop. How about classical?" I find Vivaldi in my playlist, and the sound of *Four Seasons* fills the greenhouse. I continue to repot. After a while, I notice that the plants are leaning slightly toward the source of the music. I grin and continue working until my mom calls for me to finish up. The store is closing.

My professional research focuses on growing plants in space, but I know that a number of botanists have investigated the effects of music on plants. Most studies in this area are poorly designed and show conflicting results. Anecdotally, however, many people believe that certain types of music—classical, jazz, East Indian—cause plants to grow faster, whereas certain other types—rock, country, hip-hop—stunt their growth. I've ignored the entire research area, chalking it up as too far-out for my scientific brain.

Now, I don't know what to think. Even though it's weird, I sense the plants are telling me everything will be all right. In my experience, plants don't communicate with people that way, but I will definitely experiment with music on another day. Maybe this is just a quirk of the cloudy day. I turn off the music and wash my hands.

I dread what's coming next.

Mom is still in the church service when I arrive at the cemetery, so I walk to the family plot. The last time I was here was for my dad's burial. A lush growth of thyme now covers his grave. Mom's work, of course.

Ben's grave is beside my dad's, which is why I hate to visit the cemetery. It still seems wrong that he's under the ground while I walk the earth. His stone reads "Benjamin Thomas Gray, born March 28, 1973, died July 7, 1987." Far too short of a life for such a lively, inquisitive soul.

The last time I saw Ben alive was on the final day of a long family weekend at a rented house in Daytona Beach. Our parents had allowed Ben and me to stay up late the previous night to look at the stars with our dad through his telescope, while Ava watched a movie with Mom. Ben dreamed of becoming an astronaut, and I planned to be a doctor. We both loved spending time with Dad. He was nice back then, a good father and husband. That night, he'd shown us the mountains of the moon, Mars, and the constellations.

It was a magical evening.

The next morning, Ben and I got up before the rest of the family. Some older teenagers were teaching him to surf, and the best waves were in the early morning. I wanted to collect seashells before we packed up for the trip home. We tiptoed out of the house together, and I went one way down the beach while he went the other.

I filled my pillowcase with shells then headed back toward the house. Halfway up the beach, I heard people yelling. Someone was lying on the sand. An emergency vehicle was beside the person, its lights flashing and siren blaring.

I began running when I recognized my family bending over the inert form. *Ben!*

He'd fallen off his board and hit his head. Most surfers did that and lived to tell the tale, but Ben had been knocked out. Nobody noticed until the other surfers saw the board bobbing around with Ben's ankle still attached to the leash. They rushed to help, but it was too late. Ben had drowned in full sight of a dozen surfers, a lifeguard, and an old couple walking the beach. Whereas I'd been far away, searching for seashells instead of watching out for my brother.

We three siblings had been taught to take care of each other, but I hadn't done it, and my brother had died. Dad never confronted me directly about my failure, but he didn't forgive me either. When I was older, I realized he was probably angrier at himself than at me. He'd been sound asleep instead of doing his duty when his only son had died.

For the first years after Ben's death, my mom stayed at the nursery most of the time, Ava retreated to her room, where she read books and wrote angry poetry, and I became obsessed with taking Ben's place as an astronaut. I left home as soon as I graduated from high school.

Thirty years later, seeing Ben's gravestone in all its solidity still feels surreal.

Mom approaches and places her hand on my shoulder. We spend an hour talking about Ben, reliving pleasant memories. How he loved to make models of starships and play chess. How he had his first girlfriend the summer he died and what he might have been like if he'd lived.

She talks about how hard it was for her after Ben died and how my dad never got over it. He blamed himself for not watching him better. She understood his guilt, so it helped her be more patient with him during his long illness.

I rarely get to talk this deeply with Mom, and we have a great connection. Still, when we leave, I'm done with this difficult subject and will not return to the cemetery soon.

Back home, I lie on my bed and think about everything that has happened in the past week. Returning home was a gut reaction to overwhelming stress, but I don't fit here anymore.

I have to pull myself together and figure out what to do with my life.

It's time to call Ramón. It's been a week since I've spoken with him, and I can't put it off any longer.

Chapter 11: The Hail Mary Pass

Early the next morning, I call my husband, and he answers on the first ring. "Mia?" He sounds wary.

"Sorry I've taken so long to respond to your texts. I... I needed time to think."

"I know. Your mom's been keeping me up to date. I'm glad you made it there safe and sound." He's sounding a little friendlier.

Mom didn't tell me she's talked with him. I gave her permission to call him while I was traveling, but she must have kept it up. I'll deal with her later.

He's clearly waiting for me to say something, but I don't know how to start. He doesn't fill the silence but merely waits. Patience is one of Ramón's best qualities and one of my worst.

"Uh, how are you?" It sounds lame even to me, but it's the best I can do.

He grunts. "How am I? I'm lonely, is how I am. My wife left me. The bed is too big, the house is too big, and I can't stand the silence." He changes his tone to one of singsong politeness. "And how are you?"

I deserve that, I suppose, after opening up the subject in such a wimpy way. How am I, anyway? "Still angry, for one thing. But I'm willing to listen to your side of the story. Why did you do it?"

He inhales sharply. "You could have asked me that instead of running away."

"I'm asking you now. Why?"

"Because I couldn't lie. Not even for you. You aren't the person you used to be, and they needed to know that." He pauses. When he continues, his voice is husky. "I had to do it, for your sake as well as the overall mission. If you'd caused someone's death, I couldn't have lived with myself. Can you understand that?"

I consider his words. On the surface, they sound reasonable, but they aren't good enough. Even if Jeb had assigned me to another mission, it wouldn't have launched for years, so there would have been plenty of time for me to heal. "Maybe you were right to do what you did, and maybe you weren't. We could debate that all day and probably get nowhere. But I know that if you'd talked to me about what you told them before I found out from Jeb, it might have been different. I'd have been mad, sure, but nothing like I am now. You were chickenshit for not telling me, you know?"

After a long pause, he says, "I'm sorry. I should have told you."

We breathe in silence for a while. Finally, he asks, "Will you come home now? I've apologized. That was what you wanted, right?"

It's tempting. I know I overreacted by leaving like I did. But no, I'm not ready to go back to Houston and face the ruin of my old life. Something different needs to happen. If nothing else, I want to prove to him and Jeb—and myself too—that I'm still a capable human being, a capable astronaut.

I sigh. "It's not that simple. Broken trust takes time to heal, just like a head injury. I'm going to stay here for a while, and then I'll see." I need to give him something, though, because he did apologize. Softening my tone, I say, "I'm sorry it's not what you want, but it's the best I can do for now."

After a long, charged silence, he whispers, "Sometimes, you're impossible." His voice is quiet, but his tone is venomous.

Ah, yes, this is the man I left. The one who doesn't respect my decisions and tries to control me.

"Well, sometimes, you're not so great either."

He snorts. After a long pause, he speaks, and this time, his voice is gentler. "Can we keep talking, though?"

I'm still angry, but this feels like progress. "Okay, how about once a week? And please don't text unless there's an emergency. I'll talk with you a week from today. All right?"

"All right."

I hang up and take a deep breath as I twirl my wedding ring. I'd set some boundaries and stood my ground. It's a start.

I'm in a good mood, so I answer the house phone without even checking the caller ID the next time it rings. "Hello?"

"Mia?" I hear a squeal. "Hey, it's Darla. I can't believe I finally got you."

At last, somebody easy. No matter how much time passes between our conversations, it always feels like no time at all. "Hey, Darla. Thanks for calling. Things have been crazy since I got home. How are you?"

We settle in for a lengthy catch-up. After being best friends in high school, she and I had remained close through college, although we'd gone to different universities. After college, though, we went our separate ways. Now, sadly, our main communication is through Christmas cards. Having a lengthy phone conversation with my friend is a special treat, especially after my tough morning.

She starts. "You remember Ed and I got divorced four years ago. Both girls are out on their own now and doing fine. I'm still teaching biology at Edgewater High. That's not new. What's new is that I finally get to make my own decisions about life." She pauses. "That's the short version. I'll fill in the details when I see you. What about you?"

Most of my friends in Houston are other astronauts, but they're Ramón's friends too. My mind flits to Alice, who came to visit after she got back from the ISS and stayed all of twenty minutes before she had to go. I'd thought she was a good friend, but she talks more to Ramón now than to me. Darla is just mine.

My shoulders relax, and a big exhalation escapes my lips. "Oh. I'm here for a visit. You knew about my accident, right?"

"Of course. The entire world knows about your accident. Didn't you get my cards?"

"Yeah. But I was kind of out of it for several months. Sorry I didn't write back. Anyway, a lot has happened since then. I'll be happy to tell you about it but not on the phone. How about lunch one day?"

"Sure. Will Saturday work? I could come up there, if you want."

"That's great. See you then."

I eat breakfast, do an easy yoga routine, and check the NASA news. My grounding isn't public knowledge yet. It's time to do something about that. Enough shirking.

I phone William Mayes, the lawyer who handled my disability claim.

"Mia. Nice to hear from you. What's up?"

I tell him about being grounded even though my health is improving. "Can they do that? Legally?"

The line is quiet for a moment. "I hate to say this, but I believe they can. They're grounding you now because they think you aren't up to speed, but actually, they can choose whomever they want to go on missions, for no reason at all. I'm sorry, but I don't think you have a case." When I don't respond, he says, "If you want, I can look into it further. I might shake something else out if I work at it."

"Yeah, do that. See if you can get me into space at least once. That's all I want."

After we hang up, I stare out the window for a long while. It's only ten a.m., and so much has happened already. Ramón, Darla, William. Too many emotions for my brain to process.

I go for a walk to calm down. Walking is one thing I can do, even with a bum leg. The ground feels solid beneath my feet, and I need that solidity. Back at home, I plant the lettuce seedlings I've brought from the nursery, and I make a vow: *I will take these plants, or some like them, to space with me, or I'll die trying.*

Chapter 12: Meet the One, the Only, Carleton Friend

When Darla and I meet outside the restaurant, I hug my friend like she's a lost treasure, and she hugs me back the same way. I've taken pains with my appearance today. I got a haircut yesterday, and my hair falls softly around my face. Amber eye shadow sets off my brown eyes. Skinny jeans hug my slender frame, and three-inch sandals give me some height.

Darla looks like she went to just as much trouble. She's put on some weight, but she's tall and can handle it. Her long, blondish hair is pulled back with a barrette, and bangs nearly cover her deep-blue eyes.

"Damn, girl, you look good," she says, smiling at me.

"You too. Who'd have thought we'd age so well?"

We laugh and walk, arm in arm, into the Valencia Inn. It's still the fanciest place in town, and I love the rooms filled with books and plants. It's like being in a library that also serves delicious food. We're seated in an upstairs room that overlooks the quaint, New England–style town, unusual for Florida. No one seems to recognize me, for which I'm grateful.

After we order our food, Darla shoots me a serious look. "How are you, really?"

At last, someone I can be honest with. "I got grounded, Dar. My boss says I'm not medically fit to go to space." I can hardly stand to say the words out loud.

She reaches over and grabs my hand. "That's awful. I know how much being an astronaut means to you."

"Thanks. I agree with you, but I'm still grounded. My lawyer is looking into whether I can appeal the decision. Anyway, I'm going to get well. I'm a lot better already."

I explain about my various therapies: psychotherapy, physical therapy, occupational therapy. It's wonderful to talk with Darla and to see the caring expression on her face. I mentally chide myself for not making time for reunions during all these years.

When our food comes, Darla takes a few bites then sets down her chicken sandwich. Her expression is serious. "Do you believe in coincidences?"

I shrug. "I guess so, but I have no idea what you're talking about. Enlighten me, please."

"Sure thing. You will not believe this, and I can't get over the timing, but I've met someone who might help you."

"Help me what? Get back to space?" I laugh. "You aren't in touch with my boss, are you?"

She shakes her head. "Nothing like that. But I'm involved with a group that has hopes of going into space. You might want to talk to the leader, Carleton Friend, about it."

"What do you mean, going to space?" There are legitimate businesses with plans to go to space, but I'd recognize the name Carleton Friend if I'd ever heard it. I haven't. Oh God, she must have gotten mixed up with someone from the lunatic fringe, of which there are many. I arrange my face to show polite interest instead of disdain.

"It's a long story," Darla says, her eyes lighting up. "I can tell you a little, but you'll need to talk to Carleton for the details." She takes a sip of her unsweetened tea, makes a face, and adds a packet of sweetener. "Carleton's a psychic based in Orlando. He believes it's possible to contact intelligent life on other planets in different ways than what's being done by other organizations."

I try not to wince. At least one person buttonholes me every time I give a talk and tells me about some friend who has a brilliant idea for how to contact extraterrestrials. I nod as politely as I can manage.

"His project involves gathering a group of people who can focus their minds on a single thought and project it through the universe. If there's a response, the world as we know it will never be the same."

Darla drones on and on until I finally interrupt. "Uh, you're a biology teacher. You've got a scientific mind. How could you possibly believe such... outlandish ideas?"

She nods, grinning. "I thought that way, too, until I heard Carleton talk. I'm still surprised I've become a believer, but I have. And that's not all. He's convinced that the group's ability to focus will be more effective if it takes place in space. Believe it or not, he's got financial backing to take a group into space to try it out."

I rest my chin in my hand. "You can't be serious."

Darla grins. "I'm totally serious. This could be your ticket to space."

"I read the NASA news every day, and it's never mentioned such a group." This is one of the most crackpot schemes I've ever heard. I summon the server to ask for another glass of lemonade. I may be here a while, and I need fortification.

She's not deterred by my disbelief and continues her recital of Carleton's attributes. The way her face lights up when she says his name reveals she has a crush on him. Idly, I wonder if they're lovers. After another half hour, I glance at my watch. "I've got to go. My mom's expecting me at the nursery." This is only partially true. Mom won't mind if I hang out with Darla all afternoon, but enough is enough.

She sniffs. "You don't believe me," she says, lowering her eyes to the few french fries left on her plate.

"I'm sorry, but I really don't." I try not to sound like I think she's an idiot, but it's hard. "If this scheme had any credibility at all, I'd have heard about it."

"I won't argue with you. Just know that it's funded with private money. NASA doesn't know everything that's going on in the world." When I don't respond, she asks, "Would you at least meet him? I told him we're friends. You won't have to join his group or anything, just spend half an hour with him. If you don't like him, I won't mention it again." She reaches for my hand and squeezes it.

I gulp my lemonade and consider how to respond. Until my lawyer tells me I can go back to Houston and have a second conversation with Jeb, I'm stuck here, and I could use a friend while I'm in town. If Darla really will drop the subject after I meet this Carleton, I have nothing to lose. Unless reporters find out about the meeting. That would be bad.

"All right. I'll meet him. Once. For only half an hour. How about at your house? It'll give me a chance to see where you live. If he doesn't leave when the time's up, I will." I pause. "After that, we won't mention him again. Deal?"

She bites into her last french fry and nods. "Deal."

A few days later, I drive down to Orlando to see Darla's house. That's how I think of the trip, instead of to meet Carleton Friend. I picture him wearing striped slacks and a plaid jacket, with dyed black hair slicked back like Elvis's. How could Darla have gotten involved with someone like that? His part of my visit will last a half hour, and then I can relax with Darla.

Her house is in a pretty neighborhood close to the center of town. *Nice.* She has a swimming pool and a lovely yard filled with blooming plants. I feel a twinge of envy. Darla's house is nowhere nearly as large or as nice as mine in Houston, but if things continue the way they're headed, I might never return to that house.

I take a deep breath and ring the bell. Darla answers immediately. "Welcome, welcome." She shows me around the house, which is decorated in a beach motif.

"I love it." It's very pleasant, just like Darla. I set down my purse and bathing suit and hand her the bottle of wine I brought as a hostess gift.

"Oh, thanks. Let's eat, why don't we? Carleton will be here in a little while. I didn't invite him for lunch, so let's get on with it."

As we feast on shrimp salad, we catch up on the details of each other's lives. She shows me photos of her daughters, whom I haven't seen in years. I remember when these girls were born, and now they're grown. How could that be?

The doorbell rings just as we finish going through the photo album. Darla blushes. "He's right on time." She hurries off to answer the door and reappears with a tall man who is probably forty-five to fiftyish. He's strikingly handsome, with mocha-colored skin, nicely styled black hair, and eyes so dark they appear to be deep and limitless. I understand now why Darla is so smitten. He must have women falling all over him.

As he shakes my hand, he says in a deep, resonant voice, "I'm happy to meet you. Darla's told me so much about you."

At his touch, warmth moves from my hand up my arm and into my shoulder. I rub my hand after he lets go, and it gradually returns to normal.

We move into Darla's living room. She and I sit on the couch, with Carleton in a chair facing us. I glance at my watch. One thirty. I'll give him the agreed-upon half hour, and then one of us will be out of here. This man is entirely too good-looking to be for real.

Chapter 13: And... Things Start to Get Weird

When we're settled, Darla says, "Thanks for coming, Carleton. I'm glad you could get away."

"What kind of work do you do?" I ask, to break the ice.

"I'm a business consultant, helping groups work together. I'll be leaving for a job in Toronto later this afternoon." He shrugs. "It pays the bills so I can do my genuine work, for which I don't take money."

"And what is that?" I try to keep the edge out of my voice, but I don't succeed.

He leans forward and stares at me deeply. "I'm a psychic researcher. My passion is opening people's minds to the deep connections between consciousnesses."

"Oh. That's nice." With an effort of will, I stop myself from glancing at my watch.

He smiles. "I understand you're a plant biologist, so this type of research is probably foreign to you. But I'm sure you know that plants are partial to Vivaldi."

Instantly, an electric charge runs from the top of my head to my toes. *Vivaldi!* He can't possibly know what I experienced with my plants just a few days ago, because I haven't mentioned it to anyone except Karin. Is he quoting some research I'm not familiar with, or has he somehow gotten into my mind? He's smiling at me with soft eyes, just like Ramón does. The two men don't look alike, but they exhibit the same warm expression. I look out the window at a waving palm tree as I try to get myself under control. After what seems like an hour but is probably only a few seconds, I say, in a strangled voice, "Uh, yeah. I've noticed that."

They're both staring at me. I need to say something. "Uh, how did you two meet?" I don't mean to sound like I think they're lovers—which I do, actually—but people love to talk about themselves, and that's fine with me. I need a few moments to resettle myself.

Darla laughs. "I accidentally went to one of his lectures at the community college. I thought I was in a class on climate change. When Carleton started talking, I realized my mistake, but I was so fascinated by his research that I stayed. And then I started attending his classes." She throws him a fond smile. "I feel like a different person since I've been part of his group."

"Huh. Fascinating." This time, I look at my watch. Twenty minutes to go.

"Well, you aren't here to chitchat," Carleton says, nodding toward me. "I want to tell you about our research into connecting with consciousnesses from other worlds."

"Okay." I draw out the word, unable to hide my skepticism. I usually pigeonhole people into categories such as *weird, interesting,* or *off-the-wall.* This guy is all of the above.

He takes a deep breath. "Let me start by saying I discovered my gift early, before I was ten. My father was Navajo, but he died shortly after I was born. I might have gotten my gift from him, but I don't know. Anyway, I can... hook into another person's consciousness and sense what's going on with them. When I was in grad school, I worked with police around the country to find missing persons. I found dozens of them and a few murderers. Eventually, I began noticing sounds that I wasn't sure were made by humans. 'Space noise,' some people call the sounds."

He takes a bite of one of the cookies Darla has set out. I heard about space noise during my astronaut training, so this is finally getting interesting.

He chews and swallows. "Anyway, I believe these sounds are being made by other consciousnesses, somewhere in the universe. Over the past ten years, the SETI Institute and others have documented radio waves sent from millions of light years away. Fast radio bursts, or FRBs, they're called." He gives me a questioning look.

I've heard of the FRBs but know little about them other than that teams of researchers around the world are working to decipher them. The SETI (Search for Extraterrestrial Intelligence) Institute is a credible source for him to mention. This guy is not the mental slouch I'd expected.

"Okay, then. I've been invited to host an experiment to see if human thought waves can connect with whatever is sending these FRBs. Because of the tachyon net, it's possible we can communicate with whoever is sending these radio waves—assuming they're the product of sentient beings and not space noise. Us and them, sharing our thoughts in faster-than-light communication." A small smile turns up the corners of his mouth.

I've heard about tachyons—particles that always move faster than light—but as far as I know, they aren't real, or at least, not yet proven to exist. "Uh, so you're thinking that whoever is sending these signals is already linked to us through some kind of invisible net, and we're all part of the same system?"

"Exactly." He slaps his knee and smiles at me like I'm his star student. "So far, unfortunately, I haven't been able to telepathically connect with the beings. My single consciousness isn't powerful enough. Also, I think the Earth's atmosphere bends the thought waves enough to keep them from getting through as expected."

This is far beyond my pay grade. My head aches.

"That's where the experiment begins," he continues. "The company sponsoring the research will build a spacecraft to take a group of people about sixty miles above the Earth, where the atmosphere is thin and won't bend the thought waves much. Then we'll focus our attention on the galaxies from which the FRBs have been received and see if we can communicate with the senders. Ultimately, it's a simple experiment." He takes a deep breath and leans back in his chair. "What do you think?"

"Hold on. Who are you working with on this... unusual experiment? It isn't NASA, because I would have heard of it."

"No. It isn't NASA." He glances away and then back. "The company has asked for confidentiality. The project is still in the planning stages, and there are lots of steps before an actual spacecraft with astronauts can launch."

"Is it Space Tours, Inc.?" This is the strongest possibility, since the company embraces projects that are off the beaten path.

"I'm sorry, but I can't tell you yea or nay. The world will know before we launch but not yet." He glances at his watch. "I need to leave for the airport now." He rubs his hands on his pants legs and stands up. "I'm happy to see you, Darla. And, Mia, it was a delight to meet you. I'm starting a series of four classes at the community college on Monday evenings. I'll be happy to answer your questions then, if you'd like to join us."

He hugs Darla, shakes my hand again, and walks out the door. This time, I feel no particular warmth from his handshake, but something changes, deep within me, when we touch. The only way I can describe it is that a door of some sort cracks open inside my brain. I sit down, thoroughly disconcerted, and notice that my headache is gone.

"His work is pretty strange," says Darla, laughing. "It blew me away the first time I heard him speak. I'll leave you alone for a few minutes while I wash the dishes and pour myself a glass of wine. Want one?"

I nod and sit back on the couch, trying to process Carleton's words. On the surface, his theories sound semireasonable. Underneath, however, they're probably loony. People can't communicate with aliens thousands of light years away, at least, not without using radio waves that would take thousands of years to get through. Possibly, aliens have some technology that Earth scientists haven't yet discovered, but there's no way to test that.

Going into space to send *thoughts* to potential aliens sounds extremely expensive. I can't imagine who would pay for such crazy research. If anybody does, it must be someone with enough money that they're willing to shell out big bucks for the possibility of a return so large it would change the Earth's civilization forever. There are probably people like that in the world.

On the other hand, Carleton couldn't have known I'd played Vivaldi for my plants and that they'd seemed to like it. If he was just making a general observation, why did he say it when he did, and why did he look at me as though we were sharing a secret?

The whole thing is entirely too bizarre.

Darla returns with a bottle of chardonnay and two glasses. "Well, what do you think?" she asks, a twinkle in her eyes.

I pour myself a large serving and take a sip before answering. "The whole thing seems right out of science fiction. Have you researched him and his theories?"

"Of course. He's worked with several police departments. I'm not as sure about his space theories. I haven't been able to find out anything specifically about them. To be honest, I think he's a creative genius. He's able to pull together pieces of information that nobody else would think about and combine them in ways that seem crazy but just... might... work."

"Okay. What are his classes like?"

"Oh, not at all like the lecture he gave you. He teaches us to focus our minds and communicate better with other people. He's looking for students who might be appropriate for the extraterrestrial research, and you seem perfect. Carleton must have thought so, too, or he wouldn't have invited you to join us."

"Us? You've bought into that whole thing? You know, going into space isn't something you do on a Sunday afternoon, like going to Walt Disney World. You have to train for it a long time. And it's dangerous. The rocket could explode, and you'd be dead. Like *Apollo 1*, when the astronauts died in a flash fire during a launchpad test. Or the *Challenger*, in 1986, which I'm sure you saw. It's dangerous."

Darla sighs. "Yeah, I know. There are many negative thoughts like 'What if it doesn't work? What if it blows up?' But what if it works? Just think about that."

She has a point. Maybe I'm being too skeptical. "All right. I'll think about it. Now can we go for a swim? I've done as much heavy thinking as I can handle today."

Back at my mom's house, I punch in Jeb's phone number. I need to do this before I lose my nerve. After a long wait, he comes on the line.

"Hi, Mia. To what do I owe this call? You want to come back as a plant scientist?" He sounds friendly, but there's a wariness in his voice.

"Uh, no. I'm wondering what you know about a private company that's experimenting with putting a psychic in space to communicate with FRBs. I talked with someone today who said it was a done deal. He wouldn't identify the company, though."

After a pause, Jeb laughs. "What have you been smoking? I've never heard of anything like that. It's certainly not NASA. Do you believe it?"

"I don't know." I sigh. "It's pretty far-fetched, but he sounded like it'll be funded after some initial tests."

"There are lots of crazy people in this world, and at least half of them have some half-baked idea for getting to space." He grunts. "Is that it? I've got a meeting in one minute."

"Uh, no." I take a deep breath. "I wondered if you'd consider doing another evaluation on me in, say, three or four months, like you originally promised. I'm getting so much better—you'll be amazed."

"Jeez, Mia. You know I won't change my mind about that. I've got to go. Take care of yourself." The line goes dead.

I sit on the porch and stare at my phone for a long moment. I did a foolish thing, being so vulnerable with Jeb. Truly, I invited his response. Everyone knows he doesn't change course that easily. I'll have to show him I'm better, not tell him. Or else sue him and convince him that way.

My shoulders slump as I mentally replay my mistake. *Damn that Ashley*.

Chapter 14: There Might Be a Pony in There Somewhere

I'm floating outside the ISS in my space suit, a pistol-grip tool in my hand as I work to tighten some loose bolts. It's an awkward job, but I'm halfway through when another person in a space suit approaches me on my left. I realize, to my horror, that it isn't the Chinese astronaut who accompanied me outside an hour ago. The strange astronaut comes up beside me, and I turn to face him or her.

I think it's a man, but I'm not sure why, since everyone looks alike in the EMUs. This one has his gold visor open, but all I can see are his eyes. They're dark, like limitless space, and I could fall into them and never emerge. I grab the truss and hold on for dear life, even though I'm tethered in.

My mouth opens to speak, but no words emerge. The astronaut stares at me with an unreadable expression. Maybe anger. Or sadness. Whatever it is, I can hardly breathe. I don't know why I'm so afraid of this person, but being in his or her presence terrifies me. A scream emerges from deep inside, but...

I gasp and sit up, sweat pouring down my chest onto my stomach. The nightmare, again. Fortunately, I didn't scream. At least, I don't think I did. My arms are wrapped around a pillow so tightly, though, that my biceps ache from the strain. I drop the pillow and turn on the bedside light, placing my feet on the floor.

I stand, following Karin's instructions to allow the fear to flow down my body and drain from my feet. After a few moments, I'm able to breathe normally and think about something other than my terror.

This iteration of the dream was slightly different. Karin told me to speak to the person while I was in the dream, and I'd opened my mouth to speak, even though no words came. I've never gotten that far before.

Also, this time, I'd seen the person's eyes. They seemed vaguely familiar, but I couldn't place them. And I couldn't read the person's expression.

Ramón has brown eyes like those. Could they have been his? Maybe. But I'd had the dream many times when we were in bed together, and the person hadn't *felt* like Ramón.

And then it hits me. Carleton has dark eyes. Maybe it was him. I shudder. But if it was him, he'd appeared even before I'd met him. I have no idea what he could be trying to convey.

No. Too creepy. Couldn't be.

A glance at the clock tells me it's nearly six a.m. I might as well get up, because I'll never go back to sleep. I pull on shorts and a T-shirt, drink a little water, and head outside. This time, I decide to walk instead of run. After I warm up, I might try running for a block and see what happens. But walking is fine too.

The sun rises in a mostly clear sky as I amble toward the lake. A few small clouds cover the giant orange orb, and they turn bright yellow as the sun rises above the trees. I stand and watch, transfixed by the beauty unfolding before me. After a while, I try running, and my leg doesn't ache. I speed up, and still, I feel all right.

After a block, I return to walking. I will not blow this improvement by pushing too hard. Next time, I'll run a little farther. Today, I'm just going to enjoy being alive.

For the first time, I don't need a pain pill when I get home.

During our Skype appointment later in the afternoon, I tell Karin about the dream and my experience running. She smiles. "That's great, Mia. You're making progress."

"And let me tell you what happened yesterday." I relate the experience with Carleton and how shaking his hand gave me a warm, fuzzy feeling. "And he mentioned that plants liked Vivaldi. Do you remember me telling you how I played Vivaldi in the greenhouse and the plants leaned toward the phone? How could he have known that?"

Karin's eyes grow round. "I don't know. It's weird, I agree. Will you go to his classes?"

"Don't know yet. What do you make of the dream?"

She waits a long time before answering, and when she speaks, her voice is soft. "I want to tell you something I've noticed about astronauts. Many of them are... changed... after the experience of going into space. You know, Edgar Mitchell started the Institute for Noetic Science after walking on the moon. And others have turned to art or writing or religion, when they weren't particularly drawn to those things before going into space."

"Well, that doesn't include me, because I didn't get there. Yet."

"I know, but the effect might arise merely from the act of preparing to go to space, allowing yourself to move into the unknown, rather than the actual time spent there. The dream might be telling you to look into yourself more deeply. Those eyes were really deep, you said? Well, maybe there's something deep you need to find out about yourself." She laughs. "I'm digging pretty deep myself here. Might be horseshit, but there might be a pony in there somewhere."

We laugh about the old joke. "Just think about what I said, will you?" says Karin. "I also find that many brain injury survivors change the way they think and the way they live after recovering. I don't know whether that includes you or not, but I think your subconscious is trying to tell you something."

"Well, if that's true, whatever it's trying to tell me scares the bejesus out of me."

"I know. But you're getting closer. I can tell."

The call from my lawyer comes in as I'm parking my car at the community college.

"Mia, hi, how are you?" William's voice booms from the speaker.

The man will talk for an hour if I let him, and he'll charge for every minute. I don't have the time or patience for that. "Good. But I'm late for a meeting. What did you find out?"

He sniffs. "Not a lot. It's the same as I told you before: NASA can choose who goes on missions. HR told me that crew members must be free of medical conditions that might impair their ability to take part in spaceflight. I'm afraid the NASA physicians have determined you have a condition that might impair you. Unfortunately, there's no appeal for that decision."

I turn off the ignition and sit back in my seat. "So that's it, then?"

"I hate to say it, but I think it's time for you to move on. There are many things you can do besides being a space explorer."

"But that's what I am. I'm a space explorer. I grow plants in low-gravity situations while I'm exploring space." My words sound curt and clipped, so I try to tone them down. "Thanks for trying, though. Email me your bill, will you? Got to go now."

I sit in my car for a few moments, trying to push away the depression that threatens to overwhelm me. As crazy as it sounds, Carleton's project is my best chance for getting into space.

Chapter 15: Learning to Breathe

I slip into the classroom just as Carleton starts speaking. The chairs have been arranged in a big circle, so I can't hide in the back row as I'd planned. Darla saved me a seat near Carleton, but I shake my head and take an empty chair on the opposite side.

About thirty people are in the circle, far more than I'd expected. Most are women—some young, some much older than me—and nearly all of them wear pretty sundresses and makeup. That's odd. Most women in Florida wear T-shirts and shorts when they can, with makeup only for work and Sunday school. Every woman's gaze is fixed on Carleton. Then I get it. He's a sexy man, for sure. Too slick for my taste, but apparently, these women have high hopes. *Interesting.*

"Welcome, everyone." Carleton looks around the circle, holding eye contact with each person for a few seconds before smiling, nodding, and moving on. When he's finished, he continues. "I know most of you, but there are a few new people. I'll have you introduce yourselves in a minute. First, I want to explain the purpose of this class."

He glances down at his lap and takes a breath then looks up and speaks. "Because I teach other classes here, the college allows me to use this room. But this is not a sanctioned class of the community college. You won't get a grade, and I won't check attendance. Our goal this semester is to increase our ability to hold a focus for progressively longer periods of time. In four classes, I'll teach you exercises to help you do that. In late November, I'll choose six people to join me in a simulated space voyage that will take place during December. I'll tell you more about that as we go along. Let's get started, shall we?"

He asks people to introduce themselves, telling just their names. "We don't care what you do for a living, how many degrees you have, or anything else about what you do. Instead, we care about who you are on the inside. You can share more about the other part as we go along."

When it's my turn, I say my name, and nobody reacts. I'm used to introducing myself as "Mia Gray, astronaut," and having people be impressed. Without the last part, I'm ordinary. According to my lawyer and my boss, I must get used to that.

Thomas, the middle-aged man next to me, looks like a pleasant person. I nod at him and smile.

After the introductions, Carleton says, "Next, I'll go around the room and lay my hands on each person's head for a few seconds. I've found that it helps people clear out the extraneous thoughts and allows them to concentrate more fully. I'll ask each of you for permission before I place my hands on you. If this doesn't feel like the right thing for you to do tonight, please say no. I never force anyone to do anything."

I watch as he goes around the circle and asks each person if he can touch them. They all agree. Carleton closes his eyes and gently places his hands on the person's head. After a few seconds, he shakes out his hands and moves on. Everyone looks calmer afterward.

I don't know whether or not to do it. This entire scene is far too New Agey for my tastes. But when it's my turn, I say yes. There's nothing to lose, after all.

His hands come down gently on the top of my head. At first, nothing happens. Then a peacefulness overtakes me, as though I'm walking beside a mountain stream on a warm morning. I can almost hear the tinkle of the water as it splashes over rocks. Can almost feel the warmth of the sun and almost sense a deer watching me in the field across the stream.

I don't notice when Carleton removes his hands. Eventually, I open my eyes and see that he's nearly completed laying hands on everyone in the circle.

Well. There are no more thoughts swirling in my head. No thought loops. No depression. Virtually no identity. Just clear, open space.

Back at his seat, Carleton waits for a few moments before speaking. "Today, we're going to concentrate on breathing. Some of you know the exercises I'm going to teach you. If you do, feel free to go into them and ignore my words."

He teaches us several ways to focus on our breath: counting to four on the in-breath and the out-breath, saying the words "peace" and "love" with each inhalation and exhalation, and feeling the breath travel throughout the body so it can heal stuck or painful places.

Part of astronaut training included breath techniques, but these are different. For a while, I'm able to focus on my breath without getting lost in thoughts, and it feels wonderful. Eventually, I think, *What time is it?* and *I'm tired of sitting* and *I need to pee.* I try to push the thoughts away, but my awareness gradually returns to the hard chair.

I hear voices in the hall, which means that students from other classes are leaving. I glance at my watch, and two hours have passed. *Seriously?* That doesn't seem possible. Looking around the room, I see other people opening their eyes and checking their watches or phones. I sit still and enjoy the feeling of peace that remains with me.

Eventually, Carleton says, "That's it for tonight. Please practice the techniques this week. Next week, we'll move on." He looks around the room. I feel an electrical charge in the group, and people seem to be waiting for something. Carleton hesitates then says, "Emily, do you have a few minutes?"

Emily, who's probably in her late twenties and dressed as if for a party, blushes and nods. She gathers her things and walks out the door with Carleton.

Several other women, including Darla, glance at one another and raise their eyebrows. I think I know what might be happening, and it has to do with sex. But I don't dare ask Darla about it until I have more evidence. I might offend her.

Darla comes over, smiling. "Well, what did you think?"

"I, uh, I have no thoughts." Shaking my head, I rub my face and roll my shoulders as I slowly come back to myself. "We talked about going out for a beer, but I think I'll head home. Call you tomorrow?"

She nods. "That's fine. It hit me hard the first time too. Drive carefully."

I sit in my car for a long time, trying to figure out what just happened. I feel different in a way I can't define. More open or connected, maybe. The door that cracked open when I met Carleton has opened a little wider, and it's now wide enough to walk through. I'm afraid of what I'll find if I do that.

Back at the house, I sit in my bedroom and focus on my breathing again. Time passes. Suddenly, I remember something. The memory comes as a vision, playing out in front of my closed eyes and open mind.

The alarm clock goes off, and I lie in bed for a few moments to get oriented. I'm tired from not getting enough sleep but eager to start the day. I dress in my flight suit for the talk I'm going to give at the high school. Ramón has already left for work, so I pour myself a bowl of cereal and read the news on my tablet.

Holy shit, that's the morning of the accident! After trying for a year, I have finally remembered something from that day. But what I remember is the mundane part, not what's important. Not anything about the accident. I relax and try to go back into the scene. What happened after that?

I try, but nothing comes. Or, rather, my mind can fill in the gaps based on other days, but I can't remember anything specific to *that* day.

Still, some memory has returned! I want to call someone. Karin, maybe. No, it's too late to call her. The same for Darla. Ramón? If things were normal between us, I'd call him for sure. But not now. And my mom is sound asleep.

There's no one to tell right now, so I pull out my journal and write it all down.

Chapter 16: Is This a Cult?

In the morning, I try to remember more about the day of the accident, but nothing comes. Disappointed, I head out for my usual walk-slash-run to the lake. Afterward, I sit on my favorite bench and try to make sense of last night's experiences.

To be sure, something wonderful happened—my mind stopped its chatter for a couple of hours, I concentrated like never before, and I was calm and peaceful. Recovering even a minor memory from the day of the accident was fantastic progress. But what caused it? Carleton's laying on of hands, maybe, or the meditation.

The longer I analyze what happened, the more I doubt my experience. After a while, what had felt wonderful begins to seem sinister. I hope I'm not being entrapped into joining a cult.

I need to talk to someone. Definitely not my mom, who'd think the devil had possessed me. I call Darla and leave a message, asking her to call during her lunch break.

She calls back at noon. As soon as I hear her voice, I ask, "Is this a cult?"

She laughs. "And hello to you too." After a moment, she says, "You can't be serious."

"I looked it up on the web, and there are a bunch of definitions. They all talk about veneration of a particular figure. That could definitely be Carleton. And then there's a system of beliefs that other people think are suspicious or dangerous. My mom would probably think everything he said last night was dangerous. But I don't know. What do you think?"

"It's not a cult." Darla speaks slowly and thoughtfully. "There's nothing negative or suspicious about what Carleton teaches. It's not traditional Christianity, that's true—more like a way to reach a higher plane, or to relax deeply. That's all."

"But—"

"Let me finish. Carleton is a powerful person. There's no doubt about that. He's like a shaman, I think. A medicine man, or healer. People do flock to be around him. But if it doesn't feel right to you, don't come back again. I'm sure he'd tell you that too. There's no pressure."

After a moment, I release my held breath. "Okay, thanks. The experience was pretty strong the first time, like you said." I laugh, self-consciously. "Thanks for calling back. See you next week."

With that settled, I turn to other things. I hate to admit it, but I miss doing research. I decide to conduct some experiments at the nursery. For the first one, I'll plant zinnia seeds in the simulated Martian regolith. Astronauts traveling to Mars will need beauty almost as much as they'll need leafy green vegetables during those long months. And flowers grow quickly, so measurement will be easy. I'm excited to undertake something my preaccident self would do.

I'll have two experimental conditions. For condition A, I'll place planters containing zinnia seeds in one greenhouse, where I'll play classical music for an hour a day. Condition B will be in another greenhouse, with the same conditions, except without music.

I've just finished planting the seeds when my phone rings. *Ramón.* Seeing his name pop up on my screen gives me a jolt of dread and anger, as well as curiosity. I brace for whatever the encounter will bring.

"Hi," I say. Previously, I'd have greeted him with something like "Hi, sexy" or "Hi, babe," but neither of those is appropriate now.

"Good time to talk?"

"Sure." I tell him about my experiment, and he listens closely.

When I'm finished, he says, "You would never have undertaken something so offbeat before. What's up?"

"I met this... shaman, I guess I would call him, the other day." I tell him about Carleton. It actually feels good to talk to Ramón. He used to be my best friend. Darla, as good as she is, doesn't know the full me. And my other friends seem to have disappeared.

"I've never heard of this guy," says Ramón. "I wonder if he's putting you on. Sounds like he's trying to get in your pants."

I don't feel the slightest pull toward him in that way and get no vibes he's interested in me, but I might be the only woman from the class who doesn't. "Nah. I don't think so."

There's a long pause. I take a breath. "So what's up with you?"

"Jeb offered me the command of Kairos."

My heart sinks. The Kairos mission, scheduled in four years, will involve doing flybys of the moon and then traveling into deep space for two months before returning to Earth. I desperately want to be on it.

"Congratulations." I try to keep from sounding as desolate as I feel.

He sighs. "I know. Ironic. Me and not you. I haven't given him my answer yet."

I try again to sound excited. "You'll go. Of course you'll go. It's the chance of a lifetime."

"I'm not leaning toward doing it." His voice sounds heavy, sad. "I don't feel right taking it when you wanted it so much. But that's not the only reason. I'm tired of training all the time. I want a normal life."

I wonder what that is. Being an astronaut is normal if you're a space explorer. "Huh. Your choice. But I think you should do it."

"Noted." Silence. Then, "When are you coming home?"

This is the big question, and it's in the back of my mind almost every waking moment. "I don't know that I am," I say slowly. "I may need to do something entirely different. Houston may not be the right place for me anymore." If I can't get my old life back, I don't think I can stand being in Houston, even if Ramón stops being so controlling. But I hadn't planned on saying anything to him just yet.

"Could you include me in this decision? I'm hanging out in the cold here."

My head pounds like somebody is banging it with a shovel. "Look, I can't talk about this now. I've got to go. Have a good week." I hang up, not waiting for any logical arguments against my fragile feelings or plans.

The blackness that has hovered above me for the past year descends abruptly. I'm not the first astronaut to be grounded for health reasons and not even the first woman to never get to space. The Mercury 13 women in the early 1960s were trained and qualified but weren't allowed to fly. That must have been even more depressing than my situation.

I've reached the limit of being strong. Logically, I know I need to buck up and get my emotions under control. But first, I need to grieve my loss. Really grieve it, without telling myself to buck up before I'm ready.

I leave my mom a note saying I won't be home tonight and drive to an isolated motel, where I rent a room for the night. When I open the door, the musty smell and cheap decor remind me of the room where I spent one of the blackest nights of my life on the trip from Houston. But anywhere that I'm safe and alone will suffice, because I need to cry until I can't cry anymore, with no one telling me what I ought to do or how I ought to feel.

After my breakdown at the motel, the week passes without drama. At a family gathering, I actually enjoy being with Ava, who has been friendlier since I've been working at the nursery. I exercise every day, pleased that my stamina is slowly returning. And I paint and redecorate my bedroom, finally dealing with the last of Ben's possessions. There are several sketchbooks in which he'd drawn pictures of rockets. Seeing them gives my heart a pang. I'll keep those. And some old science fiction novels about space travel, which I'll reread before donating. Finally, I throw away the *Star Trek* posters I'd appropriated after his death.

I try not to make the room too "girly" in case Ben is watching from wherever he went after he died. I paint the walls a bright yellow, hang navy-blue curtains, and buy cheerful red cushions. I feel better after exorcising the old and bringing in the new.

When that's finished, I enjoy meditating in my cheerful bedroom. My ability to calm my mind improves daily, although no new memories surface. I'm not sure what to make of Carleton, but his meditations seem to help. I'm thinking more clearly and not running as many thought loops as before the class. In addition, I've stopped whining so much about my lot in life. But no matter how many times I chastise myself for not being satisfied with these wonderful gifts, I can't force myself to give up my dream of seeing the sunrise from space at least once.

In our next therapy session, Karin congratulates me on my progress and asks to take the session in a different direction. "I'm wondering what led you to become an astronaut."

"Ah, you know that. Don't you want to help me recover more memories?" I'm dying to know what really happened the day of the accident. After all, Karin was assigned to me for that purpose, so it shouldn't be a big deal.

"Humor me, please. When was the first time you thought about being an astronaut?"

Sighing, I relent. "After Ben died, I guess. He'd planned on applying when he got old enough. We were all so sad after his death that I decided to honor him by taking his place. And it was the right decision. Ben would have been a good astronaut, but I am... was... too. I don't think I could have picked a better profession for myself."

"But you didn't apply right away, did you? You got your PhD in plant biology first. Have I got that right?"

I take a long breath. "Well, I did a lot of stuff to improve my chances of being selected. I got my private pilot's license and my scuba certification while I was still in high school. And I exercised every day for a couple of hours. By the time I went to college, I was tired of pushing so hard. I stopped flying and diving, and I discovered I liked biology better than astronomy and physics." I hesitate. "After I got my master's degree, my dad pulled me aside and demanded that I follow through with being an astronaut. He said Ben was disappointed in me, and so was he. So I took a job in the lab at NASA and got my PhD while working there. When I was thirty-six, they opened a new astronaut class, and I applied. Frankly, I couldn't believe that they accepted me."

"Ramón encouraged you to apply, right?"

"Well, yeah. We were dating when the call for applicants came out. With his support, I applied. You know the rest." I grin. Maybe now she'll help me recover my memories.

Karin nods. "Now that you're older, do you really think Ben would have been disappointed if you hadn't become an astronaut?"

What does that have to do with anything? I want to protest, but she's a great therapist, so I play along. "Oh gosh, I don't know. I've never thought about it."

"Give it some thought now. I'll wait."

"Well," I say, after a moment or two, "not really. He'd have understood that my being an astronaut wouldn't bring him back."

Funny that I hadn't realized that before. I've done my best to get to space, not only for him. For me too. And I almost made it. Being hit by a car wasn't my fault.

"How do you feel, at this moment?"

"Relieved, I guess. And sad. I wish Ben had lived. We could have both been astronauts, like the Kelly brothers. We weren't twins like them, but we could have had so much fun. And maybe we could have gone on a mission together. That would have been great."

"Good job, Mia. Sorry I have to leave it like this, but our time is up. Think about what we've talked about, and we'll meet next week."

Oh. *Damn.*

Chapter 17: The Inner Smile

On Monday evening, I sit between Darla and Thomas for the second class. Carleton follows the identical steps in his introduction: staring into each person's eyes for a few seconds, giving a brief talk about the purpose of the class, and then laying his hands on people's heads.

I've decided to test out whether it was the meditations or Carleton's hands that unleashed my repressed memories. When it's my turn for the hands, I shake my head, so he moves on to Thomas. I remember how peaceful I felt last week after he touched me and wonder if I've made the wrong choice, but it's too late now.

When he's finished with the others, he begins his lecture. "Tonight, we're going to talk about connection. Our ultimate goal is to contact whoever or whatever has been sending short radio bursts from far away in the cosmos. But before we do that, we need to contact our inner selves. Specifically, tonight, we're going to focus on having our internal organs smile at each other."

I roll my eyes. The weirdness just keeps on coming. I take a few breaths and decide to go along, for now.

He has us sit on the edge of our chairs with our backs straight and feet flat on the floor. He tells us to think of something pleasant that causes us to smile and then send the smiling energy from our heads to our hearts. We're to picture our hearts filled with gratitude.

It's a little strange, but I can do it. Then he has us move the smiling energy to our lungs, liver, kidneys, and finally, to our spleen.

By the end of the exercise, I'm having trouble following his directions. They're too strange for me. When we're finished, he asks us to find a word, a phrase, or a symbol that describes how we feel now and remember it.

Even though I didn't do all that well tonight, the word that comes to mind is *clean*. I feel clean on the inside, or at least cleaner. Several others use the same word, and I nod to them.

"Practice your breathing meditations and the inner smile meditation this week. Next week, we'll move on." He glances around the room. "Uh, Betty, would you mind staying after class? There are a few things I'd like to talk to you about." She's another young woman, maybe twenty years younger than he is. They walk out together.

I glance at Emily, who was chosen last week. She hunches her shoulders and hurries out, head down, before the others.

I stay in my seat while the rest of the group gathers their things and quietly leaves. Soon, only Thomas, Darla, and I remain.

"Phew," I exclaim. "That was pretty odd. How was it for you two?"

"Strong," Darla says, and Thomas agrees.

We sit quietly for a few minutes. Finally, Darla laughs. "Does anyone want to get a beer? I need to decompress."

"I'm in," I say.

"Sure," says Thomas. "That is, if you don't mind me tagging along. I know you're friends."

"You are most welcome," I tell him. A little tingle runs down my spine when I look at Thomas. He's not that good-looking—his short brown hair, blue eyes, and the dimple in his chin aren't extraordinary. But I have the impression that he's solid and dependable, and those are qualities I value. Also, I won't mind talking with a man who isn't Ramón and who doesn't remind me of anything in the past.

We end up at a local sports bar that is filled with life. It's just what I need. I'm tired of merely working and being with family. The sound level isn't overly loud, so it doesn't hurt my ears, and I feel younger than I have since the accident.

We order beers and talk about our experiences with the healing smile exercise. I have the feeling that their experiences were stronger than mine. Maybe Carleton's touch made the difference. We struggled with different organs, but we all feel better afterward. And then the talk turns more personal. I give Darla a hard look when she suggests we share what we do for a living.

Thomas is a civil engineer, designing roads and bridges for the ever-increasing roadway system in the Orlando area. I don't mention that I'm a grounded astronaut, just that I'm a plant biologist on an extended visit with my mom in Valencia.

Darla talks briefly about being a high school biology teacher. She loves her job, but her days start early. She finishes her beer quickly and prepares to leave. Before she can say goodbye, I ask her, "What's the story with Carleton and a different woman leaving with him every night?"

She sits back down. "As far as I can tell, he picks the person who did the best each week to go out for a drink with him."

I take that in. "Does he ever pick the same woman more than once?"

"Oh, yes. Often, in fact. He's picked me five or six times over the past year."

"What do you do after the meeting, if you don't mind my asking?"

Darla blushes and looks away. "Oh, it's just a drink and a talk about the session. Carleton has this special bar where he likes to go to decompress."

"Nothing else?" She isn't telling me everything. I can tell. I hate being pushy in front of Thomas, but this is the best time, when the subject is fresh.

"No. Of course not. What are you implying?"

Darla's tone is harsh, so I know I can't push any more. "Nothing. Just trying to figure out the lay of the land. Sorry to keep you."

"Okay." She shakes off her attitude and gives us both brief hugs before hurrying off.

I turn to Thomas. "Has Carleton ever picked you to go out for a drink after class?"

He smirks. "Of course not. Just the women. Why do you think they're all dressed the way they are?"

"Ugh. Do you think he's having affairs with all of them?"

He shakes his head. "I don't ask. I just get what I need from the class and go about my life."

Although probably not illegal, Carleton's behavior is definitely unethical, since he's the teacher. It turns my stomach. I'll have to consider whether I want to continue with the group because of it.

"Why did you join the class?" I ask.

He considers. "I'd just gotten out of a relationship and needed something deeper in my life. When I heard Carleton interviewed on a local radio show, I thought I'd try it. He's a little out-there, but I like him, and I feel better after his classes." He smiles and shrugs. "I try to ignore the thing with the women." After a few moments, he continues, "Here's a new subject. Are you married?"

"Separated," I say without an instant's hesitation. "For a while now. What about you?"

"Divorced for a couple of years."

We discover we have a lot in common. Neither of us has kids. We both love to run, bicycle, and read science fiction novels. We talk for another hour.

When we finally part, I give him a hug and a peck on his cheek. There is definitely something here I want to check out. And it feels great to have someone's arms around me, if only for a second.

Driving home, I feel more alive than I have in a long while. Even though I still harbor doubts about Carleton's project, I have high hopes of being selected for it. The whole thing is a very long shot in terms of getting to space, but it's all I have at the moment. I'll work on other possibilities as they arise.

And then there's Thomas. Starting fresh romantically is sounding better and better. Still, a pang of sadness cuts through me at the thought of hurting Ramón. I'm injuring him already just by being in Florida, and I don't like the idea of causing him further pain.

But... the thing with Thomas was just a hug and a peck on the cheek. Nothing big and nothing bad, nothing to feel guilty about.

It's great to feel like my regular, upbeat self again. Most of the good feeling is probably from the evening's clearing of toxic emotions. My organs—and my emotions—aren't exactly clear, but they are better, and I'm gaining the skills to heal myself even further.

Well, maybe a smidgeon of the good feeling is from having an attractive man look at me with interest.

The next morning, I take my mom to visit a commercial realtor. Becky was in my high school class, and we reconnected last week at a local restaurant-slash-bar where people gathered to watch the sunset over Valencia Lake. When Becky told me what she did for a living, I knew it was time to act. My mom has been trying to sell the business just by talking to friends, but it hasn't worked. Even though she'll pay a hefty commission, getting a realtor seems to be the only option if she really wants to sell it. I talked to her about it, and surprisingly, she agreed.

Becky's office is downtown, and I drive around the block several times before finding a parking spot. Mom and I walk to the corner, where we wait for the light. Something about the experience sends a chill through me. When the walk signal blinks and I hear the *beep-*

beep-beep coming from the box, my foot refuses to step off the curb and into the street. This happened once before, when Ramón was with me, and he'd rubbed my back and whispered soft words in my ear until I could cross the street. Now, my mom is halfway across the street when she glances over her shoulder and sees me stuck on the street corner.

She backtracks and stands beside me. "What's wrong, honey? Is it the signal?"

I nod. I'm sure my face has turned chalky white, and I'm afraid I might faint if I try again to cross. Mom looks around. "There's a bench right over there. Why don't we sit for a minute? Becky won't mind if we're a little late."

I nod, and we walk away from the corner and sit on the bench. I drop my head between my knees until I'm less dizzy. When I sit up, Mom hands me a bottle of water. After a few swallows, I feel stronger.

Jeez, just last night, I thought I had the world by the tail. And today, I can't even cross a stupid street. I try to chuckle, but nothing comes out.

We sit for a few moments as I watch the corner. The cars stop for the red light, and most of the pedestrians wait for the walk signal before venturing into the crosswalk. Even when they don't, cars stop for them.

I remind myself that Ashley wasn't a typical driver, at least, not in this small town in Florida. "We can go now," I say, giving my mom a slight smile. "Thanks for taking care of me."

She hugs me. "Oh, honey, that's what moms do, don'tcha know? I've heard that trauma responses come back when you least expect them."

I give her a sideways glance. "Since when did you become a trauma expert?"

"Since my oldest daughter became a trauma survivor. I can read, you know." She grins.

"Let's do it." I walk to the corner, wait for the walk signal, and keep my eyes moving as we cross the street without incident. Afterward, I breathe a sigh of relief. I hope that doesn't happen again.

At the realty office, Becky ushers us into the conference room and offers us water or coffee before we get down to business. "I've looked at the property and pulled some comps for you." She pushes over a few pages. The land is more valuable than the business, just as Ava had said. But with the mortgage on the land, we likely won't get paid enough to end up with anything at all after forty years of ownership. I struggle to take in the harsh reality. Mom rests her face in her hands for a moment, and I put my arm around her. When she lifts her head, her eyes are dry, though dull.

"Are you telling me I have to close my business in order to sell the land? That the business is worth nothing?"

"Pat, I'm not telling you anything. I'm just showing you what other properties similar to yours have sold for. We could sell your land for development because it's close to town. If you're interested, I can approach a couple of developers who're looking for land in your area. That might bump up the value a little."

"No." Mom's voice is steely. "I'm not ready for that. Since Mia's been here, things are a little better. I still think I can find a buyer for the business. Or maybe Mia will stay and run it. I won't sell unless the buyer intends to keep the business open."

"Mom." I try to keep my voice gentle. "You know I won't stay here. We talked about that."

"Yeah, but you've been here for three weeks already, and I don't hear you talking about going back to Houston. You have to do *something,* and it may as well be running the family business."

We stare at each other for a long moment. I clear my throat and glance at Becky. "Could you give us a few minutes please?" She nods and leaves the room, saying she'll be down the hall in her office when we're ready.

When the door closes, I speak, as gently as I can. "Mom, my life is too unsettled to take on running the business permanently, or even on an extended temporary basis. I'll be going somewhere else before long, even if I don't know yet where it will be. I've enjoyed visiting you, but staying isn't in my plans."

"Oh. I thought—"

"I know I said I might stay forever. But I know now that's not true. I promised to tell you what's going on, and I haven't done it. I haven't decided yet what my next step will be, so I didn't know what to say. Sorry."

Mom sips her water and stares out the window at the sidewalk, where groups of tourists walk by. "All right," she finally says. "You can get her."

When Becky comes back in, Mom speaks immediately. "I'm sorry if this doesn't fit your plans, but I want to sell the business as a working business. Surely, there is someone who wants to own a nursery. This is nonnegotiable."

"All right. I like a client who knows her mind. Does it have to be a nursery, or could it be something similar? Like, I don't know, a flower farm? Or a landscaping business?"

"Either would be fine. As long as I make a little from the deal, I can manage. Maybe I'll sell the house and move into a condo. It's a bit much for me to handle anyway. But I want to leave a legacy for someone. Other than my family, that business has been my life. Unfortunately, neither of my kids wants it. But I hope someone else will."

The truth is hard to hear. I pat her hand and tell her I'll stay a while longer. "I don't know for how long, but I'll do my best to help you while I'm here."

"All right."

We leave the office with a signed contract. I hope we won't be in limbo for long.

B ack at the house, I check my email and am surprised to find a brief note from Jeb. *I got this message from a contact at Space Tours, Inc. today. They're looking for a few astronauts to take paying passengers. In my mind, it would be more like a flight attendant, but their requirements aren't as stringent as NASA's, so you might qualify.* He forwarded the note from the company's executive vice president.

Ouch. I start to get angry at his words about the requirements not being stringent but realize this might be just the opportunity I need. It isn't what NASA trained me to do—not by a long shot—but at least it would allow me to go to space. *Hooray!*

The company is taking applications through the end of the year. I'll apply, of course, even if I'm not super excited by the opportunity.

Hmm. I wonder again if Space Tours, Inc. is funding Carleton's project. They have a lot of money and are leading in the race to take private passengers to space. But there are at least three other companies that could be involved. That is, if the project really exists. I don't doubt Carleton's sincerity—not much, anyway—but I'm unsure what to think about his project. It still seems completely farfetched.

On the other hand, I *really* like the exercises I'm learning in his classes. I definitely feel better after doing them, and they're having an effect. My headaches have decreased in intensity, if not in frequency, although I have high hopes that will be next. My leg is stronger, and I can now run—actually, "running" isn't the right word; it's more like a slow jog—all the way to the lake and back. Best of all, my thoughts and words come more easily. Nobody has told me recently I'm slurring my words. And I can now work all afternoon in the nursery, waiting on clients and ringing up sales, without feeling overwhelmed.

I'm definitely improving. But I won't beg Jeb to take me back, at least until my leave of absence is over. I send him a thank-you email and head to my bedroom to do my meditations.

Chapter 18: Telepathy Isn't Merely a Psychic Phenomenon

I slip into the chair between Thomas and Darla ten minutes before the third class, and we're sharing details about our weeks when Carleton walks in. The room instantly quietens as people close their eyes and presumably begin meditating. I do the same, allowing myself to relax from the long drive through rush hour traffic.

Carleton goes through the now-standard practice of staring into each person's eyes. He then begins the laying on of hands. This time, when it's my turn, I say yes. His hands settle gently onto my head, and a soft warmth spreads through my head and down my body. This experience isn't as intense as the first time, but it's quite pleasant. There is no stream, no field, and no deer—just a quiet peace.

When he's finished with everyone, he clears his throat and begins. "You're all doing extremely well with focusing your attention and clearing out the garbage in your ethereal bodies. Now we'll start working with telepathy. Telepathy is the ability to understand what other people are trying to transmit to you using only their thoughts, and the ability to transmit something in such a way that your selected recipient can receive it."

He waits until people nod. "Telepathy isn't merely a psychic phenomenon. There has been a great deal of scientific research done in this area. Both the U.S. and the Russian governments explored it for decades, with statistically significant results in many of their experiments."

He glances around the room. "There's nothing mysterious about telepathy. Brain-to-brain communication is common. For example, can you tell when someone is looking at you from behind? Can you tell who's on the phone before you pick it up or look at the readout? Can you tell when a family member needs you? These are common experiences with telepathy. Not everybody can do this without training, but I believe that anyone with an open mind can learn it."

I feel a thrill. I often know who's calling as soon as the phone rings—and sometimes even before. Ramón used to tease me about it. And my mom knew, even before Ramón called her, that something bad had happened to me. She'd left a message on my phone: "Is everything all right?"

However, if I have any ability in this area, it's not consistent. I regularly miss some things I should have known. For example, I didn't know my mom was having health problems before Ava told me. And I hadn't known that I shouldn't walk across the street that day in Houston. Even so, I'm eager to explore this new world.

Carleton continues. "No need to be nervous. I'll walk you through it. Now, allow yourself to relax in whatever way works for you."

In a few moments, he asks us to gather in groups of four, preferably with people we don't know. I find three other women about my age, and Carleton hands us sheets of paper with spaces for the transmitter's name, the receiver's name, and what message they receive. He also gives us five playing-type cards. Each card has a symbol on it, including a cross, a star, a few squiggly lines that he calls a wave, a circle, and a square.

We first decide who is to be the transmitter. That person chooses a card and stares at it with the intention of transmitting either an image or the word describing the shape to the others. When the rest of us think we've received the message, we're to either draw it or write the word on our paper.

We try it, and each person takes a turn as transmitter. When it's my turn, I choose the cross. Because I'm not religious, I transit the word "plus sign" instead of "cross."

When we've all taken a turn, we compare notes. I accurately received two messages, but only one woman accurately received my "plus sign."

Well. Obviously, I'm not as great at this experiment as I thought I'd be. I hadn't failed, exactly, but I also didn't excel. Maybe Carleton won't choose me for the simulation. I shake my head. This entire class is so weird that failing might actually be better than succeeding, especially since I now have the possibility of Space Tours, Inc.

We switch groups and try again. I'm surprised to note that sometimes I receive the message clearly, other times it's garbled, and in others it doesn't come through at all.

By the end of the session, I'm not sure how well I did. Everything went so fast that I lost track. This was probably Carleton's intention so people weren't consistently discouraged or elated about their prowess.

He tells us to pair up with someone and practice during the week. We don't necessarily have to use the shapes from the cards; instead, we can substitute whatever comes to mind. Each person should write down what we transmit and the time we send the message and then write down what we think we receive. Bring the notes to class to next week, and we'll compare them then.

At the end of class, his eyes rest on Darla, who is already smiling at him. "One more thing. Next week will be our last session before we choose the crew for the simulation in December. Darla will be my assistant in coordinating things for the project."

The congratulatory murmur that comes from some students has a distinctly male pitch. The women stare at one another with questioning glances before gathering up their things and quickly leaving the room.

Darla walks up to Carleton, and the two talk. Thomas and I share a glance. "Do you want to go out for a drink again?" he asks.

"Sure. I need one after that."

We go to the same bar, order the same beers, and watch a different baseball game. At least, I think it's a different game. They all look alike to me.

"So, what do you think?" I ask.

"About what?" He smiles, and it's a very nice smile.

"Telepathy."

"It's interesting. About as far from my job as it's possible to be. But I was thinking about you this past week. Could you sense it?"

My face gets hot. "I thought it was just me thinking of you."

Our laughter has a warm, friendly feeling.

I have to tell him before this goes any further. "I, uh, I sort of didn't tell you the whole truth about me last week."

"You're still living with your husband."

"Oh, no, that's not it. We're separated. But when I said I was a plant biologist, it wasn't a lie, but it wasn't the entire story."

"Okay. What is the entire story?"

"Well. Actually, I'm an astronaut. Was. I guess."

He looks thoughtful and then nods. "I *knew* your name was familiar. I figured you must be a newscaster or something like that." He pauses. "An astronaut. Did you go to the space station?" When I shake my head, he thinks for a moment. "Something happened to you, though, didn't it? Something bad, I think, but I can't remember what it was. Sorry."

"I got run down by an SUV when I was crossing a street in Houston. It was definitely bad." This was the big reveal. Now it's up to him, and I don't know what I want him to say. I'll have to get used to doing this, I suppose, but for now, I want to bite my fingernails as I wait for his reaction.

"Oh, God, I'm so sorry, Mia. Sorry it happened to you and sorry that I didn't put two and two together. Things are falling into place now. Uh, you grew up around here, didn't you?"

"Yeah, in Valencia. After a year of recovering from the accident, I got grounded. I'm told that I won't ever be an astronaut again." I struggle to keep my voice even as I speak those terrible words, although I can't look him in the eye. I'm embarrassed that I got fired from such a prestigious job. So I stare at the table and draw little circles in some spilled beer.

"Whoa. That's tough. Give me a minute, will you, to process it?"

I nod. It's a lot to take in, I know. I turn my attention to the TV and watch a batter strike out. The crowd goes wild, both on the television and in the room. "What just happened?" I ask, gesturing toward the TV.

"It's the Tampa Bay Rays against the Toronto Blue Jays. A big game."

"Oh. Thanks." Ramón is probably watching the game. I sit up straight as a thought comes to me. What if he's watching it at a bar like this one, with someone of the opposite sex?

No. No way. I push the thought away and watch the next batter swing and miss.

Finally, Thomas says, "Hard times hit all of us. But your hit seems particularly hard. I'm sorry. And now you're back home, trying to figure out what to do with your life."

"Yeah. You're good, you know? Most people wouldn't have put all that together so fast."

"I'm not your typical engineer. I hear that every day, but not in such a positive way. Thank you."

We watch the game for a while longer, until Thomas says, "I don't hold your half-truth against you. In your place, I'd probably be careful who I told too. Listen." He pulls his chair closer to mine. "I'm working on that new highway that's going in east of Valencia, and I have to be up in your area on Friday. Would you like to have lunch with me, maybe around noon?"

"Yeah, I can make that." Apparently, I hadn't alienated him with my confession. And he hadn't asked me to sign a picture of myself to give to his mother. He had definitely earned some brownie points.

We arrange to meet at a restaurant on Valencia's main street and then go our separate ways. As we hug goodbye, he whispers in my ear, "Until Friday."

I smile and nod, grateful that he hadn't added an endearment. Especially one in Spanish.

Back at home, I sit on my bed and consider the evening. I'm not sure how I feel about telepathy. It doesn't seem relevant to my life, and I have no idea how well I did with it. But I like how I felt after Carleton's healing touch: calm, peaceful, even happy.

I meditate for a few moments, using my breath. A picture emerges as soon as I settle into the meditation, and I'm both watching it and experiencing it.

I pack a bag with some handouts for the kids and then drive toward the suburbs, using my phone to guide me. Despite the phone's directions, I'm almost late, and when I arrive, I find that the school's parking lot is full. I chastise myself for not leaving earlier while driving up and down the streets, looking for a place to parallel park. Every spot is filled with what I assume is a student's car. When I was in high school, hardly anyone had cars. This is a different world, I remind myself.

Finally, I see a spot I can just get into. I pull into it, hoping no one dents my car while I'm gone. Grabbing my purse and my bag with the handouts, I get out and lock the car. The school is several blocks away, so I'll need to hurry.

And then my mental screen goes blank. *Wait, come back! I need to know what happened next.* But try as I might, nothing else comes.

I blow out my breath. My brain seems to be jerking me around, doling out memories like playing cards. I don't know if I'm in a game of bridge or hearts or crazy eights, but I wish the dealer would finish passing out the cards so I can know why I walked in front of that car.

Given what I now know, it must have been an accident. In my hurry, I didn't see the car as it rushed toward me. But I'm usually too observant to make a mistake of that magnitude, regardless of how late I am or how much I'm hurrying.

Carleton's classes have opened my mind more than anything else. There's only one more class. If I don't get the answers I want then, maybe I can request a private session.

What a strange situation. I still have mixed feelings about Carleton, but I can hardly wait for next week to see if I can finally get some answers.

Chapter 19: Having Lunch Isn't a Mortal Sin. Is it?

The week passes quickly. My zinnias have sprouted, or at least, the ones that listen to the classical music. The other group is already slightly behind. I add some broccoli seeds to the experiment. I'm not likely to publish this research, but I enjoy using my education for something more challenging than selling tomato plants.

Every morning at six thirty, I send Darla a telepathic message. I'm not sure what I receive back, but I think a lot about the ocean during the time I'm supposed to be receiving. Considering that I rarely think about the ocean otherwise, maybe I'm tuning into Darla's thoughts.

Lunch with Thomas is uneventful. Without a mysterious class beforehand and the hustle and bustle of a sports bar, sitting in the area's only pho restaurant is pretty tame. We talk about his work and how he became an engineer.

He asks why I applied to astronaut training. "I was working as a plant scientist at NASA. I liked the work, but it wasn't like being a space explorer. When my boyfriend told me about a call for a new class of astronauts, I threw my hat in the ring. But I never expected to get in. I wasn't in the military and, frankly, wasn't a male. Oh, there were female astronauts but not as many at that time." I shake my head. "Wonder of wonders, they chose me for an interview. And then another. And then I was in. I guess they liked my science background. I was already growing food for space travelers, so I could combine my interests. Which I did until... you know the rest."

He nods. "Sounds interesting."

We slurp our pho and continue talking until his lunch hour is over. He picks up the check and smiles a goodbye. "Until Monday," he says as he walks out.

After he leaves, I glance around the restaurant and am appalled to see my sister's face frowning at me. Ava slides out from the booth where she's sitting with a female friend and plunks down in Thomas's seat. "I think the whole town probably saw you and him flirting. Was that what you wanted?"

"Oh God." I rub my mouth with my napkin. "Give me a break. We weren't flirting. We're in a class together. He's working in the area, so we decided to have lunch." Shaking my head, I say, "You're making way too much of it. In case you're wondering, no, I am not sleeping with him. He's a friend, and I like him as a friend. Get off my back."

Ava squints and then pats my hand. Her voice is gentler than I'd expected it would be. "Look, I'm fine with it. You're a grown woman, and you're separated from your husband. For Christ's sake, you're living with Mom. It's only natural to want to hang out with a nice-looking man. But I bet Mom won't be as understanding. She'll say you're still married and you shouldn't date until you're divorced. I know it's crap, but if I were you, I'd meet him somewhere that you aren't likely to run into family or friends. I won't tell her, but she still might hear about this."

Shit, she's right. Ava and I have done nothing but argue ever since Ben died, and now she's being understanding. Something is off. "How come you're being so nice to me?"

Ava laughs. "I don't know. I guess I was always jealous of you."

"Yeah, but—"

She raises her hand. "Hear me out. I've thought about this a lot. After Ben died, you were Dad's favorite. Not that that was so great. He was harder on you than me. And then you went off and had this brilliant career, while I was stuck at home taking care of Mom and Dad."

She rests her chin on her palm and looks away.

I brace for a storm. This topic never gets resolved. She shrugs and gives me a small smile. "I like my life and all, but at least some of the time, I would have preferred yours. Now you're just a regular person with your own problems. Not a star anymore. We might try being friends. What do you think?"

I gaze at her suspiciously. "What's the catch?"

She shrugs. "No catch." She starts to slide out of the booth. "Never mind. Forget I mentioned it."

What is wrong with me? I reach out to catch her hand. "I'm sorry. I'd like that."

She sits back down and pulls her hand away, looking pensive. "I was thinking. You should write about your experiences, both the astronaut stuff and also your recovery from the accident. Lots of people would come out to hear you talk if you wrote a book."

"I don't know. I don't enjoy talking about that hard stuff. Or writing about it. Too painful."

"Well, you need to find something interesting to do with your time besides helping Mom and watching TV. You look more like a trapped animal every time I see you." She pauses. "I know. You could help at the store." She grins at the incredulous look on my face. "Okay, not that. I've got it." She snaps her fingers. "You could volunteer at the Extension Program. They're trying to get people to grow native plants, and they always need volunteers. There are probably some eligible men there too."

"Ha! And then I might go out to *lunch* with one of them. And give you the chance to yell at me again. I don't think so." In spite of myself, I experience a tiny glimmer of interest. "I'll think about volunteering somewhere while I'm here. I *do* need more of a personal life. But really, Thomas is just a friend."

"Whatever you say. Hey, let's go out and have a few drinks some night. How about tomorrow?"

"Sure."

I leave the restaurant, both stunned and thrilled that my relationship with my sister has turned around so unexpectedly. We've never been on the same side of anything since we were kids.

J ust before closing time, I look up to see my mom standing before me, arms crossed, a solemn expression on her face.

"What's up?"

"I just heard from a church lady that you had lunch with a man today. At the pho restaurant."

I sigh. "Yes. I know. What's the problem?"

Her eyes widen. "Honey, you're a married woman, even if you aren't living with your husband right now."

I stand and face her. "Oh, good grief. What is this, 1950? It was just lunch. He's a guy I know from my Monday-night class. I don't see the problem."

"Honey, this is a small town. And you'll always be a pastor's daughter, even though your father's deceased. Besides that, you're a celebrity. You have to keep a squeaky-clean reputation. You can't be seen having lunch with strange men."

This is one of the most ludicrous conversations I've had in years. It reminds me of the time when I was fifteen and got caught making out with a boy in the choir room. "Look, I had to deal with that kind of bullshit when I was in high school. If you haven't noticed, I'm forty-two, and I don't have to deal with it now. If you don't like how I live my life, I'll be happy to move in with Ava. She won't mind who I have lunch with. Or better yet, I'll just go somewhere else."

Mom heads out the door as fast as her bad hip and knee will allow. At the door, she turns around and takes a breath. "I'm sorry. I just want you to get back with Ramón. He's a good man, and he calls me several times a week to ask if you're okay. You won't talk to him, so he calls me. Are you going to get back together?"

I sigh. "I don't know. Sometimes I think so, and then I change my mind. I'll tell you when I know."

"Well, don't leave him waiting too long. He's a handsome man, and there are plenty of single women out there who'd snap him up in an instant." She purses her lips. "What will he think about you having lunch with a man?"

"You have no business telling him that—or reporting about my life at all. He's not my keeper, and I'm a grown woman. I'll deal with this."

I pull out my phone and call Ramón, but he doesn't answer. After the beep, I say, "Hey, it's me. You need to stop calling my mom. I don't want to put her in the middle between us If you have something you want to know about me, you can ask me. Got that?" I hang up.

Mom is still standing at the door, her eyes wide, but she doesn't say anything.

"Okay, that should stop things," I tell her. "If we get divorced, I *hope* you'll side with me instead of him, even if you like him better. Everybody thinks Ramón walks on water, but I'm your daughter, and I'm not so bad either."

I put my hands on my hips and glare at her.

Mom limps over to me. "Oh, honey, I would never side with him against you. I'm sorry if I gave you that impression. I realize he's a bit... heavy-handed about being in charge, and it makes sense that you needed a break from him. But I guess I'm a bit old-fashioned."

"A little? Huh." We hug. Afterward, I say, "You know, you might want to start dating yourself. You'll see that having lunch with a man isn't a mortal sin. It's just lunch."

"Dating, me?" She laughs. And then she looks thoughtful. "It's only been seven months since Frank died. I can't even think of such things now. Maybe later."

"Well then."

An hour later, my phone rings. Ramón. As soon as I answer, he says, "I would prefer to talk to you, but you keep hanging up on me. So in order to find out anything about you, I have to call Pat. Do you see the problem?"

God, he's right. "Here's the thing. You can't keep putting her in the middle. Please don't call her again. I promise I won't hang up on you. Okay?"

"All right."

"So, what do you want to know?"

Ramón answers in that Spanish-tinged accent that only comes out when he's furious or making love. It is definitely the former this time. "You know what I want to know. When are you coming home? I either need a date when you're coming home or a date when I'll know for sure you aren't. You can't keep me in this limbo. It's been over a month, *Chica*."

I consider. "What if I don't have a date? I'm feeling my way through a lot of conflicting emotions, and I don't think I can name a date when everything will be settled. You know?"

"If you don't want to sleep with me right now, I'll move into the guest room. We can go to counseling. We can't do that unless you come home."

I feel the anger draining out of me. I hate it when he's right. "I don't know what to tell you. Right now, I don't want to go back to Houston. It's where I got run down by the SUV and where I lost my job. And it's partly you, because you have everything I've ever wanted-ed. What am I supposed to do, be a housewife?"

Silence. Then, "God, Mia, everything isn't black-and-white. I can't imagine you ever being only a housewife if you don't want to be. You have lots of options. If you don't want to come back to Houston, what about if we move somewhere else? I miss my family in New Mexico. We could move there, maybe buy a ranch, and just live for a while. I like my job, but I won't mind retiring, to tell the truth. By the way, I turned down Kairos."

"No shit. Really?"

"I just don't have the heart for it. Too much stress. I'll be forty-nine in January, and I'm ready to do something else."

I take a breath and picture a stream and a deer. After a moment, I'm more in control. "It's your life and your decision. I know it's my problem, but it kills me to think you can just walk away from what I want so much." I pause. "How about this? If I get chosen for Carleton's project, it will take place in the first two weeks of December. What about if I let you know what I've decided after that? Maybe things will be clearer then. I know it's not what you want, but it's what I'm offering."

He agrees, reluctantly, and we hang up on a calmer note.

I sigh. All this people stuff is hard. I'd much rather deal with plants. And I am absolutely certain, if I hadn't been before, that I could never live in Valencia again. Will I never outgrow having been a pastor's daughter?

Sheesh.

Chapter 20: The Simulation Revealed

By the time Monday rolls around, I am going out of my mind with boredom. Ava was right. I need more in my life than hanging around the nursery and watching plants grow. This past week, I updated my resume and applied to Space Tours, Inc. I won't hear from them for months, though, so I need an adventure of some kind.

Let's see. I could try skydiving again. No, it's too dangerous. Something safer. I know, I could ride a bike across the country and give out seed packets to warn people of global warming. Nope, my leg's not strong enough. *Damn!* I hate that my adventure options are so limited. I'll give it more thought.

This morning, I watched from a kayak as a rocket launched from Cape Canaveral. I considered driving to the cape to watch it up close, but I wasn't sure I'd make it back in time for the class. Right now, that class is keeping me afloat, especially since it's helping to recover my memories, and I can't miss it. So I paddled out to the middle of Valencia Lake, where I could see a large patch of open sky. I watched launches from there as a kid, so I knew I'd be able to see the rocket as it roared toward the heavens.

The day was perfect: cool, clear, and windless. But as often happened, the launch was delayed for some reason that I wasn't told. While I waited, I paddled around the lake, looking for alligators but seeing none and glancing upward every few seconds.

Liftoff, at last! I looked up to see the supply rocket flash through the afternoon sky. This was not a crewed flight. Still, I couldn't suppress a thrill when it rose up, up, up until it disappeared from view.

Every flight that didn't explode was a tribute to scientific knowledge and engineering genius.

Even so, I wanted to cry. As fun as it was to watch launches, I wasn't ready to give up my dream of being on one of them. I paddled around the lake until I was under control and then drove down to Orlando for the class.

Now, in the classroom, I greet Darla and Thomas. I haven't seen Darla since last Monday. She had a family gathering over the weekend and wasn't available to hang out with me. At least, that was what she said. Maybe things are getting hot and heavy with Carleton, and that was the real reason. But I don't ask. Everyone has the right to a little privacy.

We compare notes about the telepathic messages we transmitted and received during the week. Sure enough, Darla had sent me thoughts about the ocean. Actually, it was a lake, but water, anyway. She received my transmissions, but she thought I was sending the number six when it was actually fifteen. At least she got the number part. That's amazing progress, considering we're new at this entire experiment.

After the greeting and the head-touching, Carleton begins his speech. "As you know, this is our last meeting before interviews for the simulation project we're calling 'Auriga.' That is the constellation some fast radio bursts have been traced to. Hopefully, we'll be able to telepathically contact whoever or whatever is out there. But that's for later. Tonight, we'll send energy waves to each other, and we'll do that with our hands and our minds."

He divides the class into groups of seven or eight. One person stands in the center, with the others forming a circle around her or him. The center person is to relax while the others try to tune in to that person energetically.

A middle-aged African American woman named Sheila with whom I haven't spoken before stands in the center of my circle.

Sheila's dark-brown face is wrinkled, her body sags like she hasn't exercised in years, and her fingers are stained from nicotine. On the other hand, she's wearing a pretty blue pantsuit and has jangly Southwestern jewelry around her neck, on both wrists, and on most of her fingers. She looks lively and interesting.

I tune in to her as well as I can. It takes a few moments to calm my mind and begin to sense the woman standing before me. When I do, I sense that something is wrong with her heart. I don't know how I know that, but my thoughts are drawn to her heart.

Carleton tells us to hold our hands in front of us with our palms facing the person at the part of their body that we've identified. We shouldn't touch the person. Whether we're a foot away or three feet, it doesn't matter. If no place particularly calls out to us, we can send them energy generally.

Confused, we all turn to look at him, so he shows us how he does it. He holds his hands near a man's shoulder. He appears to be beaming energy through his palms and toward the shoulder. There's nothing to see—no rays of light, no colors pulsing from his hand to the man's shoulder. But I sense energy moving, although I can't describe how I know that.

After watching for a while, I stand in front of Sheila and hold up my palms so they're facing the woman's heart. I feel a slight pulsing in my hands, and soon, they become warm.

Two other people also beam energy toward Sheila's heart, while others beam it at her lower back, and two send generalized energy. After a few moments, we all lower our arms to our sides.

Next comes the debrief. Sheila describes feeling like she was a Christmas package, all tied up with bows. "I felt like the most special person in the world." She has heart problems and problems with her back. "But I feel wonderful now. Thank you so much."

The people who transmitted energy all had unique experiences. I felt warmth flowing through me. Another woman saw an aura around Sheila. A man just sensed that her back was messed up. Another had no idea why she was drawn to a certain place.

I'm next. I stand in the center of the circle, close my eyes, and try to relax. Slowly, I feel warmth spread throughout my body. It's strongest at my forehead, where I hit the pavement. Tender fingers seem to massage my brain ever so gently. At one point, I peek and see that my colleagues are focusing their energies all around my body, not just at one place.

And then it's over. I feel warm and happy. People stare at me with curiosity. "Okay. Here goes. I had a terrible accident last year—a car ran me over and smashed me into the sidewalk. I noticed you were aiming all over my body. It felt great, but I can't help wondering what you felt."

People tell me: "You seemed depleted all over." "At first, I went with your head, but then I felt like your right leg needed help, too, so I moved there." "I honed in on your face and sort of patted the energy field."

"Thank you," I say, tears streaming down my cheeks. "You weren't wrong. I have been very depleted. I broke my leg in a bunch of places, and I smashed my forehead into the pavement."

We switch roles. With practice, I grow more confident in my intuitive hunches about where to place my hands. I learn to pull energy in through my head and move it toward the person with my palms, or at least, I think I do. Truthfully, I could be imagining the whole thing. But if it's my imagination, I'm proud of myself. I've never thought of myself as a particularly creative person.

All in all, it is the most amazing experience I'd ever had, and that's saying quite a lot.

At the end of class, Carleton talks about next week, when he'll be interviewing applicants for the Auriga Project. A representative from the funding company will be there to help with the interviews.

He draws in a breath. "The principal thing that's being tested in this first simulation is whether seven people can stay inside a closed space for two weeks and still get along. We'll spend a lot of time meditating and sending energy out to various parts of the universe. And everyone will have chores to accomplish. But make no mistake, spending two weeks inside a small building with virtual strangers will be arduous."

He locks eyes with each of us then nods. "To make sure that everyone takes this mission seriously, the funders have added a stipulation. If you accept a position on the crew, you must agree to stay in the dwelling, no matter what, for two weeks. The funders will award everyone who makes it through the entire time ten thousand dollars for their trouble. Anyone who insists on leaving early will give up their award and repay up to three thousand dollars in expenses. Is that clear?"

Gradually, excited whispering replaces a surprised silence. Carleton hasn't mentioned money before. Earning ten thousand dollars for two weeks' work, no matter what it entails, will ease many people's lives, especially since it comes just before Christmas. After a moment, though, the implications of possibly having to repay the money become clear, and disappointment replaces excitement. Several people leave, frowning and shaking their heads.

Carleton gives us more details. The simulation will take place in a geodesic dome near Crestone, Colorado. The altitude there is about eleven thousand feet, so if people can't deal with high altitude, they shouldn't apply. The funder will provide all food and other necessities, along with airline tickets. Ultimately, it won't cost participants anything, as long as they're prepared to stay for the entire two weeks. Participants will receive their checks a week after they return to Orlando.

Finally, he says that anyone interested in learning more about the project should come to next week's meeting. He glances around and asks Sheila to join him. As much as I'm revolted by the custom, I'm pleased he chose Sheila. Thomas and I exchange knowing glances.

When everyone else has left, Darla asks if we're up for a trip to the bar. Thomas immediately says yes, but I'm not so sure. I'm eager to get home and meditate, hoping to retrieve the last memories of the accident. On the other hand, I bet Darla knows more about the project than Carleton told us tonight.

I decide to go. I hope the memories will still be accessible when I get home.

Thomas sips his beer then wipes his mouth with a napkin. "Ten thousand dollars. That part sounds great. But being charged three thousand if there's an emergency—I don't like that."

I agree, but before I can speak, Darla interjects, "The funder has threatened to cancel the next part of the project—taking us to space—if anyone leaves early. Carleton didn't tell you that tonight, but it's true."

Huh. There's no point in participating in the simulation if the possibility of going to space is off the table. I'm sure *I* can do two weeks inside a dome, but I can't vouch for anyone else. Suddenly, the project looks less appealing than it did when Carleton first mentioned it. I ask Darla, "You're going? Have you got the time off from teaching?"

She nods. "I'll get a sub. Already talked to the principal, and it'll work. He thinks it'll make a great story to share with the kids after I get back."

"Help me understand. If one person leaves, does that mean the others won't get paid?"

She thinks for a moment before shaking her head. "Good question. I'm not sure. You should ask Carleton next week."

We focus on our drinks and our own thoughts for a while. Finally, Thomas asks, "Why didn't he tell us about all this earlier? Up till tonight, he hadn't mentioned money. Not that money's a bad thing, but I'm surprised he's just now mentioning it."

"Ah, yes," says Darla. "He didn't know about it until a few days ago. He thought the participants would get a free ride. No reward for doing it but no fine for leaving either. The funder has been adding conditions recently. I'm not sure Carleton would have proposed this project if he'd known all the conditions they'd impose. But now he's trying to make the best of it."

I tune out the conversation and focus on my welter of confusing emotions. Excitement is strongest. I'm bored and reluctant to return to Houston, so this could be the adventure I've been seeking. Contacting extraterrestrials is a long shot—ridiculous, really—but I wouldn't mind a couple of weeks of relaxation in the Colorado mountains. And a chance to get to space, if that aspect of the project continues.

Fear of the unknown creeps into my awareness. I don't know who's sponsoring this project or what new conditions they might impose. The money is an enticement, I have to admit. I've spent all my settlement money and am watching my savings dwindle. Conversely, this entire project is a pig in a poke. It might be dangerous in ways I have no idea about yet, especially since the funder is so insistent that nobody leaves early. If it's not dangerous, why have that stipulation?

After a few moments, suspicion takes over. Maybe the people in Carleton's group—maybe even Carleton himself—are pawns in a larger scheme that has yet to be revealed. I'm not at all sure I want to participate in something that dicey.

How quickly things change. Less than an hour before, I'd congratulated myself for having some talent for telepathy. And I'd thought I would be part of a momentous experiment that would not only send me to space but could also change the nature of the human experience. Now, I'm a shill in some kind of con. I can almost feel steam rise out of my head.

I slam my beer mug down on the table, and half of the liquid sloshes out, so I rush to mop it up before it spills on my lap. When that's done, I ask Darla, "What do you know that you're not telling us? Do you know who's behind it? Or is this whole thing a fraud?"

She shakes her head. "I've spent every free minute online for the past week, researching who might be behind the funding. I've got it down to four companies, but they're the ones you'd already suspect, so it does no good." She names them off, and I nod in agreement. One thing is for sure: NASA isn't behind this scheme. The government would have sent out requests for proposals, and the entire world would have known about it. Everything would have been aboveboard too. But private businesses play by different rules.

She eats a potato chip, looking thoughtful. "Here's what I know. The company—we call it Alpha Company, for simplicity's sake—has built a geodesic dome that will be the site of the simulation. Constructing it has been a rush job, but it'll be finished before our group moves in. You might not know this, but there are similar projects going on around the world. Let's see—there's one in Utah and another in Hawaii. And a huge one in Dubai. Alpha Company will probably use our dome for other simulations after they complete our project. That much, at least, is on the level."

I shudder every time she says the word "simulation." It reminds me of the SAFER sim that I failed so many times. I wonder if something like that will happen in this simulation.

"What does the place look like?" asks Thomas. "You got pictures?"

"It's high on a mountaintop in the Rockies. I've seen pictures, but I don't have any to show you. Carleton insisted the air must be as thin as possible to give us the best chance of contacting other sentient beings. I don't understand it, honestly. But if we're able to document that we've sent out and received telepathy waves while we're in the dome, receiving funding for the actual experiment in space will be a piece of cake."

"So that isn't assured even if everyone stays for the entire time?" asks Thomas.

"We don't have to contact aliens during the simulation, but it has to work otherwise, as Carleton said tonight. Even so, Alpha can pull the funding after the simulation if they want to."

"Huh. Pretty good deal for them," I say.

"True that."

The conversation gradually flags. Before long, we all leave for home.

In the parking lot, Thomas pulls me aside. "Would you like to see *A Christmas Carol* with me on Friday evening? I hear there's a good production here in Orlando."

"Christmas? Already? It isn't even Thanksgiving yet."

He laughs. "I know. Christmas seems to come earlier every year. But what do you say?"

I hesitate. This sounds awfully much like a date. Am I ready to date? "Sure. Sounds like fun."

"Great. I'll call you later, and we'll set it up. See you then."

Chapter 21: The Warning

As soon as I get home, I prop myself up in bed and try to meditate. Even though I use all the techniques Carleton has taught us, nothing happens—I can't center down, can't calm my mind, and definitely can't access any memories. The problem is that I can't stop thinking about the simulation and whether or not I'll apply. After an hour, I give up.

Then I discover that I can't even sleep.

I toss and turn all night, trying to decide what to do. Toward morning, I fall into a light slumber and have the space dream again. It's all familiar, even to my sleeping self. The astronaut who comes up beside me, wearing a space suit. His dark eyes. This time, his expression is compassionate rather than angry. I try to speak, but nothing comes out. And then something new happens. The man shakes his head at me!

I jolt awake, heart pounding, sweat streaming, like always. But this time is different. Instead of just staring at me, the mysterious man actually communicated. He seemed to be trying to warn me about something, but it wasn't clear. I wonder what it could be as I put my feet over the edge of the bed and push them down onto the tile floor.

Was he warning me about Carleton? That seems the obvious answer. The man must be telling me not to get involved with Carleton's experiment. Why not? I don't know. Maybe his action reflects my own doubts and fears about the project. In that case, the spaceman could represent my unconscious self, as Karin has suggested several times.

I try to sort it out in my half-asleep state until daylight arrives. I'm exhausted, demoralized, and anxious, so a day off—or at least a morning off—sounds exactly right. I can't take the entire day off, because I have to visit my plants this afternoon to water them and turn on the music. I've started sitting with the ones in the experimental condition for half an hour too. While I'm there, I send them good feelings. I don't know if they respond, but it's the most peaceful part of my day.

I get up, wander around the house, and try to relax. But my mind won't shut down. It reminds me of the months after the accident when I constantly experienced thought loops about Ashley. This is the first loop I've run in weeks, but I'm unable to stop my mind from going around and around about the simulation. The damn cow is chewing its cud again.

When I sit with the plants in the afternoon, I don't bother trying to send them positive energy. I'm unable to be that clear. Instead, as a way to stop the thought loop, I think about the positive things in my life. The list includes spending precious time with my mom and sister, learning to meditate, an increased level of physical healing, reconnecting with old friends and making new ones, and being able to think more clearly than I have since the accident. I even feel better about Ramón. He'd been trying to help when he was bossing me around all those times, even though he often went about it in the wrong way. And I've recovered some of my memories. Some are better than none, but oh, how I wish I had all the information about that terrible day. Maybe the rest will come soon.

Regardless of what happens with the plants, I leave the greenhouse feeling better.

During my Skype meeting with Karin on Wednesday, I start by describing my experiences in Carleton's classes.

"This is wonderful! I had no idea you would take to something so out of the ordinary."

"Thanks. But let me tell you the rest." I describe Carleton's new rules for the simulation participants.

Karin frowns. "Surely, you aren't thinking of doing this. There must be something dangerous or unsavory about this thing. After all, being somewhere for two weeks shouldn't be such a big deal that they would need to charge people so much money if they leave."

"My thoughts exactly. I probably won't do it. But I need to do *something*. I'm going out of my mind with boredom."

"That's the way healing works. You weren't bored until recently, were you?" When I shake my head, she continues. "Up till now, you were too exhausted from dealing with your injuries to have enough extra energy to be bored. Boredom is a positive stage in the healing process. Now you have to figure out your next steps in life. I hope you end up doing something gentler with yourself than being an astronaut or a... guinea pig for an anonymous business, but it's your life. I'll probably support whatever you choose." She pauses. "What else do you have for me today?"

I describe how the spaceman had shaken his head at me. "What do you think?"

"I'm glad the dream has moved on a little," she says after sipping some tea. "It shows you're less stuck than you used to be. As for what it means, that's for you to say. What was your first thought when you woke up?"

Hmm. I try to remember, but nothing is clear. "Uh, I think I figured the person was warning me not to do the experiment."

"And how did that feel?"

The emotion is easier to access. "I was a little angry at him for telling me not to do it but not telling me what *to* do. I'm at such loose ends right now that I could use any input." My laughter has a hollow sound.

"Okay. Think about it some more. Try journaling about it too. In fact, try meditating on the dream and ask the person what he or she wanted. Write down the first thing that comes to you."

"Oh. All right. But when are you going to help me recover my memories?"

"You're doing fine on your own. I don't want to rush the process. Remember that we tried for months to find them but nothing happened? They're coming back in their own time and at their own pace. I think you're doing great."

"But I still don't know what happened."

"You know part of it. Try journaling about it, and maybe the rest will come."

After we hang up, I try meditating and journaling about the dream and the accident, but nothing comes to mind. Nothing at all.

Screw it. I have other things to do in my life. Sheesh.

On Friday evening, I have to force myself to drive to Orlando. It's my first date in years, if *date* is even the correct term, and my entire body is trembling in terror. Part of me wants to turn around at every interstate exit and rush back to the safety of Valencia. But another part wants to spend time with Thomas and see what happens. I drive so slowly that I end up being late.

When I park, I realize that my wedding ring is still on my finger. Is it appropriate to wear it on a date with another man? No, I don't think so. I pull it off and stash it in the ashtray that no cigarette has ever sullied. My hand feels naked without the ring, but I ignore the feeling.

Finally, I locate his condo and knock at his door.

He opens it, smiling, and invites me inside. The condo overlooks a water feature on a golf course and is decorated beautifully in modern décor. *There's more to this guy than I thought.* I'm afraid he'll offer me a drink and then make a pass, and I won't know what to do. Instead, he suggests we leave for the restaurant right away since we're a little late for our reservation.

"Sure," I say, feeling lighter.

He chose an Italian restaurant in the same neighborhood as the theatre. At the table next to us is a group of twentysomething guys who are apparently at the beginning of a bachelor party. They drink several carafes of chianti, their sound level increasing after every carafe. We watch at first with amusement and then with frustration as the rowdy bunch drowns out our attempts at conversation. We eat our dinner quickly and leave.

At the theatre, we find our seats and breathe sighs of relief at the blessed quiet. The play won't start for a few moments, so we have a while to talk. I tell him about the experiment I'm conducting with my plants, and he tells me about his job. It's a regular conversation between friends, and I relax. I like this man.

Finally, the play starts. Thomas has told me that his cousin played Tiny Tim in local productions when they were kids, and his parents forced him to watch it every year. He claims to have the whole play memorized. During a scene with the Cratchits, he leans over and whispers, "This Tiny Tim is so much better than my cousin."

It's all I can do to not burst out laughing.

Afterward, we go back to his condo. This time, he offers me a glass of wine, and I'm happy to accept. We sit together on his couch and listen to *Moonlight Sonata* on his stereo. I slip off my sandals and relax into the cushions. "Mmm, this is wonderful," I say, smiling at him.

"Yes, it is." He moves closer and puts his arm around me.

Oh God, this is it. I have to decide what to do—or not decide and let things happen as they will. The moments pass, and I don't get up and leave, so when he leans in for a kiss, I reciprocate. *Ah, yes.* It's been a long time since I felt a man's mouth on mine. I'm in heaven.

We kiss for what seems like a long time. For once, I don't question my motivations or feel guilty. I just experience the bliss of an uncomplicated kiss.

Until it becomes complicated. His hand slides down my face and down my neck and rests on my sternum. And then it moves farther down. I stiffen, remove his hand, and sit up, looking around blearily.

He immediately scoots to the far end of the couch. "I'm sorry, Mia. I moved too fast, and I made you uncomfortable."

"Yes." There's a long pause as I try to figure out what else to say. I feel around for my shoes then slip them on. "I need to go anyway. It's getting late." I set my empty wineglass on the coffee table and stand. "Hey, it's all right. I really do need to go. And yes, things were moving too fast for me."

He stands, too, looking embarrassed.

I give him a weak smile.

As I walk toward the door, he says, "I hope I didn't ruin things forever. I'm very attracted to you, but I'll go at whatever pace you want."

Suddenly, everything is clear. I take a deep breath and turn toward him, hoping I can say what I need to say without crying. "Thank you for a lovely evening. I really like you, too, but I'm not ready for a relationship. I need to figure out what to do about my marriage before I get involved with anybody else, even somebody as great as you. I'm sorry if I led you on. Can we be friends and see how it goes?"

He nods, taking a deep breath. "Of course. You tell me what you need. I can be your friend, even if that's all it ever is. It's rare that I meet someone I'm so compatible with."

I step forward, and we hug. "Good night. I won't forget this evening."

"Me neither. By the way, I'm going to the meeting on Monday. What about you?"

"Don't know yet." I open the door and step into the cool night air. "I'll play it by ear. Take care."

When I get into the car, I slip my ring back onto my finger. Yes, that feels right. I don't know what will happen with Ramón, but whatever it is, I'll deal with it before starting something else.

Driving home, I know I made the right decision. But sometimes it sucks being a grown-up.

Chapter 22: The Worst Thing I Could Do

When I walk into the classroom on Monday evening, I see that Thomas has saved me a seat. I wonder if being with him will be awkward. I decide to play it cool, so I smile as I sit down. "How did you know I'd come? I only decided this afternoon."

He grins. "If you hadn't shown up, I could always invite some other pretty lady to sit next to me."

Not awkward, then. We laugh, and he pats my knee. "I'm glad you came. It costs nothing to listen to what he has to say."

"My thoughts exactly."

The room fills with people. Almost everyone from our class is here, along with a dozen people who must have been from Carleton's other classes. Someone has set the chairs up in rows, like a regular classroom. Carleton, Darla, and a man I don't recognize sit at a table in front.

When everyone is settled, Carleton stands up. "As you know, we're here to interview for the Auriga Project crew. Let me introduce you to the people at the table. To my left is Darla Whitcomb, whom most of you know. Darla will act as my assistant in facilitating this project. To my right is Curt Rowell, who is the representative of the company funding the project. He'll help conduct the interviews and decide on the crew members."

Curt gives us a small smile then writes on his legal pad. He looks like the quintessential bureaucrat: fiftyish, button-down shirt with a pocket protector and pens, short brown hair parted on the side, and reading glasses perched on his nose. His sour expression articulates better than words that this isn't his idea of fun. I would bet he sits in an office and doesn't regularly deal with people. I feel a stab of sympathy.

Carleton continues. "You all know what this project is about: the power of focused thoughts. We have three goals. Ultimately, we're trying to contact extraterrestrials through our focused thoughts. We don't really expect that to be successful during this simulation, but we'll try it. We'll also send thought messages to a receptive person a few miles away to see if we can establish a connection. Finally, we'll have electronic instruments set up outside the dome to measure the force of our thoughts. That's it."

He glances over at Curt, who doesn't look up from his legal pad, and then continues. "You know about the requirement to remain in the dome for the entire two-week period. This experiment is costing Alpha Company an enormous amount, and they only want participants who are as committed as they are. You must make up your own minds about whether you want to do that. I'll respect your decision either way."

He answers questions for a few moments. Finally, the room falls quiet. Carleton smiles. "We'll conduct the interviews in the classroom next door. Darla will escort you in one at a time. The interview probably won't take more than a few minutes. Okay, let's get started."

After Carleton and Curt leave, Darla gestures for the person nearest the door to come with her. The rest of us spend the next hour chatting and wondering what's going on in the interviews. Unfortunately, no one comes back afterward to fill us in. I wonder if they've been spirited away by aliens and stifle a giggle.

Eventually, it's Thomas's turn. He waves at me when he leaves, but he doesn't come back either. Something must be going on that I'm not aware of, or else he would have come back to tell me how it went. If I don't see him, I'll call him afterward to see what happened.

I'm last and more than a little nervous by the time Darla appears. She ushers me into a classroom where Carleton and Curt sit behind a small table. A single chair sits in front of the table, so I drop into it, willing my hands not to shake.

Apparently, Curt knows I was—am—an astronaut. "Do you think you'll go back to NASA soon?"

Ah, he doesn't know they grounded me. *Good.* That speaks volumes for Darla's and NASA's ability to keep a secret. "Depends on how things go. I'm exploring other options. This project is one of them."

Carleton speaks up then, saying that he's looked at everyone's scores in the telepathy class and mine are in the top ten.

"Thanks," I say, surprised and pleased to know I didn't fail.

After another ten minutes of softball questions, Carleton asks, "So, are you interested in participating in the project? We'd like to invite you to join us."

Huh. That was fast. "Uh, I'm not sure."

Curt leans forward. "If you'll allow us to use your name in our promotional materials, we're prepared to double the amount of your reward."

I sit back in the chair and consider his offer. It feels slimy somehow. Even if NASA would allow me to do that, I wouldn't think of asking them for permission. I pick up my purse and begin to rise. "I do not want my name associated with this project. If that's a requirement, cancel my application."

Curt blushes. "No, it's not a requirement. We won't be doing any promotions for the simulation until it's over. I was thinking about the next phase, where we actually send people up to space."

"Oh," I say, sitting back down. "That's different. I'd like to decide about the two phases separately, if that's okay with you." When they nod, I continue. "I have a question. If one person leaves early, will the others still get paid?"

Some sort of nonverbal message passes between the two men, but I don't catch it. Carleton clears his throat. "I've asked that same question. I understand that it depends on the reason a person leaves, in addition to how many people remain in the dome."

The whole thing is a crapshoot, then. None of us will know what conditions we'll face in the dome or how dedicated the other participants will be. *Damn.* I wanted an adventure, but I'm not sure if this is the best one.

I have another concern to resolve with them before making my decision. "As you know, I'm a plant biologist, and I'm involved in some experiments that will be ruined if I stop them. If I'm to take part, I'll need to bring my plants. There will be four good-sized pots and two grow lights and a few other things. Everything would need to be transported in a way that the cold doesn't kill them. Is that possible?"

Carleton and Curt look at each other, clearly surprised by this question. Carleton defers to Curt, who thinks about it for a full two minutes before he answers. "I think there will be room for the plants, and we should be able to set everything up for you. Of course, there'll be electricity and heat in the dome, so that won't be a problem. We can transport the boxes and plants in the Jeep that we'll use to transport the participants. It's heated."

He nods. "Yes, we can accommodate those requests. We will expect all participants to do chores, so your chores could be the maintenance of your plants. You realize, though, that we're allowing this because of your celebrity status. Other people won't be allowed to bring in so much."

Put-up-or-shut-up time. "Okay. Great. Will Darla and Thomas be among the crew?"

"Yes," says Carleton. "Darla is going as my assistant, and Thomas has accepted our invitation."

That would make it fun. Still, I know what my family will say: that I'm nuts for even considering this crazy project. And the spaceman had shaken his head at me.

On the other hand, I'm bored out of my mind, and two of my friends will be there. What are two weeks, after all, in the big scheme of things? "I'll look over the contract, and if it's okay, I'm in."

Carleton shakes my hand. "You won't regret it, Mia. Curt will email you the contract tomorrow. We'd like to know your decision by Friday, because if you bow out, we'll offer the option to someone else."

I walk out in a daze. *Oh my God, what have I done?*

Thomas waits for me outside the building. "They wouldn't let me come back in the classroom." He smiles. "Well?"

I take a deep breath and whoosh it out. Suddenly, this whole thing is real. "I hear you're going."

"Yeah. I need to use up some vacation days by the end of the year, so I might stay in the area for a few days and go skiing." He shrugs. "What about you?"

A sharp gust of wind whistles around the side of the building, and I shiver. "I need to look over the contract first, but if it's okay, I'm in."

"Cool. It's going to be fun." His face lights up.

"It'll be something," I say, suddenly dubious. "I hope it's fun."

As I drive home, I wonder if he's gotten the message that I want to be only friends. And then I wonder if I've gotten it.

When the contract arrives in my inbox, I read it through and see nothing new or problematic. It's a simple form that goes over the requirements: appear in Crestone at the agreed-upon time, stay in the dome for the entire two weeks, get along with people, take part in the telepathy exercises, and afterward, keep the details of the project confidential until given the authorization to speak about it. Money to be awarded upon completion of the two-week simulation in Colorado.

I think about it for an hour then sign the document and send it back. *All right, here we go.* This is not nearly as exciting as preparing for a space mission, but it's far better than anything I've done in the past year. And I won't have to quarantine beforehand. The whole thing will be a quarantine. I laugh at my joke.

Only later do I tell Mom that I'll be leaving for a while after Thanksgiving.

Mom is furious when I tell her about the simulation. Even after I explain my reasoning, she's convinced I've been seduced by the devil. She refuses to talk to me about it or about much else after that.

Ava is only slightly less scandalized when I tell her over drinks as we watch the sunset by the lake. "Is this just a way to spend more time with Thomas? If it is, surely you could spend your money on something a little more fun than two weeks cooped up on a mountaintop with a bunch of strangers."

"No, it's not about Thomas at all."

"Then, what?"

Valencia is experiencing its first cold front of the season. The wind blows fiercely over the lake, and my nose is running like a faucet. Despite the country band that plays valiantly on the deck outside the restaurant, most people have moved inside. I shiver. "Can we go inside and have this conversation? I'm freezing."

"Coward." But we move inside and find a table where we watch the sunset through the window. "Don't change the subject."

"Oh God, Ava, there's a bunch of reasons. I'm bored out of my skull staying here. I don't want to go back to Houston if I can't be an astronaut. The trouble is that I don't know where to go or what to do yet. And I don't know what to do about Ramón. I told him I'd give him an answer after the simulation. This will give me some time to decide."

Ava huffs. "It seems like you always have to live on the edge. Danger attracts you. You've been doing that ever since Ben died, you know? You weren't like that beforehand."

"I was twelve before that. You don't know what you're like before you're twelve."

"True. But this feels like you're trying to do what Ben would have done. He was the risk-taker in the family. Not you."

"Oh, stop trying to psychoanalyze me. I get enough of that from my therapist."

"Okay. It's your life. Maybe you'll write a book while you're stuck on the mountain. It's what I would do. On second thought, can I go with you? I could use a vacation."

I laugh, and we sip our wine in companionable silence as the sun dips slowly beneath the surface of the lake. The cold front has brought high clouds that become neon orange as we watch. A thought comes unbidden: *There really are ways to watch beautiful sunsets that don't involve rockets, weightlessness, or danger.* I have to admit I like this one.

"Mom's shitting a brick, you know," she says.

"Yeah. I know. Even more reason to get out of town for a while."

Things are even worse with Ramón. He just sighs and says, "I guess that's it, then? With us?"

Why does everyone think this is the worst thing I could do? "No. Not necessarily. Think of it as a two-week mission. That's all it is. Much better than six months at the space station. I'll be back by mid-December. I promise we'll talk then."

Long pause. My stomach sinks. He seems to be building up to something important, and I'm afraid he's going to give up on me. On us. Finally, he clears his throat and speaks a little hesitantly. "You know, Crestone isn't all that far from Santa Fe. I'll be there for Thanksgiving with my family. You could come, too, and I could fly you to Colorado afterward."

Huh. That's an interesting offer, but something about it doesn't feel right. "Sorry, no. I have a meeting about the simulation a couple of days after Thanksgiving. Please tell your family hello for me and that I'm sorry I'm not there."

"No problem. I didn't really expect you to come." We hang up shortly after that. We're drifting apart, and I'm sure we both know it. There are no more Spanish endearments and no loving words of any kind. We might have shared our last Thanksgiving together. That thought makes me want to cry.

Thanksgiving is a grim holiday in our household this year. Mom and I cook, and Ava's family comes over for dinner. Mom is still furious with me, so cooking in her small kitchen is an awkward experience for both of us.

As we pass the food around the dining table, I reflect on the changes in our family in the past year. The main one is that my dad is gone. As much trouble as I've had with him over the years, things don't seem right without him at the head of the table.

Ramón and I have visited my family several times at Thanksgiving. He always makes everyone laugh with his goofy astronaut jokes. (What is an astronaut's favorite place on a computer? The space bar.) And he makes the best fried polenta with chorizo, roasted chili cornbread, and pumpkin flan I can imagine. Unfortunately, I've never learned to cook these delicacies. My family's Thanksgiving dishes are ordinary compared with the Ramírezes'.

I feel a twinge of regret that I didn't take Ramón up on his offer. I'd stretched the truth when I told him I couldn't come. There really would have been time for me to go to Santa Fe if I'd wanted to. I could picture it: his family would be polite to me, but that would be all, and I'd be so embarrassed I'd want to sink under the table. Besides, his cousin Brenda would be there, and she's always disliked me. She's best friends with Ramón's first wife, Deborah, to whom I apparently don't measure up. I haven't met Deborah, but Ramón texted me she'd be at the family dinner.

Great fucking shit. I shouldn't be surprised about Deborah. Lots of women will be after Ramón if he turns out to be available. Deborah would likely have an inside track since she was the one to dump Ramón. She might have had second thoughts about the divorce, even though it was ten years ago.

I eat a bite of sugary sweet potato, but it sticks in my throat. A sip of tea helps, and I try to think cheerful thoughts. The problem is that I can't think of any.

Ava's sons, Jacob and Shawn, are the only cheerful people at the table. Both boys load up their plates and dig in. After his first helping, Shawn asks, "Where's Uncle Ramón?"

Dear child. He's only twelve, and he doesn't know what's going on. "Oh, he's with his family in New Mexico. He wasn't able to make it this year. Maybe next year."

"How come he's in New Mexico? Isn't he from the real Mexico?"

Ava tries to shush him, but he glances at her with confusion.

I laugh. "No, sweetie, his ancestors came from Spain hundreds of years ago. They aren't new immigrants. His family still speaks Spanish and keeps some Spanish customs, but believe me, they're all-American."

"Oh," he says. "I still wish he was here. Last year, he gave me a model rocket."

"Yeah, I know. He's a great guy. I miss him too." I really do miss him, I realize.

My mind flits back to last year, which was the absolute worst holiday ever. My leg was still in a cast, so I couldn't travel. Even leaving our house was hard. And my mental processing moved so slowly that, by the time I'd grasped someone's meaning, the discussion had moved on to something else. Noise bothered me too much for me to be in a restaurant, so Ramón had made dinner for the two of us, cooking a tiny turkey and all his special dishes. I couldn't eat much, but I gave it my best shot.

Afterward, some of his buddies came over to watch football, so I cleaned up the kitchen. It took me all afternoon, but I was proud to have actually accomplished something. That was rare in those days.

Ramón rose well to the occasion of being a caregiver, at least, at first. As the oldest of four children, he was used to the role. But he hadn't really wanted to be a parent. And that was what he'd become to me: a parent. Maybe he hadn't liked it any better than I had.

If we're together next year, I'll fix a special Thanksgiving dinner for the two of us. It doesn't seem likely, though.

My mind is a welter of confusion, sometimes moving in one direction and then taking a one-hundred-eighty-degree turn. *Divorce him. Return to him. Try to get my job back. Figure out something else to do.* The confident woman I've always been has disappeared, and I have no idea how to get her back.

Although I haven't had a headache in a couple of weeks, my head starts to pound during the meal, and the pain is as bad as it has ever been. I can't eat more than a few bites. As soon as I dare, I excuse myself and go to my room, where I spend the rest of the evening lying on my bed and staring at a small black beetle as it climbs the wall, falls down, and climbs back up again. I consider smashing it, just to put an end to its eternal climb.

Instead, I just watch.

Chapter 23: It's Rarely the Things You Think about That Get You

We meet at Orlando International Airport for our flight to Denver. I check to see who made the cut besides Darla, Thomas, and me. I recognize two of the women who Carleton had left with after class, but it takes me a moment to remember their names: Emily, the pretty woman in her twenties, and Sheila, the older woman with the Southwestern jewelry. There's another woman I don't know, so she must be from one of Carleton's other groups. I introduce myself. Suzie is about my age and perky, and I like her instantly. I'm happy with the selections and look forward to getting to know everyone.

Carleton and Curt are also here, of course. Curt smiles at me and winks, and I'm surprised to discover he has a personality. I won't flirt with him, but maybe hanging out with him won't be so bad. Carleton, on the other hand, looks like he's lost his last friend. There are circles beneath his eyes like he hasn't slept, and his expression is grim.

I pull Darla over. "What's up with Carleton? He doesn't look happy."

She glances at him with soft eyes then shakes her head at me. "I don't know. He was fine last night. Maybe something happened this morning. I think all the responsibility for this trip is getting to him. He'll be fine once we arrive and get settled."

She pulls me farther from the group, into a quiet spot, and flashes me an enormous smile. "I want to tell you something, but it needs to stay a secret until we get back. Okay?" After I nod, she continues.

"Carleton asked me to marry him last Saturday, and I said yes. We're going to announce our engagement after we get back from Colorado. He doesn't want to do it beforehand, since some of the women have crushes on him, and he's afraid it'll make things more difficult. But I've been bursting to tell you. Isn't that wonderful?"

I hug her and try to act excited. Darla is in love, and that's always a wonderful feeling. Cynically, I wonder if the feeling is as mutual as she seems to think. As I recall, Carleton didn't exactly discourage those other women. But it isn't my problem. I congratulate her and promise to keep her secret.

When we rejoin the group, I notice that everyone but me seems to be loaded down with luggage. Carleton hadn't told us to pack lightly, but I did anyway, except for my plants. The others have packed lots of clothes, books, snacks, and games. I brought a couple of books to read, but that's it in terms of entertainment. Maybe the others will share.

As I think on it, packing so lightly might have been a huge mistake. Carleton emailed us on Thanksgiving to say that we couldn't bring any electronics to the dome. He thinks they might interfere with our thought transmissions. We'll have to leave our phones and every other gadget at the retreat center where we'll be staying for our first few nights in Crestone. Yet another restriction that I didn't know about. I was pissed but mostly disappointed that I wouldn't be able to talk with my family for two weeks.

Now, the thought of fourteen days with nothing to do drops on me like a lead balloon. I race into a store and buy a couple of novels and a sudoku puzzle book. Carleton said we'll be busy scanning the heavens, so maybe there won't be that much free time. I'll make do. But I'm going to miss my phone terribly.

And then another wave of irritation rolls over me. Jeez, even when they're in space, astronauts get to speak to their loved ones. For a few moments, I consider backing out. But no, I made a commitment, and I'll stick to it. Nobody said I had to be happy.

On the plane, I'm stuck in a middle seat between Thomas and a gigantic man who's headed home to Denver. It's a good thing I'm small. I remind myself that I've endured much more cramped spaces in my life and I'll survive a few hours on a commercial flight.

Thomas and I chat for a while before I ask him, "Why are you doing this, really? It's not... because of me, is it? Because I—"

He shakes his head. "Spending time with you will be fun, for sure. But I heard you when you said you weren't ready for a relationship." He pauses. "No, it's an adventure, and I've had precious few of them in recent years. Also, I want time to reflect. I've been daydreaming about joining the Peace Corps or something like that, but I've always been too busy to give it serious thought. Now I can."

"The Peace Corps? Why?" *Hmm.* I wonder if I could do that.

He sighs. "Because I'm sick of spending my time building roads and bridges for the masses who are constantly coming to Florida. It makes me crazy to cover up so much good land just so people can drive from one theme park to another. In the Peace Corps, I could build roads for poor people to take their produce to market or bridges so people could see their friends without having to cross raging rivers. It's a lot more meaningful."

"That sounds great. What's kept you from doing it up to now?"

"Fear, I guess—fear of change, for one thing. And fear of running into a dangerous situation I can't handle. Fear of not being able to get another job when I come back. You name it, and I've got it. Fear is my thing, I guess." He shrugs and looks down at his hands.

"I understand. That's something we have in common. When I first learned I was going to the ISS, I was thrilled. Then I started thinking of everything that could go wrong. The rocket might explode. I might get hurled out into the vast nothingness of space until I ran out of air and died." I shudder. "Things like that. But my husband finally told me it's rarely the things you've thought about that get you. Boy, was that the truth. It never crossed my mind that an SUV would hit me instead of a meteor."

We're quiet for a while.

Finally, Thomas says, "Thanks. I'll add that to the mix in my thoughts." He reaches over and squeezes my hand. "I'm happy to have you for a friend, Mia."

"Same here." We smile then pull out our phones and thumb through the options.

The plane lands at Denver International Airport exactly on time, and we're picked up by a van and a driver for the trip to Crestone. There's a little trouble loading so much luggage along with my plant boxes, but the driver eventually jams everything into the van's cargo area. I'm relieved I didn't bring my experiments. Despite Curt's assurance that they'd stay warm, at the very least, the move would traumatize the plants. I gave my mom instructions for how to care for them in my absence. They'll be fine. Instead, I packed lettuce seeds, small pots and trays, a bag of potting mix and some simulated Martian regolith, fertilizer, and grow lights. And my lab notebook. I'll start over and see what will happen in two weeks. Not much, I suspect, but it should keep me busy.

In the van, Curt sits up front and fiddles with his phone, but the rest of us pile into the back seats. Now that we're almost there, the general mood is lighter, and we all laugh and chatter during the four-hour trip. Carleton sits between Darla and Sheila, but he doesn't say much and seems less excited than the rest of us.

Snow is new to several people, as are mountains. Their oohs and aahs are contagious, and soon, we're all exclaiming about the stupendous views. As the van makes its way over passes and through small mountain towns, I reflect on the adventurers who settled these wild places. Of course, the Arapaho, Utes, Apaches, and other tribes had been here for a thousand years or more. Following the buffalo must have been a grand adventure for them. But when white men killed the buffalo and pushed the native people onto the driest, least hospitable land, mere survival became their adventure, although I doubted they thought of survival as an adventure. The land is hard, and it will crush people who aren't just as hard. The mountain views are lovely, but the soil is dry and rocky, fit only to support a few cattle or sheep.

After several stops for food and pee breaks, the van finally pulls off of Highway 17 and onto the straight two-lane road that will take us to the village of Crestone, nestled at the foot of the Sangre de Cristo Mountain Range. I'm tired and overstimulated, and I need a nap. Fortunately, bedtime isn't too far away.

Maybe the altitude is getting to me. Crestone is at eight thousand feet, and the dome will be even higher. Altitude hasn't bothered me in the past, but my body is different since the accident. Things I hadn't noticed before are now problems: loud noise, alcohol, flashing lights, fast conversations. I'll have to pay attention to how I tolerate the altitude.

The van winds around the streets of the village that is composed of a general store, a couple of restaurants, a lumber yard, and many art galleries. Eventually, it stops in the parking lot of the East Valley Inn, which is a beautiful two-story retreat center overlooking the valley.

We tumble out, shivering in the chilly mountain air. As soon as the driver unloads the luggage, everyone but me grabs their suitcases and runs inside. I stamp my feet on the couple of inches of snow on the sidewalk. I'm glad I brought seeds instead of plants. The plants would have shriveled up and died from the shock of entering this severe climate.

I focus on what is in front of me—the Rocky Mountains. Snow on enormous peaks just beyond the town glows in the starlight. Stars twinkle above, so bright they almost make up for the lack of sunlight.

I see the Milky Way, something I can't see in Houston or Valencia. The sight is postcard beautiful and nearly takes my breath away.

I wonder if my leg has healed enough for me to ski. Maybe, but if I break it again, I might never walk again. Also, the neuropsychologist warned me that my brain was fragile, and another nasty fall might kill me. Nope, no skiing for me. But snowshoeing is nearly as much fun and considerably safer.

The smell of burning pinyon pine fills my nostrils with delight. I haven't smelled this sharp, deserty aroma since my last visit to Santa Fe, the winter before my accident. It brings back happy memories of walking around the city with Ramón and making love in the tiny bedroom in his parents' house, with its handmade furniture and paintings of the desert. Happier days.

When I can't stop shivering, I go inside. The front door opens into a large room that's decorated for Christmas with strings of lights and pine boughs, with a giant log fire in an open fireplace. Ah, so that's the source of the pinyon smell. I don't see any other guests beyond the ones in our group, who huddle in front of the fire, laughing and talking. Apparently, this place isn't as appealing to tourists in the winter as it probably is in the summer. Too bad. So far, everything about Crestone is glorious. My fatigue has vanished, and I'm awake, alert, and ready for whatever comes.

We make our way into the dining room, where a buffet filled with Mexican dishes awaits us. I've missed authentic Mexican food. People in the South don't care for as much spice as in the West. I eat with relish, my tongue burning from the chili peppers.

"Okay, crew, we'll meet back here at seven in the morning," Carleton says when we've finished eating. A few people boo about the early hour, and he reminds us we're on mountain time now, two hours earlier than eastern. "You'll be awake, I bet. Enjoy your night."

My room is spartan but comfortable. I change into pajamas and check my phone. I'll be without a phone for two weeks, so for now,

I'm glad to have it. There are voicemails from Ramón, my mom, and my lab assistant, Toni. It gives me a warm feeling to know that people care about me.

It's too late to call anyone back, but I listen to the messages. Mom said, grudgingly, that she wished me well and she'd be praying for me. That was a step up from the cold hug she gave me this morning. And then she said the realtor had scheduled a showing with someone "appropriate" in a few days. She'd tell me more if it worked out. *Yay!* It'd be the first showing.

Toni called to tell me she was researching the effect of intention on plant growth. I'd told her about my experiments, and she was excited to find a new research direction. She'd get back to me after pulling together all the studies in the area.

Ramón's voicemail was particularly sweet: "I hope your trip goes well. Feel free to call me anytime, day or night, if you need me."

No endearments, but I can't expect any, given how hard I've pushed him away. Maybe he's just being a loyal friend, concerned about my welfare. Before I left, I asked him how his Thanksgiving had gone, but he responded with a noncommittal "Fine." I wanted to ask about Deborah, but I bit my tongue. They divorced because Deborah wanted children and Ramón didn't. As things turned out, Deborah hasn't remarried, hasn't had kids. That means she's available again. It's none of my business, but I'm dying to know if anything happened between them.

For the first time, I wonder if he was right to side with NASA against me. Maybe I wasn't in as good a shape back then as I'd thought. I'll add it to the list of things to think about while I'm in the dome. There should be plenty of time to consider everything.

If things go well, I might take a trip to Houston and surprise him when I get out. Or even better, we could come back to Crestone together and rent a house for Christmas.

Just thinking of the possibility makes me smile.

Chapter 24: Into the Dome

I get up early and go for a walk in the predawn mist. Another couple of inches of snow fell during the night, but I'm fine in the boots and coat I bought before we left. I pass fields of rabbit grass, a desert plant that holds down the soil. Forests of cottonwood trees indicate that a creek is close. A dog sits in the middle of the road, completely unfazed by my presence or the pickup that carefully drives around it.

For the first time in a long while, I'm in a good mood—an actual good mood. In Houston, during the long months of my recuperation, I'd been angry, depressed, and disillusioned with the world. And for most of the two months I've lived at my mom's house, I've been putting one foot in front of the other, trying to keep from falling into an emotional pit. Now I welcome the good mood, as if meeting an old friend.

Being an astronaut isn't all puppies and rainbows. I worked hard every day for years, memorizing formulas, understanding how rockets worked, diving in a forty-foot pool to practice weightlessness, and so many other things. The hard work didn't bother me as long as a trip to the ISS was in the offing. Now, I wonder if it was worth it. Maybe, like Ramón said, there are other things to life that I haven't thought about in a long time.

Do I really want to go back to that?

Yes. Kairos is the carrot I've longed for. That mission would entail more years of training, more memorization, more simulations. I yearn to be part of humanity's first venture so far from Earth. It won't be easy, but everything in life is a balancing act between pain-in-the-ass fear and heart-stopping wonder.

I sigh and turn back toward the inn. Crestone's deep-seated peace invites me to go deeper into my thoughts than I have since the accident. In the two weeks ahead, I'll have little to do but think. I hope I'll come out with a decision about Ramón and a plan for what to do next with my life. As an added benefit, I might actually understand what the spaceman dream is about. If not that, maybe the memories will return and I can stop thinking about the accident. Karin will be proud of me if I pull that off.

Back at the inn, I pour myself a cup of coffee and join the group that has already assembled. Everyone except Curt, who is nowhere to be seen, sits on meditation cushions that are arranged in a circle. When we're settled, Carleton smiles and says, "Good morning. You all look refreshed. I want to tell you the plan for the next two days, and then we'll talk about the dome." He looks refreshed too. The mountain air must be good for all of us.

I haven't sat on a meditation cushion before. My knee doesn't like to bend out to the side, at least, not for long. My neck isn't great without back support either. I will need a real chair with a back if this goes on for long. Looking around, I see that I'm the only one squirming. *All right, then.* I'll call on some of my famous discipline and sit on the infernal cushion.

Carleton smiles at me, seeming to understand my discomfort, but he doesn't offer a solution. I stiffen my spine and straighten my legs in front of me. That's better.

"I want you all to be outside as much as possible today and tomorrow. On Saturday morning, as soon as we finish breakfast, Suzie will ferry us over to the dome. Once we're sealed in, you won't be outdoors again for two weeks, so enjoy yourselves while you can. For the next two days, we'll have a Jeep at our disposal, with Suzie as our driver. Talk to her if you want to go anywhere. She'll be our Crestone contact, so she won't be joining us in the dome."

All eyes turn to Suzie. She nods and smiles as if to say it's fine with her.

Carleton continues. "She used to live in the area, so she'll be a great contact person. Besides having her as our driver, we'll send her messages telepathically every day. She's a good receiver, so we're hoping she'll receive everything we send. And if we have an emergency, we'll contact her, and she'll come to us right away. Questions?"

None.

"Okay. Part of the reason we're here early is to make sure that no one suffers from altitude sickness. If you do, we need to know about it before we leave for the dome. It's a potentially dangerous health problem, so please tell me if you experience headaches, nausea, shortness of breath, dizziness, or cough. Sometimes, the symptoms go away after a day or two, but if not, you'll need to get to a lower altitude."

Everyone nods. Altitude sickness is like having a brain injury, I realize. Aside from shortness of breath, I've had all those symptoms during the past year. So far, I feel fine.

"In terms of what there is to do around here, you can hike or snowshoe right from here. The front desk clerk can check out snowshoes to you. Also, the Great Sand Dunes National Park isn't far. Suzie will organize a trip if you want to go. A couple of hot springs are a few miles away too. And there are a number of spiritual centers in town. The front desk clerk can arrange a tour, or you can check them out by yourself. You're on your own until Saturday morning, so have fun. And get used to these meditation cushions. We'll be using them much of the day once we're in the dome."

He smiles, stands up gracefully, and saunters out of the room. The rest of us stand and stretch as we compare notes about how we'd like to spend the time. It all sounds great, but so does sitting by the

fire and watching movies on my tablet, perusing social media, and listening to music. None of that will be possible in the dome.

I end up doing everything. I snowshoe on a winding trail then
soak in hot springs for hours, only leaving because Suzie insists. With
Thomas and Darla, I walk up the amazing dunes and slide down on a
piece of cardboard, grinning and hooting all the way. And I visit half
a dozen spiritual centers. Exploring them isn't something the old me
would have done, especially since I was raised in a strict evangelical
church, but branching out feels good.

I consider asking Suzie if she'll change places with me for the du-
ration. But I signed a contract, and I'll honor it.

I'm in the last group to go to the dome. After shoving my belong-
ings into the Jeep's hatch, I squeeze into the back seat with Sheila
and Thomas. It's the first time I've ridden in an SUV since one ran
me down, and the experience is creepy. Fortunately, it's not an Explorer. Still, I can see that it might be difficult to spot a short person
standing in the road over the hood of the vehicle. I'll be happy to get
back to my Tesla when this is over.

Suzie drives out of the town and up the unpaved mountain road
behind it. The road, narrow to begin with, gets smaller every hundred yards as it winds around and up. For the first few hundred yards,
the dirt is relatively smooth. Then the rocks begin, and the potholes,
and the icy patches. After jumping and jolting so much that I grab
on to the handhold above my head, I understand why locals buy such
giant vehicles. There are rocks in the road that my car couldn't clear.
And the Jeep's large tires don't slide on the icy patches.

Okay, I won't complain about SUVs again, as long as they stay in
their proper places. I can do without them on city streets, but they
make sense in outback Colorado. Suzie seems comfortable driving

the Jeep, and I understand why she chose to remain behind. She can quickly drive up to rescue us if something goes wrong.

We travel about a mile past the last house and then past a small campground. The trees get smaller and more twisted as we approach tree line. Finally, a large, dome-shaped building rises on the left side of the road. It's nestled in a small, relatively flat field. It resembles a movie spaceship that has recently landed or a tennis ball that has been cut in two and one half smashed into the ground. It won't surprise me if ETs step out of the building, their bony fingers pointing at us. Instead, Carleton and the rest of the party come out to welcome us. No ETs. Not yet, anyway.

I stand back and assess our temporary home It's wide and tall and whiter than the snow that surrounds it. The snow is patchy and dull in places, whereas the dome is so bright it hurts my eyes. The builders probably applied the adobe mud with a hand trowel, because it's lumpy and makes the building look like it has measles. At the top is a large skylight, and the adobe surrounds it like lips puckered for a kiss. My misgivings melt. Maybe it won't be so bad to spend two weeks in this quirky tennis ball.

The building seems to be completely off the grid. Just north of the structure, a bank of solar panels stands low to the ground. Various insulated pipes stick out from the walls, and one leads to a steep, rock-covered area that might be a leach field. An electrical box is attached to the outside of the building. *Hmm.* How can we reset an electrical breaker if we can't go outside? Even the ISS allows astronauts to go out to fix things.

A small lean-to is attached to the south side of the building. I open the door and peer inside. Several of the pipes end up here. They must connect to the water well. I see a gas furnace too. The last thing in the lean-to is a generator. Good idea. It will provide electricity if the solar power fails in a storm. So far, so good.

When I've finished my outside inspection and go inside, I see that someone has carried in my suitcase and boxes. I'll thank that person later. For now, I stand in the doorway and take in the space where I'll be held prisoner for the next two weeks. No, it's not helpful to think of it as being held prisoner. Rather, it's the place where I can relax and refresh. *That's better.*

I've been in cylinders designed to be shot into the sky but never a dome. A series of doors leading to bedrooms stands open around the perimeter of the lower room. "Cubicles" is probably a more accurate term, because a quick glance shows them to be tiny, maybe eight feet by five feet. I count seven cubicles and a bathroom. A spiral staircase leading to the second floor stands in the middle of the room. Beside it is a long dining table and chairs. Scattered around the room are a few other chairs and a couple of couches. The small kitchen is opposite the front door. I see no windows downstairs, only glass window blocks. They let in some light but not much. Glancing up, I see the second floor is filled with windows, and the light filters down. I can put my plants up there.

"Here's your room," says Darla, who has come up beside me. She gestures to the first room to the left of the front door. "I put your stuff inside."

"Oh, thanks." There is just enough room for a single bed, three small shelves for my clothes, and a tiny bedside stand. No chair. The roundness of the dome makes for no square corners. An opaque window block brightens up the back wall, and a lightbulb hangs from the ceiling. That's it. No closet and no pictures or decorations of any kind. As spartan as it is, it's still slightly larger than my room in the space station would have been.

"It's fine," I say, smiling at Darla. "Where's yours?"

"At the far end." She gestures to the fourth room on the left. "The bathroom is opposite me."

So Darla won't be bunking with Carleton. Interesting. "What's upstairs?"

"Our meeting space."

I walk over to my boxes. "What about my plants? Where do they go?"

Thomas comes over and grabs one. "Let me give you a hand. There's a table upstairs for them. You'll like it."

I climb up the steep spiral staircase and enter a beautiful area, one complete with shiny wooden flooring, cheerful throw rugs, small but clear windows high up the walls, and a couple of long tables where I can set up my plants. Two exercise bikes take up one section of the room, and three small desks have been pushed together near the stairs. In the center is a big open area where the meditation cushions are stacked.

"It's nice," I say, plunking down a box on one table. Thomas deposits the second one beside it. Before I can begin unpacking them, people start to gather on the first floor, and we join them. Carleton and Curt are standing, and everyone else finds seats.

"Now that everyone is here, you're free to go," Curt says, nodding to Suzie. He holds up a walkie-talkie, and so does she. "Suzie will be available if we have a problem. But we won't." He smiles at her. "As long as you keep it with you at all times, you can relax and enjoy yourself."

She turns to us and waves goodbye. "I'll pick you up in two weeks. Have fun."

"Oh, and close the door behind you," says Curt.

"Sure thing."

"And lock it. I have another key if we need to get out."

She holds up a bronze house key and walks outside, closes the door behind her, then turns the key in the dead bolt. Lights flash on a keypad near the doorknob.

"I've set the combination," says Curt. "It's written on an envelope that will be on my desk in case of emergencies, along with the extra key."

A wave of nausea grips me as I stare at the closed door. There will be no leaving except in case of emergency. Someone sucks in their breath like they're holding back a sob, but I don't look around to see who it is. We probably all feel the same way. We listen as the car starts and drives slowly down the road.

When it's gone, the quiet is overwhelming.

Carleton speaks. "Okay, here we are, folks. It's exciting to begin a new venture, isn't it?"

I reluctantly tear my gaze from the front door, aware that the others are having trouble looking away from it too. "Exciting" isn't the word I would choose. "Tense," maybe. Or "creepy." I shake my head. I'll try for exciting.

He continues. "Suzie will receive our thoughts every day at ten a.m., three p.m., and seven p.m. She'll record what she thinks she receives, and we'll write down what we send. When we leave, we'll compare notes." He nods to Curt then sits next to Darla.

Curt smiles. "Now that we're here, crew, I have some things to tell you. I am vice president of new programs at Space Tours, Inc., and I want to welcome you to our first moon adventure simulation. We call this venture Sim City."

A loud murmur rises from the group as we exclaim our surprise. Sheila whispers to me, "I knew there was more to it than telepathy."

Space Tours, Inc., is where I've applied to be a flight attendant-slash-astronaut. *Interesting.* I whisper my agreement.

"There are structures like this nestled in various out-of-the-way places around the world," continues Curt, "but mostly, they're preparing to colonize Mars. That isn't our mission. We want to take tourists to the moon. It's closer, easier, and safer. And far, far cheaper."

He grins like a kid on Christmas morning. "Our company has three approaches to moon tourism. The first is to take tourists for a flyby near the moon. We've already done that three times, and it thrilled the passengers." He nods as the group hums with excited noises. Then he holds up his hand for silence. "Second is a lunar circumnavigation. That's scheduled for some time in the next six years, maybe in conjunction with a NASA flight. Finally, our most important project is to land people on the moon for anywhere from a few days to a few weeks. You're our first simulation group. If this goes well—and I don't doubt it will—there will be other simulations here. In the next one, we'll add another building with a covered walkway between them. And others, too, as we go along. Hence, the term 'Sim City.' This is going to be big, folks."

He smiles. "After everything checks out, our engineers will build a dome like this on the moon where people like you can come to decompress and enjoy seventeen percent gravity, get massages, and enjoy the view. We plan to have this project up and running within ten years."

I'm familiar with experiments in moon tourism. At least, I knew about the flybys but not the moon habitation. I wonder if NASA is aware of this simulation. One of the first things I'll do when I leave will be to call Jeb and tell him about it.

I turn my attention back to Curt, who looks more relaxed than I've seen him. "We don't want the press involved until we've completed this initial simulation. But they'll be waiting for us when we walk out of here. Much of the world's population will be eager to go for a vacation on the moon. At least, the rich ones will be. And there are plenty of them." He chuckles.

We digest his words in silence for a few moments. Finally, Emily raises her hand. "What about the telepathy project that we came to do? Is that not happening?"

Curt gestures to Carleton, who stands up, his expression strained. "Yes, we're doing it. To be honest, I didn't know about this other piece until shortly before we left Orlando. Until then, I thought we were only doing the telepathy project I laid out for you." He takes a breath. "Curt has assured me we can still complete our experiments."

He pauses and looks around the room. "There will be plenty of time for questions as we go along. For now, here's the schedule: You can sleep as long as you want and have breakfast when you want, as long as you're on the cushions by ten o'clock. Emily will teach a yoga class every morning at seven thirty, and you're welcome to take part, but that's up to you."

All eyes turn to Emily, who blushes and nods.

"At ten o'clock, we'll send a telepathic message to Suzie, and then we'll work on other projects. You might not have noticed, but we placed a random-number machine inside the small shed out back. It will generate random numbers and keep track of them on both a thumb drive and a paper log. For a few minutes, we'll try to make the numbers change from random to sequential. And when we're finished with that, we'll scan the heavens with our minds, a section a day.

"We'll work from ten to noon and then take a break for a few hours. We'll regather from three to five and take another break, and the last session will be from seven to nine in the evening. The rest of the time is yours."

When he's finished, Curt stands up. "Now I'll give you a tour and tell you some things that will make life easier for everyone. Please follow me." He leads us to the bathroom, and we peek in. It's small, but it has the essentials: sink, toilet, shower. "The toilet is a composting one. Read the directions on the card posted above it, and you'll get the hang of it. Fortunately, we won't have to empty it while we're here." Several people curl up their noses, but he ignores them.

"To save water, I set the shower to turn off after one minute, and it won't turn on again for ten minutes. We have a well, but we're pretending we're using a water tank, just as we would on the moon. In this scenario, there's enough water for two weeks as long as we don't waste any. If you plan on washing your hair, I suggest you put the shampoo on in the sink and then step into the shower to rinse it off. If you do it quickly, all will be fine." He glances at our concerned faces. "There are seven of us, so I've programmed the shower for seven minutes throughout the day. Outside the door is a list of available times, so you can sign up for when you want to take your shower." He nods toward the bathroom door.

Sheila's face is bright red. She raises her hand. "Curt, are you for real? I can't take a shower in a minute, much less wash my hair. Have you ever tried to wash Black hair in a *minute*? Maybe it'll work for y'all's hair, but it sure as shit won't work for mine."

Curt shakes his head. "If you were on the moon, you'd be happy to get a shower of any kind. Up there, water is the scarcest resource there is, except for air. You'll just have to figure out how to make it work."

She frowns and opens her mouth to continue her protest.

I lean over and whisper, "Let's see what other surprises he's got in store for us before we complain too much."

Sheila nods, her face set in a grim mask.

Curt leads us to the kitchen area. "We've stocked the kitchen with premade meals that are like what one would eat in space." He opens a cabinet that's stacked with bulging bags. "You'll get the hang of it quickly, I'm sure, and there are directions on the bags. As you might have noticed, there's a tiny refrigerator and freezer for ice and fruit. On the moon, electricity will be precious, but here, we'll heat food in the microwave." He glances at me. "Is that what astronauts use on the space station?"

I glance around, but no one looks surprised to hear that they have an astronaut in their midst. Looking back at Curt, I say, "It's a little different, especially since there isn't any gravity. This should be much easier."

He laughs. "Well, we would have added weightlessness to the experience if we'd been able to figure out how." He looks around. "There should be enough food for everyone to eat their fill. And we have filtered water for drinking, so feel free to make tea or coffee. Just please don't waste water. We're measuring our usage, and we want to keep it to a certain minimal level. Otherwise, I'll have to ration it. We don't want that to happen, now, do we?"

He sounds like a stern preschool teacher. Like scolded children, we shake our heads in unison. He walks to a cabinet I hadn't noticed. "Here's your treat. I stocked this cabinet with enough wine for each person to drink a bottle a week. Your names are on the bottles. You'll each have a red and a white. There are also four six-packs of beer and a bottle of whiskey for you to share. There isn't enough alcohol for you to get drunk and stay drunk, so make sure you ration it so you can enjoy your time here. And don't hog the drinks you're supposed to share, or things could get ugly."

Even though I'm not much of a drinker, having access to alcohol is the best thing I've heard so far. Everything else seems pretty restrictive. The rules make sense, though, as a simulation of a moon voyage.

He leads us toward the dining table. "We can use this both as a Ping-Pong table and for eating. I hope you all retain your fitness levels and maybe even improve them. You probably saw the bicycles upstairs. Please make use of these activities often."

He glances at Carleton. "Is that everything they need to know for now?"

Carleton nods. "I guess so. Let's unpack and get settled, and we'll meet upstairs in half an hour."

Chapter 25: First Contact!

Standing still as statues, we all stare at one another, probably thinking the same thing: this will not be easy, especially the shower part. I'm already nostalgic for the hot springs I soaked in yesterday. Sighing, I go to my room and unpack. When I've found places for my clothing and toiletries, I push my suitcase under the bed and lie down. The mattress is firmer than I like but tolerable. After a few moments, I get up, climb the spiral staircase, and begin unloading my boxes of plant supplies.

With the big overhead window, there will be adequate light, but I unpack the grow lights anyway. I set up the containers and add small bits of the special fertilizer I'd taken from my lab in Houston. Finally, I plant the lettuce seeds, water and fertilize them, and write notes to myself explaining what to do with the trays. The experimental group is to be sent good intentions, while the control group is to be ignored as much as possible. I don't have enough space to separate the boxes very much. Nor do I have music to play for them. This will have to do.

I don't expect to complete the project while we're here. I'd asked to bring plants primarily to see if they'd let me do it. Two weeks isn't long enough to achieve any results, but we might see some little seedlings sprout. Greenery always makes life more bearable.

Before long, we gather on the meditation cushions. I'm not happy on this hard cushion, but I'll deal with it later. After our usual introductory exercises, we send a telepathic message to Suzie, followed by visualizing the random-number generator putting numbers into sequence.

We end with the main event: trying to locate intelligent life in the universe. I figured we'd use our imaginations to visualize the stars and planets. Carleton, however, has a big surprise for us. A large piece of equipment sits in the middle of the floor, covered by a close-fitting case. With a grand flourish, Carleton pulls off the cover to unveil a digital projector. He explains that he borrowed it from the University of Colorado. When he closes the window shades, the room is completely dark. He turns on the projector, and I draw in a breath. Seeing the stars and planets spread out above our heads and along the surface of the dome makes the entire experience come to life.

"Okay, people, here's the deal. These are pictures from the Hubble Legacy Field, which took photographs over a sixteen-year period. The photos we'll explore here include the area from which fast radio bursts have originated. I've divided it into twelve quadrants, and we'll focus on a different one each day for twelve days. If we want to return to certain quadrants when we're finished, we can do that. This is the first quadrant. Take a look." He waits while we stare at the shining stars and planets nested in the dark space. Using the controls, he travels deeper into that section. "It probably won't look any different to our uneducated eyes than the other quadrants, but we'll systematically go through them all and see what happens."

"What, exactly, are we supposed to send out?" asks Darla, frowning.

"Personally, I'm going to send out the word 'friend.' Not only is it my last name, but making friends is what I try to do in my life. I'd love for you to join me in sending out that word, but if that doesn't work for you, feel free to send whatever message you want."

His theory base seems disturbingly vague to me. Assuming that the tachyon net is how we'll contact other beings, it makes little sense that six people's thoughts will be stronger than one person's. I also don't see how sending the word "friend" will be any more effective than sending, say, "*Star Wars*." Contact is contact, whatever word we use. Or not, in all probability.

I fear that Carleton hasn't thought all the way through this project, but the time for detailed questions and skepticism is long past. I'll be a team player and do my best.

Instead of projecting skepticism, I try to make my mind neutral and focus on the quadrant Carleton indicated. This area includes stars and planets that are relatively close as well as some that are farther away than I can imagine. I repeat the word "friend" while visualizing it as a radio wave that spreads out and intensifies as it flies across the universe. Nothing happens, as far as I can tell, but the whole effort is relaxing. Expanding.

In a few moments, Thomas speaks in a quiet voice. "I think I've got something." We stop concentrating and gape at him. He's sitting with his legs crossed, back straight, and eyes closed. "I feel that my mind is being caressed by another being far away. Really far away. I sent out the word 'friend,' and I got back 'yes, friend.' I'm still in connection. Carleton, what do I do now?"

I stare at Thomas with my mouth open. I'd thought that Carleton might profess to sensing something, or maybe one of the others, but not Thomas. He's too down-to-earth to claim that he feels something just to get attention. If he says he has something, he does.

Carleton squats beside him. "Can you point at the location?"

Without opening his eyes, Thomas points at the far-left portion of the quadrant.

Carleton sounds calm when he says, "Okay, everyone, let's join Thomas in placing our focus where he pointed."

I try, but I'm too excited to focus. Suddenly I'm forced to consider if this could be real. I've never believed Carleton's woo-woo theories, but Thomas has just rocked my entire foundation, and I don't know what to think.

After about five minutes, Thomas says, "It's gone." He opens his eyes, takes a deep breath, and stretches. The rest of us do the same as we stare at him.

"Tell us exactly what happened," says Carleton. He sounds calmer than I would have expected, given that his entire premise has just been validated—at least, to a point.

"I was thinking the word 'friend' and focusing my mind in different areas of the quadrant. For a while, nothing happened. And then I sensed that someone—or *thing*—had heard me and was sending a response. I'm not sure it knew that specific word, because what it sent back wasn't exactly the same word. It sounded in my mind something like 'flttt.' I know, weird, but it felt friendly, so I stayed with it. Nothing else happened. It didn't get stronger while everyone else was focusing on that area. And then it pulled away. That's all I know."

Darla, sitting beside him, reaches over and holds his hand. So does Sheila, on his other side.

He lies back on the floor, shaking his head. "That was the most bizarre thing that's ever happened to me."

Carleton moves behind him and holds his head in his hands for a minute. When he lets go, Thomas sits up. "Thanks, guys." He glances over at me and raises his eyebrows.

I wink back my congratulations.

Carleton sits back down. "Ladies and gentlemen, we may have just witnessed the first contact with intelligent life on another planet. Congratulations, Thomas."

Part of me wishes I'd been the first one to make contact, but if it couldn't be me, I'm glad it was him. Everyone gathers around Thomas, sending him energy. After a few moments, we drop our hands. "Thank you," he says. "Now, if you don't mind, I'm going to my room and write all this down. After that, I may take a nap."

We clap as he descends the staircase. Journaling seems like a good idea. Curt gave us all notebooks when we arrived so we could write about our feelings and experiences during the simulation. This will be the first notation in my journal and in many others', I figure.

We go to our rooms silently and close our doors.

Chapter 26: Reality Sets In

Several of us gather for lunch at one o'clock. I eat a packet of tuna salad and an apple, while Thomas chooses a packaged steak. "It's better than I expected," he says, grinning. The others laugh as they taste the new food.

"How does it feel to have made first contact?" I ask.

He frowns and bites his lip. Finally, he asks me in a low voice, "Could I have been hypnotized or something? And who would have done it? I don't recall being hypnotized. But after thinking about it, I'm not sure contact really happened."

I set down my apple. "I honestly don't know. If you were hypnotized, so were the rest of us. But you were the only one who sensed a response."

Just then, Curt comes out of his room and sits at the table. "I heard about what happened. Congratulations, Tom." He opens a packet and pushes something vaguely greenish into his mouth. "The only problem is there's no proof that anything really occurred. Whether you were hypnotized isn't the relevant question. More appropriate is how do you prove anything at all happened, except in your imagination? SETI sends out radio waves and can objectively analyze any data that comes back, but whatever happens on the inside of your mind is purely subjective. It won't convince anyone. Unless a flying saucer sets down in the field." He chuckles. Glancing at me, he adds, "You should know that, being a scientist."

I blush and watch as the others exchange glances. Curt's intrusion on a private conversation demonstrates that we won't have any privacy during the weeks ahead. Apparently, anything that's said at the dining table is fair game for anyone else to comment on. That's going to take some getting used to. I don't like Curt much, but I can't argue with his logic.

I've been aware of the problem of objective verification ever since Carleton first mentioned the project, but I haven't brought it up. I considered the project merely an adventure that would allow me to take a break from my life and possibly get to space. Now my scientific mind is at war with my desire to believe that Thomas did what he said. Curt's right that there is no objective proof that anything happened, but his comment sounded pretty snarky. I lower my eyes and keep eating.

Thomas clears his throat. "I prefer to be called Thomas, if you don't mind. I don't know about objective proof All I know is that I've never felt anything like that before." He pauses. "Maybe those beings were waiting for a message from us, and that's their cue to drop by. We *should* keep a lookout for flying saucers, like you said." He grins and turns back to his steak.

The festive mood ruined, we eat silently, and one by one, we place our empty containers in the trash compactor and go elsewhere. I glance at my watch. Two o'clock. There's an hour until the next session, and I need to do something to keep from going stir-crazy. Time is already dragging.

"Hey, anybody interested in Ping-Pong? I see the paddles and net over here." I fumble through a stack of things on the shelf. "And here are the balls."

"Sure," says Thomas. "But beware. I'm the king of Ping-Pong."

"Oh yeah? We'll see."

We spend an enjoyable half hour batting the ball back and forth. My eye-hand coordination isn't what it was before my accident, and my legs don't move as quickly. I'll need to practice more, for sure.

Well, I have nothing but time. We finish our last game, which he wins, sweaty and laughing. Curt challenges Thomas, and he accepts.

I look around for Carleton but don't see him, so I knock on his bedroom door.

"Come in."

He's reclined on his bed, and he's created a minimalist desk by cutting up a cardboard box and placing it over his lap. He's writing something in a notebook. When I come in, he closes it and sets the box aside. "How are you?"

I'm not sure how much insulation is in the walls, so I speak softly. "Curt brought up a good point. How do we document that Thomas made contact when it's all subjective?"

He leans his elbows on his legs and tents his hands over his mouth. "I'm playing it by ear, pretty much. I'll document where in the grid the contact took place and at what time. When we get back, I'll forward the information to SETI, and they can determine if they received any fast radio bursts at the same time. That's all I know to do. Do you have any other ideas?"

Carleton seems different from the way he was before we came. Less confident, more tense. More... depressed, maybe. What happened to our fearless leader?

"Uh, no. That seems good." I kneel on the floor. "Is everything all right?"

He sighs and glances away.

I wait.

Finally, he looks back at me. "Everything's falling apart. You heard Curt. I didn't know any of the rules until right before you did, and by that time, it was too late to cancel. He isn't at all supportive of what we're doing. In fact, he makes fun of it. This project won't go any further—that's for sure—no matter what happens. I can't believe I was such a poor judge of character. I wonder what else I missed."

He hesitates. "There's more, but I don't want to get into it right now. Thanks for asking, though. I really appreciate your support."

I hate seeing this side of him. "Listen, all you say might be true, but you're still in charge of this project. You can tell Curt to shut up when he starts in on how stupid the whole thing is. And maybe SETI will have the evidence to validate your ideas. Don't leave us leaderless with that jerk. Okay?"

He nods and gives me a wan smile. "Thanks, Mia. I needed that."

I glance at my watch. Only ten minutes before the next meeting. "See you in a few."

By nine o'clock, we're all more than ready to quit. No one makes another presumed contact, and six hours of sitting on a meditation cushion, trying to concentrate, is exhausting. I pour a small portion of wine into a glass and sit on a couch on the lower level. Emily and Sheila join me. This is a good time to get to know them.

"Uh, what brought you two here?" I speak quietly to keep anyone else from barging in on our conversation.

They glance at each other and shrug. Finally, Emily responds. "Frankly, I needed a break from my kids. My husband is babysitting while I'm here. It's the first time he's had their full care, and he can't even call me when he has a problem. I love it." She sees my questioning look and adds, "Ian is two, and Jessica's four. They fight all the time." She smiles. "That's not the only reason, of course. I feel like Carleton has something important to teach me. Also, I'm a freelance writer, and I'm helping him write his book."

"He's writing a book? What kind?" Maybe that was what he was writing when I barged into his room earlier.

"Oh, you didn't know? It's about his ideas for telepathy with other consciousnesses. Essentially, it's what we're doing here, but he's worked out the theory base and the physics involved. I don't under-stand all that. I just help him put together his sentences."

"Are you planning on working on it while we're here?" Sheila asks her.

"If he wants to. Doesn't matter to me. I'm going to teach a yoga class every morning, and if anybody wants to come, fine. If not, I'll do it by myself. And I've got a suitcase full of books I've been saving to read. I can't imagine being bored." She laughs.

I sip my wine. "What about you, Sheila?"

"Ditto for what Emily said about being attracted to… Carleton's work. I feel like I've grown so much since I've been following him. I'm a bank teller, so it's not like my life is all that exciting. Spending two weeks in his presence, without dozens of other people hanging around, seemed too good to pass up." She glances away, a shy expres-sion on her face. "But also, I figured it would be a good time to quit smoking." She holds up her hands, showing us nicotine-stained fin-gers that are shaking slightly. "I've smoked for twenty-five years, and my doctor warned me I might not last very long if I don't quit. I've tried before, but I never make it more than three days. Now I won't have a choice." Her smile is tight, and she taps her feet on the floor.

"You're a brave woman," I say. "Cold turkey? Not even a nicotine patch?"

"Yup. I'll get through it. There's no choice."

"I imagine you'll spend lots of time on the exercise bikes, then." We laugh.

Emily claims to be happy without her kids, but I imagine she'll be climbing the walls—just like Sheila—before long. My life is far easier than theirs, and I'm grateful.

"What about you?" asks Emily.

"I had a nasty accident last year, so now I need to figure out what to do with my life. I thought being held prisoner in a dome might help me come up with a plan."

Sheila scratches her cheek. "You were an astronaut, right?"

For the first time, I don't bristle at the use of the past tense to describe my career. *That's interesting.* "Yeah. But now I'm grounded, at least from NASA. Space Tours might hire me, though. I guess that was why they included me in this group. Job interview of a sort."

"Wow," says Sheila. "I've never even been in the same room with an astronaut before. Would it be an imposition to ask you about it?"

I consider her request. On the one hand, I want to bond with my new friends. On the other, I don't want to be "the celebrity." I've had enough of that. "Thanks for asking. I'd rather not talk about that part of my life. Not yet, anyway. But I have other interests besides being an astronaut. Mainly, I try to grow plants in space. That, I'm happy to talk about anytime you want." I laugh. "You might get sick of that topic, though."

"Not at all," she says. "It sounds fascinating."

That breaks the ice. We chat about our interests for two hours. At midnight, we notice that the lights are off in the rest of the dome. I realize I missed my shower appointment at ten o'clock. *Damn.* I try it anyway, but the shower won't turn on, so I wash up as best I can and go to bed. This schedule is going to take some serious getting used to.

I wake up later than usual the next morning, gritty and stinky and irritable from missing my shower. I'll have to wait until ten o'clock in the frigging night to try again because the other time slots are taken. I didn't sleep well either. The too-firm mattress doesn't fit my back, and I'm used to sleeping with an open window. That won't happen again for weeks. And now I can't go for my regular walk and run. Worse, I can't even tell what's going on outside. The foot-square window block in my bedroom shows that the sun is shining, but that's as much as I can see through the wavy glass.

Two weeks of this will not be easy. *Shit!*

I dress and stagger into the kitchen. At least someone made coffee. I pour a cup and sip it while listening to the yoga class upstairs. I should have gotten up early enough to do the class. Maybe tomorrow. Or the next day. Or the next. Time spreads out before me like an unbroken highway to the other side of the solar system.

Sheila emerges from her bedroom, looking as ragged as I feel. She gives me a strained smile and pours herself a cup of coffee.

"Did you sleep well?" I ask.

"Hardly at all. You?"

"Better than that but not well."

We sigh and sip our coffee.

"I'm used to reading the news on my tablet," I tell her. "I knew I wouldn't be able to do it here, but I figured I'd appreciate that the world would go on without me. Now I realize it might just drive me crazy to be so out of touch for so long."

"You and me both, sister."

Curt comes out of his room, looking rested and cheerful. "Morning, ladies." He fills a cup with water and sets it in the microwave to heat while he readies a tea bag. He glances down at our shoes. "I forgot to mention yesterday that you'll need to leave your shoes at the door. No street shoes in the dome. Did you bring slippers?"

Blood pounds in my ears. "Another set of rules, Curt? Why didn't you tell us all of them at once? And what will you do if I choose to wear my shoes inside? Throw me out in the cold?"

We glare at each other. I feel like I'm back in Jeb's office, going nose to nose with my stubborn boss. I stand up, ready to move into his space and see what will happen.

He chuckles, good-naturedly. "I guess I can't do anything about it if you choose to wear your shoes. But the place will get filthy, and you'll have to live with that, because I don't think there's a vacuum cleaner. Banning street shoes seems like a way to keep it relatively clean."

I glance down at my tennis shoes. They probably have dirty soles. God, I hate it when jerks are right. I take a deep breath and sit back down. "Oh, all right. I brought some slippers. I'll change after breakfast. But in the next simulation, bring a vacuum cleaner. Seven people in a contained space for two weeks will be messy, even without outside dirt."

"Duly noted. I'm already making a list of things we need to include next time." He smiles, sits down, and begins reading what looks like a large technical book.

Sheila and I glance at each other and shake our heads.

By the time we gather in our circle to start the day's telepathy session, I'm feeling a bit better. Three cups of coffee helped. I chastise myself for being such a wimp.

For two hours, we sit on the uncomfortable cushions and try to concentrate. "Try" is the operative word, because it isn't easy. The bloom has definitely worn off of this rose, and it's only day two of the simulation. My leg aches from the awkward position on the cushion. I might need to use a chair sooner rather than later.

After lunch, I ride the exercise bike for an hour. I've never been a fan of indoor cycling, but this is better than nothing. I pedal and watch the sky, which is bright blue, the color some call "Colorado blue." The deep blue reminds me of the color of the Earth as I've seen it in the simulations and all the webcams. I feel a pang at the thought of never seeing it from the ISS, but the pang isn't as strong as it used to be.

There are four windows on the second floor. Beneath a good-sized skylight at the top of the dome, I see the sky and the tops of the surrounding mountains. Underneath it, three smaller windows capture three separate views. One is of the mountain right beside the dome, which seems closer than I remembered. The second gives a view of another mountain, farther away but still close. The third reveals the San Luis Valley—not its floor but a small part on the other side, near the San Juans.

Watching the sky gets me thinking about the weather forecast. A big storm is brewing, and it may hit us in about a week. It's supposed to be the first significant blizzard of the season, dropping maybe three feet of snow. Before that, we might get minor storms but nothing major. As someone in Crestone told me, the weather in the mountains is so changeable that nothing might happen at all. After all, winter hasn't really set in yet, even at eleven thousand feet. The day we arrived, the temperature in town rose to fifty degrees.

I've never lived around snow and don't know that much about it. I learned to ski because Ramón liked it, but being cold and wet isn't really my thing. I prefer to wander through the European countryside, seeing unusual plants and visiting forests and arboretums. As I pedal on the exercise bike, I remember our wonderful honeymoon.

We'd married in August, two years after we met. It was a small wedding, limited to family and close friends. We aren't the first couple to both be astronauts, but it isn't common. If we'd invited more people, the press might have swamped us. The ceremony was in a small Catholic church near the home we'd just bought. My dad was angry that I hadn't asked him to officiate, but neither of us wanted him. He was just too judgmental. The priest had agreed to perform the ceremony if we would raise our children Catholic. That wasn't a problem, given that children weren't in our plans.

It was a sweet, simple ceremony. I wore a short beige dress, and Ramón wore a tux. We recited the vows we'd written. Afterward, we flew to Rome for a two-week honeymoon.

I miss the people we were before my accident, when I was an up-and-coming astronaut and Ramón was a loving partner, not a hovering parent. At the thought of the accident, I expect the usual anger toward both him and Ashley to surface, but it doesn't. Instead, what comes is *Oh, get over it, Mia. Enough anger and grief already. Bad things happen to everybody.*

I startle, surprised by this unexpected response to my usual thought loop. Maybe I *have* grieved enough and whined enough, and it's time to move on. But how? That's the question I hope to answer in the next days.

Letting go of my anger and self-pity is a good place to start.

The afternoon and evening sessions go smoothly, without excitement. I'm disappointed, but it's a reality of our situation. Things will go up and down. We're settling in for the long haul.

However, seven people going up and down the tight spiral staircase is taking its toll. The curved handrail has become loose and wobbly. After the evening session, when we're all standing around with wineglasses in hand, Thomas asks Curt, "Where's the toolbox? I'll tighten the bolts on the staircase. That way, we won't have to be so careful."

Curt takes a deep breath and bites his lip. "I... I looked for it, but I didn't see one. I'm afraid the builders might have left it outside."

"What?" We all speak together, incredulous. Immediately, we search for the toolbox. It isn't under the kitchen sink. Nor under the bathroom sink. Nor in the utility closet with the broom and mop. Nowhere.

When we're positive that it's missing, Thomas clears his throat. "I think we should go outside and look for it. We're likely to need it for more than just this. They built this place in a hurry, and it's got some problems. This is one of them."

I hold my breath, waiting for Curt's response. It comes quickly. "No can do. We agreed not to open that door for any reason until we leave to go back down the mountain."

The room becomes quiet as others pick up on the tension.

"How would it hurt?" asks Thomas, his voice louder. "It doesn't negate the simulation if we run around to the shed and pick up the toolbox and run right in."

"This was our agreement. You signed the contract, just like everyone. For the next project, I'll make sure there's a toolbox. This time, we're just going to have to make do with what we've got."

"But why? I don't understand."

Curt sets down his wineglass and licks his lips. "Look, several simulations around the world have been ruined because people went outside for 'just a minute.' Their errands turned out to take longer than that, and then it happened more often, and pretty soon, people weren't staying inside at all. That won't happen on my watch, because we won't be going outside."

No one speaks for at least a minute as we exchange outraged glances. I brace myself to jump into the argument, but just as I open my mouth, Thomas says, "That's over-the-top rigid, Curt. But I'll do what I can with the silverware." He grins, breaking the tension.

The others laugh, probably thinking he's kidding. I know he isn't, at least not entirely. He's an engineer, after all, and he probably carries at least a multi-tool at all times. God help us, though, if we really are reduced to using the silverware to fix our problems. Or if the staircase falls down on our heads.

Chapter 27: The First Thing to Go Wrong

After a short but refreshing shower, I discover that most of the others have gone to bed. Darla is up and sees me, but she makes a shushing motion as she slips into Carleton's room. I wish her well but wonder how two grown-ups can sleep in these tiny beds. Maybe that's the point—they don't sleep. After they make love, Darla will probably sneak back into her own room for the rest of the night.

The only person left up is Curt, sitting at the dining table. I would've preferred to ignore him, but the shower has rejuvenated me, so I sit beside him. He nods at me and returns to staring into his two fingers of whiskey.

I know what I want to say, but I'm not sure if I dare. It will be an even longer two weeks if he's pissed at me. But if I can get through to him, it might make the experience better for everyone. After a moment, I speak quietly, without looking at him. "Could I ask you a question?"

"I guess." He sounds like he's preparing for another argument.

Now or never. I take a breath and turn to make eye contact. "It seems like you go out of your way to be a jerk. Why is that? You're here with the rest of us, yet you don't even try to be part of the group. You can do what you want, of course, but I just wondered."

He's silent for a long moment. Finally, he grunts. "I'll tell *you*, but I hope you'll keep it to yourself."

I nod, trying not to look too eager.

He takes a sip of whiskey and swallows. "Look, my job's on the line. Our CEO didn't want to bother with this simulation, but I talked him into it. It's a make-or-break thing for me. Headquarters is monitoring all our electronics. If we open the door for any reason, they'll know about it, and my ass will be grass, as they say in the Marines." He frowns and shakes his head. "At fifty-five, I don't know who else will hire me. But if I bring this in successfully and under budget, I'll probably get a promotion." He pauses. "There it is. I'd rather be a jerk than lose my job. It's a tough world out there."

He has a point, but he still doesn't need to be so tough on everybody. "Isn't there some middle ground? Okay, so you can't open the door without your boss knowing, and he'll immediately end the simulation. I can see that it would take something more than a loose railing to make that worthwhile. Still, I think you could do some other things that would make you part of the group instead of the person everybody loves to hate."

"Yeah? Like what?"

"Give us five minutes for showers, for one thing. Even three minutes would be a reasonable compromise. One minute is too hard, and it just pisses everybody off. We have a well, for Christ's sake, so water isn't really scarce. You can make the same point by limiting showers to five minutes, and people will like you a lot more."

He snorts. "I don't give a shit if people like me. I won't see any of you again after the simulation. And tough but clear rules make life easier for everybody."

I shake my head. "Hey, if anybody knows about rules, it's me. I can do rules, especially if they make sense." I hear my voice rising and deliberately lower it. "But your rules are more or less arbitrary. You could lighten them up and have a better chance of people staying until the end."

He takes another couple of sips of whiskey before responding in a less defensive tone. "You think I'm coming on too strong?"

"Yeah, *waaay*. Maybe you could join us in our meditations once or twice, or at least do a yoga class. You're going to go out of your mind if you don't do something with the rest of the group. Who knows, maybe you'll be good at telepathy."

He snickers. "Now you've gone too far. Carleton's project is bullshit. I'm sure you know that. But I hear you. I might join you for some other things." He thinks for a moment. "Not yoga and not sitting on your damn cushions and staring at the sky. But if you were to give a talk about growing plants in space, I'd come to that."

I've pushed him as far as I can for this night. At least I've opened a channel of communication that isn't limited to him barking orders. Maybe he isn't totally a bad guy, just someone who doesn't know how to deal with people.

"Sure, I'll do that." I stretch. "It's my bedtime. See you tomorrow. Good talk."

"Sure."

The next morning, Curt announces that, effective immediately, showers will be increased to two minutes. Everyone except me cheers. Two minutes is better than one, even though it still isn't long enough to take a decent shower. But I'd hoped for three. Still, I nod to him and grin, and he responds with a serene smile.

He must have talked with Carleton about the plants, too, because as soon as we sit on the cushions, Carleton says, "We've had a suggestion that Mia give a lecture about growing plants in space. You willing to do that, Mia?" When I nod, he continues. "I think the best time would be before the evening session. We can take a half hour from our meditation time to do other things. Unless anyone objects?"

No one does, so Carleton asks, "Tonight, then?"

I nod, unsure of what to say in my lecture, but I'll give it some thought. It shouldn't be hard to come up with something to talk to neophytes about. I did it often enough in what is seeming like another life.

"And we can use some other volunteers to give talks about topics you're experts in," Carleton says. "If not experts, at least something you're interested in. Before radio and television, people entertained each other by giving talks or playing music. Did anyone bring a musical instrument?"

No one raises a hand.

Carleton sighs. "How about singers? Anybody can sing. Emily?"

Emily blushes. "I can carry a tune, if that's what you're asking. But I'm not what I'd call a singer. I guess I could lead some folk songs one evening."

"Great." Carleton beams at her. "What about other talks? Anybody interested?"

No one volunteers. "All right," he says. "We'll play it by ear. Maybe it'll come more naturally after a few days."

The strain in the group has decreased since Curt's announcement. People smile more frequently and seem more relaxed. Also, Carleton is back to his old self, or at least on the way. Maybe Curt talked with him. Or maybe Darla's visit last night cheered him up. Either way, the group needs a leader. And it sure as shit isn't Curt.

As we walk down the stairs after the afternoon session, Sheila loses her footing and falls down the last few stairs. She screams when she hits the floor and keeps screaming. Darla helps the older woman to the nearest sofa, where Sheila holds her right foot and continues to wail.

Everyone gathers around as Darla gently pulls off Sheila's sock and examines her foot. Her fourth toe is jutting out at a weird angle, and it's already turning blue.

"It's broken," Darla says. "You must have banged it on the metal stair when you fell."

"I did. It hurts like holy hell."

The rest of us stare at each other. I've had some EMS training, although I'm not certified. The toe looks bad but not bad enough to be responsible for Sheila's hysterics. I've broken a toe before. It hurt badly—an eight or nine on the pain scale for a short while—but screaming wasn't justified. Maybe Sheila's response has something to do with quitting smoking.

Darla looks at me and shakes her head, her eyes pleading with me to do something. I realize she has no idea what to do. I squat by Sheila and grab her hand. "Look at me," I say softly. "You broke your toe. It's painful, I know, but you'll be okay."

Sheila lowers the decibel of her screaming, but she moans loudly and thrashes from side to side.

I look at Thomas. "We need ice. Will you get some and wrap it in a towel, please?"

He nods and hurries off.

I turn again to Sheila, whose face is set in a grimace. "Okay, I need to elevate your foot." I tell Emily to get some pillows. "And would somebody please get the first aid kit? I hope there is one?" Curt rushes into the kitchen. At least he didn't forget to stock first aid supplies.

When everything is settled, I ease Sheila's toe back into place while Darla holds her hand. By this time, Sheila is reasonably calm. I tape the broken toe to the third toe, elevate the foot, and place the bag of ice over it. The first aid kit has some painkillers, so I give Sheila the appropriate amount.

There's nothing else to do. "If we were in town, we'd probably want to have a doctor look at this. But I think she'll be okay." I step back. "We'll give it a day or two and see how it goes." Squatting by Sheila, I ask, "What else can we do for you?"

She looks tired, but she's under control. "Does anybody have any chocolate? I'd love some of that."

"I brought some," says Emily. "I'll get it." She rushes to her room and returns with a large chocolate bar, which she hands to Sheila like it's nothing. My respect for the young woman increases, because I'm not sure I would have been so quick to give away a favorite food—if I'd thought to bring anything. Come to think of it, some chocolate would have been nice.

"All right, people, let's give Sheila a chance to catch her breath," says Carleton. We shuffle off to different parts of the dome, leaving her alone.

Thomas and I walk to a more private area near the front door. "What do you think?" I ask. "Was this caused by the loose railing?"

"Maybe. Or maybe Sheila tripped. It's not the easiest staircase." He hesitates. "There are a lot of problems with this place." He explains that, while we were in Crestone, he talked to the owner of the lumberyard. "I enjoy hanging around local places and finding out what's going on. The guy knew about this dome. Said a crew from Los Angeles built it instead of a local contractor, and he wasn't sure how sturdy it was. He joked about it falling down around us."

"It doesn't seem that bad, really." I wonder where this is going.

"Yeah, but when we got here, I walked around and found the building inspection report. The inspector hasn't signed off on anything since October 5. Two months ago. And that was just for the foundation."

"Huh. Well, Crestone seems pretty casual about things like that. I saw a lot of buildings that might not conform to building codes. Still, that could explain the loose railing."

"I don't like to see such shoddy workmanship.'

I shake my head. "It's just one more thing that hasn't turned out like we thought. I really hope Sheila's all right, because I don't want to have another argument with Curt about opening that door unless it's truly an emergency. As of now, it doesn't look like that."

"Yeah. Hey, thanks for taking charge. You did a great job."

"Thanks." I pause. "I haven't talked with you much in the last couple of days. How are you doing with the message you got from... somewhere? The universe? Your subconscious?"

"Let's sit for a minute." We find a couch and get settled. "At first, I was floating. Euphoric, really. I was proud of being the first one to make contact. But now"—he shrugs—"I don't have the slightest idea what happened. I think I imagined the whole experience, to tell you the truth."

I think about that for a few moments. "Honestly, I don't know what to say. Maybe it was contact. Maybe it wasn't. We'll probably never know. Do you feel changed by the experience in any way?"

He sucks on his upper lip. "Maybe. Not sure yet. To be honest, I haven't given it that much thought recently. I'm used to playing computer games at night and checking my email, so I'm jonesing for anything electronic. It's hard to concentrate on anything other than that and the problems around here. If I had tools, I'd fix a lot of things." He frowns. "But, hey, I'll get through it. What about you?"

I sigh. "I want to look at my phone at least every five minutes. My hand feels weird not being able to hold it, and I'm kind of itchy, like I've gone off coffee or something. It makes me aware of how addicted I am to social media. Even worse is that I miss being available if there's a family emergency."

"Are you expecting something bad to happen?"

"No. Not at all. I just hate being out of touch, you know? I feel like I've been hung out to dry, and nobody I care about will even know. Does that sound stupid?"

"Nope. I feel the same way."

We sit in silence for a few more moments. Eventually, Thomas says, "Hey, I'm hungry. You want some supper?"

We head off to figure out which of the packets of food to try this time.

Chapter 28: A Tug at the Edge of the Mind

Curt stays downstairs to keep Sheila company when the rest of us gather for our evening session. My lecture is first. When everyone has settled on the cushions, I walk to my plant boxes.

"Let me tell you about this experiment." I talk about the experimental and control groups and ask everyone to spend a few minutes each day sending positive intentions to the boxes on the left and to ignore the ones on the right. Then I review the research studies in the field, some of which are positive for the impact of intention and others that don't show any significant results. "None of them show that positive intention actually harms plants, so it seems a worthwhile thing to try. If it works, we might have some lettuce sprouts to look at while we're here." I smile and sit down.

All eyes stay on me. Everyone is seemingly waiting for more. "Uh, maybe you want to hear about growing plants in space." Their faces brighten. "Okay, fine. Well, it's not as easy as you might think. The fundamental problem is the lack of gravity. The roots don't know which way is down, and the stems don't know which way is up. Also, water and other nutrients float, so it's hard to get it all together. A group of NASA scientists have figured out how to help the process along. They glue the seeds to little plant pillows that fit together like bookends." I place my palms together to demonstrate. "The plant pillows contain dirt, fertilizer, and other nutrients, and they wick the water so it gets soaked in. With the pillows placed under grow lights in space, the plants grow in the right direction. So far, astronauts have been able to grow and eat salads at the space station, and that's no small thing." Some people's eyes are glazing over, so I know I've said enough. "That's all for now. If you want to know more, talk to me personally."

Everyone claps, and we start the session. Same old, same old. Sending thoughts about horses to Suzie then trying to make the random-number generator put numbers in order. Finally, scanning a different section of the universe and sending out friendly thoughts. I sense that the energy in the group is waning. Mine certainly is.

Soon, I exchange my cushion for a chair, and so do Carleton and Thomas. Sitting on the chair helps my concentration, but I'm losing track of the point of the exercise. I decide not to try so hard and merely put friendly thoughts outward to the universe. I picture my thoughts as some kind of flour—maybe whole wheat—that I'm throwing by the handful out to the stars. I've never baked bread, but it's sounding like a good idea after all the prepared food I'm eating.

I'm fantasizing about whole wheat bread with raisins and cinnamon when something tugs at the edges of my mind. It feels a little like a fishing rod with a tiny fish on the line: just a little nudge. Still, it hadn't been there before. Is this a response to my friendly thoughts, or is it a dream of warm, fragrant bread?

Another nudge. Or tug. I wonder if I should say something. No, it's too small. I continue sending out friendly thoughts, and the tug gets stronger. Now I realize it's not a tug. It's a... a smile? A wave? Yes, that's it. From somewhere high and to my left. I turn to face the place, and the feeling becomes stronger.

"Uh, I've got something. It's not a word. More like a wave, or maybe a smile and a wave together."

Carleton asks me to point at the place. I do, and he jots down the coordinates and the time. "See if you can mentally wave back."

I picture myself waving to a friend, maybe one I haven't seen in a long time. Even though my body doesn't move, I mentally send a gigantic wave with both hands.

And then... I'm nearly bowled over by the force of the responding wave. So quickly? Nothing can move through the universe that fast. A thrill runs down my spine. And then something changes. I receive another wave, but it isn't completely friendly. I'm not sure how I know this, but I do. After a second or two, it halts. Whoever sent it might have thought better of it and tried to take it back. Or maybe a different being stopped the first one from waving. I picture someone holding a person's arms down by their sides so they can't wave. Yes, that feels right.

A moment later, whoever or whatever is holding the waver's arms growls—at the waver, I suspect. I hear the sound, loud, inside my head. It's shrill and angry, a little like a dog's growl but sharper, deeper. It seems to come from a hefty creature, reminiscent of a wolf, that is facing an enemy. The sound lasts for what feels like forever as it grows in intensity, and I'm overwhelmed with fear. Slowly, another thought surfaces. Maybe the growl is aimed at me. Maybe the growler thinks I'm the enemy.

Almost immediately, the growl stops—or is cut off. One instant, I'm connected to at least one other being, and the next, I'm not. Relieved but confused, I open my eyes.

Carleton is squatting beside me. "What happened?"

"Uh, would you mind turning off the projector? I don't think it was entirely friendly."

He turns it off, and everyone faces me, eager to hear what I have to say.

"Well..." I lick my lips and begin to tremble. Even though I want to tell them what happened, I can't get any more words out. Is that thing really gone? Will the growl return? *God, I hope not.* Suddenly, I'm freezing, as though I've been dipped into a vat of dry ice.

"I'll get you a blanket and some hot tea," Darla says as she heads for the stairs. By this time, my teeth are chattering. The inside temperature was fine when we first started meditating, but now I feel as though the thermostat is set to… maybe minus thirty degrees. It takes all my energy not to shiver so hard that I'll break my teeth.

At Carleton's suggestion, everyone gathers around me and places their hands near my body, beaming me energy. It feels great, but the only thing that warms me is when Darla covers me with a heavy blanket and forces my fingers to wrap around a mug of hot tea.

Eventually, after drinking the entire mug of tea, I stop shaking. I lie down on the floor, using my meditation cushion as a pillow, and snuggle beneath the blanket. It's so cozy I might never move.

Inside, I'm shaken to my core. Nothing in my life, not even waking up in the hospital with no idea of how I got there, has scared me to this degree. Something terrible happened to the being that waved to me in a friendly fashion. I know it as surely as I know that something just as horrible could happen to the Earth's population if that wolf-thing realizes where we are. And that could be the end of us.

Carleton opens the shades and, through the dome's windows, I see stars floating above me. There is no moon, so the stars look close enough to touch. I shudder. The growl came from one of those stars. I hope it's so far away that whoever or whatever made it will never bother me or anyone in our solar system.

Panic rises, and I shiver again.

Above me, Carleton's voice says, "Why don't we leave her alone for a while. Darla, maybe you could stay with her."

I nod. "Thank you."

The group troops down the stairs, and I hear them pouring their nightly drinks and murmuring. Beside me, Darla asks, "Can I get you anything? More tea, maybe?"

"Yeah. Could you put some whiskey in it too? I don't care how it tastes."

"Sure."

She returns with a mug filled with peppermint tea and something else. I sit up and sip it. The taste isn't familiar, but it's wonderful. It warms me all the way to my toes. I glance a question at Darla, who smiles. "Schnapps. I brought it with me. It's our secret."

I thank her, and we sit together and stare out the windows. Finally, she asks, "Do you want to tell me what happened?"

I force out the words, and the telling takes longer than the experience did. "That was it, really. Something bad was there, and it stopped whoever was waving at me. I sensed that it held down their arms. And then it growled, maybe at me or maybe at whoever was waving. I'm not sure, but it was hideous." I do my best to reproduce the sound but don't even come close to the horror of it.

"God, that sounds so scary. Did you shut it off, or did it just go away?"

"I'm not sure. Maybe some of both."

This time, I don't shiver when I think of the experience. The drink helped. We lie side by side under the blanket, and Darla holds my hand as I slowly relax.

"You know, Dar, I'm thrilled you're here, but mostly, I want Ramón right now. I was a fool to get so mad at him for doing his job. And now, I'm sorry I left him. So, so sorry. I may have lost my dear husband, and I'm stuck in this stupid dome and can't even call him to apologize. What if I never see him again? Or what if he goes back to his ex-wife?" I cry, hard and painful sobs.

Darla holds me until the sobs wear themselves out. "Honey, you can call him in ten days. That's not so long. From what you've told me about him, he'll forgive you. And he'll be happy to have you back. Don't fret." Darla strokes my hair.

"I hope you're right. Hey, thanks for being here for me. I'll be all right now. You can go down, and I'll just lie here for a while. It's okay if you tell them what happened. I'm sure they're curious."

"Okay." She kisses my forehead. "Let me know if you need any-thing else."

When I'm alone, my analytical mind takes over. I have no objec-tive verification of what I experienced and likely never will. Regard-less, I'm sure that whoever or whatever first waved at me had been good. That wave had felt open, pure, positive. Conversely, the being that growled was bad, maybe even evil. How terrible the waver must have felt to be forcibly stopped from showing friendliness.

My dad had often preached about good and evil, but I'd never truly understood what he meant. Now, from experiencing them both in such close proximity, I get it at a deep level. I consider the good in my life. My mom is good, even though I sometimes struggle with her rigid beliefs. The space program is good. Plants are good. Ramón is good. That was why I married him.

I've been blessed with so much good and so many good people.

Then my mind turns to the bad in my life. I'd thought Ashley was bad, but now I understand that she had a momentary lapse in judgment. It doesn't make her a bad person but a person who did something wrong, for which she surely felt terrible, and she'd paid her debt. Ramón had also done a bad thing, but so had I when I left him so impulsively. Even my dad, who had been so difficult, wasn't all bad.

I decide that, at least in my worldview, extremes of good and evil exist, but mostly, people are some of each. *I'm* some of each. I've known that since I was small. Now I understand it in a more pro-found way.

Suddenly, my life up to now stretches out before me in a long line, and I see it clearly, maybe for the first time. Other than Ben's death, which was terrible, most things have gone well for me. I'd thought I deserved all the good things that came my way, but I hadn't, any more than anyone else. I'd just been a hard worker and extremely fortunate.

That insight is going to take some time to percolate through my being. I know, though, that I will be a different person after tonight. Ideally, a better one.

I put away those thoughts for the moment and turn toward analyzing the experience itself. Like Thomas earlier, maybe someone hypnotized me into creating the wave and the growl. Who? Carleton? I guess he could have, but he seemed as clueless as the rest of us when contact occurred. Or maybe my experience was the result of the group dynamics, being isolated in the dome, or altitude. Maybe it was a combination of things.

No. No matter what games I play with my mind, I will forever believe in my heart that I didn't make it up. The experience was too real, too immediate, to dismiss as mere self-hypnosis. When we focus our minds together, I feel the strength of it, the energy within our attention. But I have no idea where the energy goes or whether it goes anywhere at all, other than floating around in the room.

The memory of the growl swirls around in my consciousness. It's extremely intense at the moment, but I know the intensity will lessen over time. Eventually, it will be like the anger I felt at Jeb for grounding me—just one of many experiences in my life, both good and bad.

Suppose I really did, by some fluke, contact another civilization? If so, it's probably not the same one Thomas contacted. His contact was friendly and even responded to him with a form of the word "friend." My experience was completely different. Maybe the being who waved at me was held captive by the wolf, and that was why everything got shut down so quickly.

My mind moves ten steps ahead in a celestial game of chess. I'm no longer the scientist or the astronaut but a fearful sci-fi junkie, and I can't stop my mind from going to the worst-case scenario. Maybe I accidentally contacted the hounds of hell somewhere in the universe and they'll visit us and hold us prisoner as they're doing with that other species. In that case, for our own safety, we should not try again to contact another civilization. Assuming the tachyon net is a real thing, we shouldn't naively assume that all communication within it will be positive.

Focusing our thoughts within our own solar system is probably safe. If there is intelligent life on any of its planets, scientists probably would have known about it by now. But beyond... no one can say, not even the *Star Trek* crew. Most scientists think the FRBs are stars exploding, but they might be wrong.

It's safer to stop this experiment immediately. If Curt insists, we can stay inside the stupid dome for the last ten days, but we shouldn't attempt to contact extraterrestrials again. It just might work, and that could be the worst thing to ever happen to the Earth. Our group could become famous not for doing good things but for bringing destruction to the entire planet.

I need to talk to Carleton immediately.

Chapter 29: So That's How It Is

Wrapping the blanket around my shoulders, I grab my empty mug and slowly climb down the stairs. That stair rail is getting worse, despite Thomas's efforts with his multi-tool.

The first floor is mostly quiet, so at least some people have gone to bed. Not everyone, though. Curt and Sheila are sitting at a small table and playing a card game. She has propped her foot on a chair, and she looks more relaxed than the last time I saw her. So does Curt. *Hmm.*

At the dining table, Darla and Thomas talk quietly and munch on peanuts. I can't hear what they're saying, but it seems to be an intense conversation by the way they're holding themselves.

"Where's Carleton?" I ask as I pour myself a glass of wine. "I need to talk to him." His bedroom door is open, and he isn't inside. Well, he has to be somewhere. Maybe the bathroom.

"He's in Emily's room," says Thomas, sounding strangled. Darla stifles what sounds like a sob.

Uh-oh. "Uh, is Emily in there with him?"

"Yep." Thomas's voice is grim.

Whoa. I bite my lip and try to think of a better spin than the one that jumps to mind. "Maybe they're working on Carleton's book. Emily told me she's helping him edit it."

"The light is off," Darla says. "They were in there when I got back from being with you. The son of a bitch."

"Oh, wow." I sit beside her and rub her back. "I'm sorry, sweetie. But it might not be what it seems."

The three of us sit in silence for a long while, the only sound the muted laughter of Curt and Sheila on the far side of the dome.

Suddenly, exhaustion overcomes me. "I'm going to bed. This whole thing is falling apart. Let's get a good night's sleep and see if we can sort it out tomorrow."

Neither Thomas nor Darla responds. Shaking my head, I head off to the bathroom. Dang, I've missed my shower again. *Figures.*

I lie in bed, trying not to think about the terrible night but unable to think about anything else. My head pounds, and my leg aches as badly as it did right after the accident. I'm so tired that I'm not sure I have the energy to even roll over in bed. Because of my wired-slash-tired state, sleep is impossible, so I run the incident with the wave and the growl over and over in my mind. Eventually, I take medicine that I haven't needed in months.

I'm outside the space station in my space suit, tightening some bolts. The project has gone well, and I'm almost finished. I'm looking forward to getting back inside and having a drink. Even though I'm clipped in, the blackness of space creeps me out. Then another person in a space suit comes around the corner of the station. The USA patch on the person's arm confirms that it isn't the Chinese astronaut I came outside with. My heart pounds in fear, and I feel sweat pouring down my chest. This shouldn't be happening.

I vaguely remember that something similar has occurred before. But this situation feels different—I don't know how, but it isn't the same.

I sense that the person beside me is a man. He pauses a few feet from me, holding on to the handrails. He isn't clipped in, which is infinitely dangerous and against protocol, and he isn't wearing a SAFER. Nothing about this encounter is normal. Who is he?

He comes closer, closer. I can see his eyes. They look familiar, but I can't place them at first. And then I do.

"Ben?" Can this possibly be my brother, grown up and hovering outside the ISS? For the first twelve years of my life, I knew him like I knew my own self, but I obviously haven't seen him since.

He nods.

"What are you doing here?"

When he answers, his voice is a deep baritone that sounds much like our father's but not quite. "Taking care of you."

"What do you mean? You're dead."

He nods, looking sad. "I've been taking care of you ever since I died. But I'm getting tired, and my powers are weakening. I'm ready to move on."

"How have you been taking care of me?"

"Watching out for you. You took my place as an astronaut, so it was only fair I watch out for you. I'm really sorry that I lost focus for a few moments in Houston."

I choke up, but there's something I've needed to say ever since that horrible day at the beach. "I'm so sorry you died. If I'd been watching out for you, it wouldn't have happened. I've missed you so much."

"It wasn't your fault, you know. Even if you'd been watching, I would have died. It was just one of those things that happen. An accident. I'm not unhappy here, but it's time for me to move on to the next phase of my life. Is that okay with you?"

"What is the next phase?"

He shakes his head. "Not for you to know, Mia-pie."

His favorite nickname for me.

He sounds sad when he asks, "Will you be all right without me?"

More than anything, I want to ask him to stay. Not to leave me again. But that wouldn't be fair. He told me what he wants—my permission to leave this realm. He's right. Accidents happen. Some of them have more consequences than others. But they're accidents, all the same. There's no use holding on to the emotions surrounding them.

Finally, I nod. Yes. I will.

He touches my helmet with his, and I see that he's smiling. After pushing himself away from the ISS, he drifts into a higher orbit. The last I see of him is his arm waving goodbye.

I wake, the familiar sweat and tears covering my face. Darla is standing over me. "Mia, sweetie, wake up. You were yelling, 'Come back, come back.' It was just a dream. You're okay now."

Oh, good grief. I've always been afraid I'd scream, but this is the first time I've actually done it, I think. I take the tissue Darla thrusts into my hand and struggle to sit up. After wiping my face, I see several of the others standing in my doorway. I must look a fright. I smooth down my hair and tell them, "Sorry I woke you all up. You can go back to bed. I'll be fine."

They disappear from the doorway, and Darla sits on my bed. "It's been a hard evening. I'm not surprised you had a nightmare. Do you want me to stay for a while?"

I shake my head. "Believe it or not, a lot of things are beginning to make sense. No, you go back to bed. I'll tell you about it tomorrow."

After Darla leaves, I lie back and think about the dream. Ben! Why didn't I recognize him before? If he really was still alive on some level, it makes sense he'd feel responsible for my safety and stay in this realm to take care of me. I was so happy to see him, see how he'd grown up, hear him talk. But he clearly was ready to move on to somewhere else.

If, as Karin suggested, I've conjured the dream-Ben out of my subconscious to stop feeling guilty about his death, I must be ready to let go of the guilt. Ben, or my projection of him, is letting me off the hook. I don't need to feel guilty anymore. He isn't angry with me and probably never was.

Tears come again, but this time, they're cleansing. I'll always grieve Ben's loss and feel sad that I let him down that day, but I can move on, just as he is moving on. Now I can focus on finding out who I really am instead of Mia impersonating Ben.

Also, I can let go of the anger toward Ashley. That was another accident. Ashley will have to live with the guilt for that one. I just have to move on with my life.

I turn on my light and sit up for the rest of the night, journaling about my feelings. At first, they're all over the place, but they even out as the night wears on. I wonder if experiencing the wave and the growl somehow prepared my mind to stop running away from the spaceman dream, or if it was merely the right time for me to get over my fears and face what was standing in the way of my next steps. Guilt and fear have always been my closest companions, and fortunately, I seem to be in the process of letting go of both of them.

As I write, another, deeper wave of understanding hits me. When I was twelve, I threw away my own dreams in order to take on Ben's and convinced myself they were what I'd wanted all along. Even so, I loved being an astronaut. I wouldn't have been nearly as happy being a doctor. Yes, it would have been wonderful to use my training and go into space and to figure out what it meant to "touch the face of God." It was a lofty goal but one I may not achieve. Admitting that reality hurts my heart, and I'm going to need to grieve for a long while. But when I finish grieving the loss, I'll find another goal that's achievable in my current iteration.

I've got time to figure out my next step. I don't have to come up with a life plan while I'm at the dome. There's another ten months before my next official meeting with Jeb. Suddenly, the pressure in my chest lightens, and my headache stops.

I can hardly wait to talk to Karin about these breakthroughs. She'll be pleased. And Ramón. With every cell of my being, I hope he'll take me back. I'll call him the second I'm released from this damned dome.

I've done well so far with what I wanted to accomplish during this trip, even though not in the ways I'd anticipated. I still wonder what happened with the accident, but it seems less important now. Maybe I'll never know, and that will be all right too. Not really, but I'll live with it.

I sleep through breakfast, yoga, and the beginning of the meditation-slash-telepathy session. When I finally straggle into the kitchen, I expect to be alone. Instead, I'm surprised to see Sheila and Curt playing cards again. This time, Darla has joined them.

I pour a cup of coffee and wander over to the card game. "What are you all playing that's so absorbing?"

Sheila looks at me and grins. "We started with gin rummy, and now, we've moved on to hearts. We're hoping for a fourth so we can play bridge. I haven't ever played before, but Curt has talked me into trying." She shrugs. "Do you play?"

I shake my head. "Never learned. But I've always been curious about it. If you're willing, I'll try it." I pause. "But first, how's your toe? May I look at it?"

When she nods, I squat and look at the foot that's propped on a chair. Not as swollen. I gently remove her sock. Yes, the toe is yellowish from the bruise, and the color seeps up her foot, but it's healing. "Can you wiggle it, even a little?"

Sheila winces but takes a deep breath and wiggles her toes. The broken one doesn't move much, but it moves. And she doesn't scream. That's progress.

I smile and pull the sock back onto her foot. "Good job. I think you can cut down on the ibuprofen now. Can you put weight on your foot?"

"Nope. I hobble around on my heel. It works, especially now that I can get my sandals on to protect my foot. But I'm not going back up those stairs. Uh-uh."

Can't blame her for that. Chuckling, I say, "You don't have to do anything but wait out our time here. But you were really excited about being part of the telepathy project. Are you willing to give that up so easily?"

Her eyes get big, and she shakes her head. "Honey, I heard what happened to you last night, and the whole thing creeps me out. Carleton hasn't paid the slightest bit of attention to me since we've been here. He didn't even come over to see how I was doing this morning. You all were the only ones. But at least Curt seems to enjoy my company." She flashes him a flirtatious smile, and he grins back.

Oh. So that's how it is. I guess she got over being mad at him. Well, who am I to question fate? I turn to Darla, who had sat quietly during the conversation, mostly staring at her cards. She looks unhappy. "Uh, what about you, Darla? How come you're not up there with the others?"

She squints her eyes and snorts. "You know why."

"Could we talk, then? Privately?"

Darla places her cards facedown on the table and stands up. "Y'all go ahead without me. This might take a bit."

We find a couch where we can talk privately as long as we keep our voices down.

I start. "Did you talk to Carleton this morning?"

"Yep. He seemed surprised that I was pissed. His story was that last night's session totally freaked Emily out. The poor thing asked Carleton to hold her for a while to soothe her fears. They laid down on top of Emily's bed, and they both fell asleep. Later, he woke up and went to his own room." She raises her eyebrows. "Like I'm supposed to believe that. He insisted that nothing sexual happened, but would you believe him? Because I'm not sure I do."

I take a breath and consider. "I don't know, Dar. It seems inappropriate, even if it wasn't sexual. Has he given you any cause to doubt him in the past?"

"That's what I've been thinking about all night. He's always out with women. He says they're just having drinks and talking about his work. I used to believe him, but now I have my doubts. Stupid me."

"Whew. That's tough." I think about it for a moment while sipping my coffee. I've never been in a similar situation, so I have no real advice for her. "I can't say whether or not I'd believe him. But we're stuck here for a while longer. How do you want to handle it until we leave? I think that's the question for the moment."

Darla snorts. "Yeah, I know. He set up this whole thing like an Agatha Christie book, you know? All these people on a train in the Alps, and somebody is murdered. Only there hasn't been a body yet. But if he keeps messing around on me, there's likely to be one, I can tell you that." She leans in closer. "I want to hear about your dream, but first, I need to tell you something that happened the day they interviewed you all for this trip."

That seems so long ago I can barely remember it. But clearly, it's important to her. "Okay. Tell me."

"Carleton got a letter from a famous physicist that day. He'd shown the physicist the first few chapters of his book, where he lays out his ideas about the tachyon net and how telepathy can span light-years to reach other planets. He explained all this to you. Remember?"

"Yeah."

"Well, this physicist thoroughly debunked Carleton's ideas. He said that tachyons are only hypothetical particles, and, if they even exist, they wouldn't work the way Carleton claims. Besides that, six people concentrating wouldn't be stronger than one person concentrating. And being in space wouldn't make the slightest difference from being anywhere else."

Darla stops to smear her lips with ChapStick. "Anyway, the guy said there might be ways that consciousnesses can communicate with each other across vast distances, but Carleton's wasn't one of them. What was worse, he said he was going to write to Space Tours and tell them they were funding a fraud." She glances at me and frowns. "We were afraid that the funder might pull the money before we even got here. I did my best to make him feel better. I told him the renowned physicist might be wrong and that tachyons are so weird that anything is possible, even if the theory base isn't clear right now. *Yada yada*. I was the supportive fiancée that nobody even knew about. Boy, was I stupid."

I lick my lips. It's incredibly dry here, and my lips have cracked. I'm glad somebody brought some ChapStick, because I didn't think of it. With her permission, I borrow some of hers. Ooh, that feels great. Now I can concentrate.

"I'm still a little wiped out, and my brain isn't working all that well today, but let me see if I've got this right. This physicist doesn't believe Carleton's ideas about telepathic communication across vast distances?" She nods, so I continue. "But something *is* happening here. Thomas experienced it, and so did I. Even if Carleton's ideas aren't completely right or can't be proved yet, *something is happening here*." I take a breath and go on. "Scientists disagree all the time. I don't think you need to be too concerned. Space Tours clearly didn't cancel the project."

"Hmm." Darla is quiet for several moments while I finish my coffee. "Okay, thanks. That was helpful. I think I've been starstruck by him up till now. Now I find that he's just a guy and a not-too-trustworthy one at that. A lot like my ex-husband, now that I think of it."

I reach over and pat her hand. "And so, here we are. What do we do now?"

After a long while, she says, "I guess I'll play along while we're here. Not make too many waves. At least, not yet. But he'd better keep his hands off of Emily, or all bets are off." She shakes her head. "What about your dream?"

The happenings of last night seem far away at this moment. "It was important, but I don't want to talk about it right now. It's all good, regardless of how it sounded last night." I smile. "Changing directions. It's eleven thirty. I was going to ask Carleton to stop his efforts to make contact. Last night, it seemed too dangerous to keep going. But now I think you're right. I'll go through the motions for the rest of the time. Like you, not make too many waves."

We sit in silence for a moment. Suddenly, I see our situation in a completely different way. "Uh, about our supposed contacts. Maybe I've got it all wrong and we aren't actually contacting anybody except our own inner minds. Whatever's in there is coming out because of the isolation and our expectations of contacting extraterrestrials. We believe we've made contact when we haven't at all." I frown. "Actually, I feel better about the project when I think of it that way. Because if there are other sentient beings out there, the odds of their being hostile are just as strong as them being friendly."

I set down my mug and massage my face for a moment. I hope I don't look as tired as I feel, but I'm pretty sure I do. "Are you hungry? I need food and another cup of coffee. After that, I'd love to get a bridge lesson."

We hug.

In the afternoon, we both return for the group session. I join in the telepathy exercises of sending thoughts to Suzie and trying to put random numbers in sequence, but I don't attempt to send my thoughts out to the universe. Instead, I think about all the things I want to say to Ramón when I see him. Mainly, it's a long list of apologies.

Darla seems to doze much of the time.

For the next three days, everyone is civil, aliens don't contact anyone, and Darla and I spend most of our free hours learning to play bridge.

Six more days before we leave the stupid "Sim City." That's doable, as long as nothing else upsets our shaky equilibrium.

Chapter 30: A Contract Is a Contract

I've been watching the clouds roll over for a couple of days. Some snow has fallen but just a few inches here and there. I wish I could see through the first-floor window blocks, but nothing comes through them except light. I can see a little of the valley through the second-floor windows. Mostly, though, I see the sky and the side of the mountain that's close to the dome. To my untutored eye, that mountain is awfully steep. Several times, I've watched mountain goats bound up and down it, making the incline seem like nothing. With the new snow, everything is white, including the goats.

I imagine inmates in other prisons also spend a lot of time gazing outside and dreaming about being out there. All I can think about is the joy of inhaling fresh air, even if it's cold. The confinement is definitely getting to me.

Some thoughtful person affixed a thermometer to a nearby tree, and it has both an outdoor and an indoor readout. During the first week, the outside temperature maxed out at around forty degrees, going down to single digits at night. Inside, we were toasty since the solar panels sent plenty of power to the furnace.

Yesterday, though, things changed. The white, thin clouds I'd grown used to turned thick, gray, and angry, and now they hang low over the mountains. I might be able to touch a cloud if I could reach outside. Without a weather forecast telling us how much snow to expect, I fear we're in for a long, hard blizzard.

In the afternoon, as we sit down for bridge, I ask Curt, "You do still have that walkie-talkie, don't you? Have you talked with Suzie since we've been here?"

"Nah," he says, smiling. "I'll call her if we need her, but I'm sure we won't. There's only a few more days now. What, are you worried?"

I shrug. "I think we're in for a blizzard. And I don't like how close they built this dome to the side of the mountain." I try to sound nonchalant when I ask, "You guys got a building permit for this place, didn't you?"

"Oh God, you and Thomas are such worrywarts. He asked me the same thing. Of course we got a building permit. What kind of idiots do you think we are?"

I let that one slide. "All right, just asking. I don't like the looks of the weather. Wish we had access to a forecast."

He gets up and walks to where he can see out the top window. "Phew," he says, sitting back down. "That really looks scary. I used to have a house in Lake Tahoe, and we saw clouds like that all winter. Yeah, they brought a lot of snow, but after the storm, the sun would come out and melt some of it. Otherwise, we'd dig ourselves out. We can do that here if we have to, but I bet it'll melt before we leave."

"Enough talk," says Sheila. "Deal the cards."

A few minutes later, Emily comes out of her room, and she's crying. "I can't stand it here anymore. I need to go home to be with my kids." She walks over to Curt. "I don't care if I lose my ten thousand and have to pay a fine. You said we could leave if we need to, and I need to. You don't even have to call Suzie. Just open the door, and I'll walk down the mountain. But please do it soon, before it snows. I'm all packed to leave, so let's get on with it."

Curt sets down his cards and scratches his head. He takes a deep breath as he looks up at Emily, who is crying and hovering over him. "I'm sorry, Emily. I really am. But I will not open the door. People in the home office are monitoring our digital lock. If I open the door, they'll declare the entire project a failure. Only a few more days, and you can see your kids. We'll all walk out together, and the van will take us to the airport. You'll be happy you stuck it out."

He glances through the windows. "Besides, the snow has already started, and I don't think you could get down the mountain before you froze to death or lost your way." He pauses. "I'm sorry, Emily. I really am. But you'll have to stay here until the time's up. Could I interest you in some cards? We can play something different. What do you say?"

I wait to see what Emily will do. Curt makes an excellent case, but I don't know if it'll work. The young woman has been increasingly emotional in the past few days. At meals, she talks nonstop about her kids and how hard it must be on her husband to care for them in her absence. And she's eating two or three times more than the rest of us. Her jeans are held closed by a safety pin now, and her sweaters strain across her breasts. It's a good thing Curt's team provided far more food than they thought we'd need, because otherwise, we'd be out.

We all try to be patient with her, but none of us have small children at home. In my experience, complaining and dwelling on problems definitely make them worse, but I don't say that to her, for fear of sounding like her mother. Earlier, Emily talked about wanting to read books, but I haven't seen her reading, not once.

She stands by Curt's chair and yells, "I want to leave *now*! This is a hostage situation, and you're holding me against my will. If you don't open that door, I'll get a knife and make you. And when I get out, I'll tell the police what you did, and they'll charge you with false imprisonment or kidnapping or something else bad. Because you're an evil man."

Curt stares at his cards with a hard look on his face. "Where were we?" he asks the card players.

I prepare to intervene if Emily assaults Curt. The younger woman is right that she's being held against her will, but her threats don't sway Curt. I remember seeing some opioid meds in the first aid kit. I might need to sedate her if she doesn't stop yelling.

Thomas peers over the railing. He and Carleton have been using the exercise bikes. In a second, Carleton rushes down the stairs.

"Emily, sweetie, I know you're upset, and you have every right to be. But you can't leave right now. I'm so sorry." Carleton's voice is smooth and caressing. Darla's face resembles a thundercloud. She can't be happy about how he's acting, but I hope it works.

He moves toward Emily and grabs her by the shoulders. She startles but then settles into his hands. Very gently, he pulls her away. "Let's get you back to your room," he croons. "I know you miss your kids. Why don't you show me their pictures and tell me more about them?" As he speaks, he walks her toward her bedroom. His arm is around her shoulders, and he pulls her close to his chest.

Emily murmurs something, but I can't make it out. When they're in her bedroom, Carleton reaches over and closes the door, not looking back at us. Quiet emanates from the room.

I glance at Darla. Her elbows are on the table, and she's resting her head in her hands. I ask if I can get her anything. She shakes her head, so I leave her alone.

I turn to Curt. "Emily's right, you know," I say, anger spilling out despite my effort to keep my voice low. "You *are* keeping her here against her will. You're holding us all hostage. That's a crime. Please call Suzie and have her come and get her. I'm serious. I'll give up my reward if you let her go, and I imagine the others will do the same."

Curt shakes his head. "No can do. A contract is a contract." He sneezes, excuses himself to get a handkerchief, and doesn't return.

Sheila grimaces then hobbles to her room, shaking her head.

I sigh. This feels like a horror movie, and soon, a monster will burst out of the basement and eat us, one by one, before we can get away. I don't know how to fix the situation, so I go upstairs to ride an exercise bike and watch the sky. I wonder if any of Emily's outburst had to do with falling barometric pressure, or if the separation from her family is all that's getting to her. Maybe it has something to do with Carleton, but that is none of my business. I'll try to keep a closer eye on the young woman. *Poor thing.*

Thomas gets on the other bike and starts pedaling. He leans toward me and says in a soft voice, "I haven't talked with you lately. How are you?"

I sigh. "It seems like these two weeks are taking freaking forever. Even winter survival training didn't feel this long. At least then I could *do* something. Here, I feel like a prisoner." I pause. "Actually, I *am* a prisoner. All of us are. No wonder Emily is cracking from the stress." Pedaling harder, I say, "Okay, enough of that. How are you?"

He glances at the sky, which has darkened even more in the past few moments. "I've been thinking a lot. It's been good for me in that way. At home, I never stop moving long enough to finish a thought. I haven't come to any conclusions, but it's been nice to have the time to go deeply into my thoughts."

We pedal for a few moments. "I know what you mean. For the past couple of days, I haven't tried to check my nonexistent phone every two minutes. And I've done some good thinking too. I figured out some stuff that's been bothering me. I have to admit it's been helpful, but I still can't wait to get out of here."

"You never told us about your experience with making contact."

I briefly describe the wave and the growl. They've faded a little in my memory since that horrible night, and I'm relieved.

"Wow." We compare our various experiences for a few moments, and then we're quiet.

"What about your husband?" He sounds hesitant, but I appreciate that he's brave enough to broach the subject.

Smiling, I stop pedaling and turn toward him. "I've had a break-through there. I hope this is okay to say, but I've realized how much I love him and want him back." This is tricky territory, given our history, but it needs to be said.

He nods, pedaling slowly. "I figured as much. Don't worry. I'm fine with it. As a matter of fact, I've been thinking about someone I recently met. I don't know if she's interested, but I'll check it out when we leave here."

I smile in relief and relax my shoulders. "That's great. I'd like to meet her sometime. Have you decided about the Peace Corps?"

"Not yet. I'll get more information when I'm home." He waits a bit. "What about you and that life plan?"

"That's the big question. I'm working up to it." After pedaling as fast as possible in order to hit my high-intensity target, I back off, breathing heavily, and settle into a slower pace. "I like the idea of retreats. I'm going to try to do one every year. But it doesn't need to be at the moon or anything simulating the moon experience. There are plenty of places here on Earth where a person could have the space and time to think. In the future, though, I'll give myself the choice of when to leave, and I'll definitely go outside whenever I like. And I want better food."

"Yes, to all of that." He nods toward my plants. "It looks like some of your lettuce plants are sprouting. That's great."

"Yeah, the ones we've sent good wishes to are sprouting. The others—not yet."

He lowers his voice. "My first job out of college was in Montana, and I lived there for ten years. I remember clouds like these, and they always dumped a ton of snow."

Shaking my head, I say, "Hopefully, the solar panels keep working. Do you know how long the batteries will work when there's no sun?"

"I think the bigger problem happens if the panels are covered by snow. Someone will need to rake off the snow if it's too much, but obviously Curt won't let us do that." He slows down his pedaling. "Fortunately, there's a backup generator. And the solar panels are tilted, so snow will eventually slide off and they'll start working again. I'm less worried about the solar panels than I am about being so close to this mountain. Avalanches don't give warning. You know?"

I remember one of Ramón's favorite sayings, that people usually worry about the wrong things. I've been thinking about the solar panels instead of an avalanche. "But surely the dome is far enough away from the mountain that an avalanche won't wreck it. There are building codes for that sort of thing. And domes are incredibly strong. I know that much about them."

"Yeah, I hope you're right." His voice sounds grim.

Chapter 31: Four Days, Fourteen Hours, and Twenty Minutes

Carleton doesn't come out of Emily's room for the afternoon session, so Darla announces that it's canceled. We'll try again in the evening. Thomas calls for a Ping-Pong tournament. Curt isn't feeling well, but Thomas, Darla, and I play while Sheila cheers from the sidelines. We don't bother keeping our voices down.

By the time Carleton appears, the rest of us have poured drinks and are sitting around the table, playing charades.

"Join us, Carleton." I point at the empty chair beside me.

He glances at Darla, who gives him a hard look. He shrugs, goes into his bedroom, and closes the door behind him.

"Huh," says Darla. "I'm not going to chase him. He can sure as hell come out and ask to talk to me if he has anything to say."

"Looks like he doesn't," observes Thomas.

"My thoughts exactly," she replies. "Man, I can't get out of here soon enough."

"Four days, fourteen hours, and twenty minutes," says Curt as he emerges from his room, coughing.

We all groan. Four days seem like four years at this point.

The snow starts in earnest by five. A light mounted on an outside pole gives us a surreal view of the falling flakes. By seven o'clock, two things have happened: the snow is at least a foot up the light pole, and Curt is really sick. He's running a high fever and coughing like he's going to hack out his lungs. His throat is so sore he has trouble speaking or even swallowing water. He lies on his bed and alternately throws off the covers when he's hot and frantically pulls them back on when the chills strike.

I've become the de facto health care provider, even though I'm relying on training from years before. Fortunately, the first aid kit is reasonably well stocked. I give Curt medicine to reduce his fever, sore-throat lozenges, and cough syrup, but none of it makes a dent in his symptoms.

"What is it?" asks Carleton when I come out of Curt's room to get more water for him.

"Flu, I'd guess," I say. "He didn't get a flu shot this year."

"But… after so long a time? I thought that comes on only a few days after being exposed. It's been more than a week, and nobody else is sick."

"It's unusual, I admit. But I can't imagine what else it could be. Maybe a different virus. I'm pretty sure it's viral, though. Came on really fast and with extreme symptoms. We should wash our hands a lot and try not to touch our faces. There's not much point in trying to stay away from him, because he's exposed all of us. Maybe if we take turns reading to him or something, it'll distract him from his pain."

"All right. I'll get that going." He smiles at me. "Thank you, Mia. I don't know why Curt's team didn't think about putting a medical person in the group. We'll definitely make that recommendation—if there's a next time. I don't know what we'd have done without you."

I shrug. "He needs to drink some more water. He's burning up."

Sheila stops me on my way from the kitchen. "Can I go in there?"

"Did you have a flu shot?"

"Yeah."

"Sure. See if you can get him to drink this water, okay? I won't mind having a break."

I go upstairs and stare out at the snow. The others are already there, even Emily, who is now quiet and withdrawn.

After a few moments of watching the snow, I ask, "How many of you had flu shots?"

Everyone but Curt, it turns out. "That's good, assuming it's influenza and not some other nasty virus."

We fall silent. "This entire project is cursed," says Emily, drawing out the last word. "We're all going to die in here."

Ignoring Darla's glare, Carleton squats beside Emily. "Would it help if you do some yoga or some meditation? Would that take your mind off what's going on?"

She shakes her head, grimacing.

Carleton looks around the group. "Let's make a circle around Emily and send her loving energy."

We move to do it. I send compassionate energy to the younger woman through my hands. She probably shouldn't have come on this trip. She might get Carleton's attention while we're here, but it can't be worth the genuine angst it's causing her to be without her family. After a few moments, she appears to be calmer, so we sit again.

Carleton asks, "What about if we go ahead with our usual program? We missed the afternoon session, and we're late for the evening one, but it might help if we stick with our routine."

Personally, I think we should make a plan for what to do if we lose power, but I don't want to make people more worried than they already are.

Everyone agrees to try it for a little while. As we concentrate on a different sector of the universe, Darla calls out in excitement. She's heard something odd. It sounds like a radio broadcast, only not in any language she understands, and there's some kind of noise behind the voices—possibly music but unlike anything she's ever heard. She describes it as something a rainbow might make, tinkling and beautiful. Actually, she tells us, her face shining, that this is the most beautiful sound she's ever heard.

I strain to focus where Darla pointed, but I sense nothing other than my own thoughts. I'd love to hear something as beautiful as what she described. That would be infinitely better than hearing another growl. Darla needs something pleasant to remember about this trip because her relationship with Carleton will probably end when we leave the dome. Come to think of it, I feel pretty done with him too. I remember Curt's comment that nothing we hear or sense can be proven. Without objective verification, we're sitting in this dome twiddling our proverbial thumbs.

Still, it's something to do. I definitely feel better, more healed, since I've been doing Carleton's meditation exercises. But now I'm ready to move on with my regular life, even if it means not going into space. Now that I understand the spaceman dream, I can live with that.

When I leave this ridiculous simulation, I'll figure out what to do next. I'd hoped to leave with a plan, but that will depend partially upon Ramón. We need to work out our next steps together. Assuming he still wants me. And I promised to stay with my mom until the nursery has sold. That's as much of a life plan as I can make right now. Given how many other things are going on, I think I'll give up on recovering any other memories about the accident. Like Ben said, accidents happen. I'll just assume it was one of those and move on.

Downstairs, Curt continues to cough, but there's nothing more I can do for him. I hope the rest of us don't get sick, because the medical supplies won't hold out.

I wonder what Ramón is doing while I'm twiddling my thumbs. If he's following the weather forecast for Crestone, he'll know we're in the middle of a blizzard. More likely, he's working so hard that he barely has time to think about me. Or maybe he's found a girlfriend, maybe even gotten back with his ex. That gives me pause. I fervently hope it isn't the case. I decide to try to send him a mental message of my love. That's much more appealing than thinking about some musician on the other side of the universe who is playing a rainbow I can't hear.

I picture Ramón on our bed, naked, waiting for me to finish with my shower and come to him. His skin is lustrous from his own shower. He's combed his hair and brushed his teeth then put on the tiniest bit of aftershave lotion because the musky aroma drives me wild. He's turned the lamp in our bedroom to its lowest setting.

I find him lying on top of the covers, waiting I can tell what he's been thinking because he's ready for me. Hard, big, and lovely.

If I was there with him now, I'd climb onto his body and fit him within my own. He would smile and whisper, "Corazón," and I would kiss him until our lips were red and chapped. We would move together beautifully. I would climax first, and then I'd collapse onto his firm chest. He would grasp my buttocks and roll me over, and then he would pound into me to finish. I would climax again with him, and it would be wonderful.

Afterward, I'd snuggle within the curve of his arm, and we would murmur sweet nothings to each other until he fell asleep. He always falls asleep before I do. I would lie in his arms, blissful at being with the man of my dreams. Eventually, I would drift off.

I decide to reach out to him and see if he picks up on my mental message. After spending a few moments deciding what to say, I begin. *I'm so sorry for the trouble I've caused, my darling. Please meet me in Crestone so I can apologize, and we can enjoy the snow together. I know what I did wasn't fair, but I love you. Please, please, please.*

I transmit the message over and over for at least fifteen minutes. I hope he'll receive it and be at the inn waiting for me when I leave the dome. I don't really believe it will happen, but it's the best thing I can imagine. Just thinking about Ramón makes me moan in frustration. Everyone turns to me.

"Is there something else?" asks Carleton.

Oops. Shaking my head, I smile. "Private thoughts. Sorry to interrupt your focus."

The group becomes quiet again. I've lost the thread of my thoughts. I have no idea if Ramón will receive my message or will care if he does. So much has happened between us that I'm not sure he'd be on my wavelength even if he tried. On the other hand, my mom has always been on my wavelength, even when she doesn't approve of my behavior. I'll send her a mental message too.

I picture her sitting on her couch and watching television. What is she watching? I don't know, and I hope my message makes it through the blast of the television. *Mom, there's a big snowstorm here, and things aren't going well. Please call Ramón and tell him to come to Crestone. I love you, and I miss you. Please, Mom, call Ramón.*

Sheila sneezes.

Oh shit. Sheila had a flu shot, so if she's sick and not sneezing for some other reason, then Curt probably isn't suffering from influenza. Another type of virus would make us all vulnerable. Maybe whoever stocked the food cabinet or cleaned the dome was sick. Viruses can linger on surfaces for weeks.

Something is definitely happening here, and it isn't good.

I'm starting to agree with Emily that this place might be cursed. I can't imagine who cursed it or why. But I do not agree that we're going to die here. Not if I have anything to do with it.

Chapter 32: What a Time to Break Down

Sheila comes down with the mystery virus. Coughing, sneezing, sore throat, high fever—the symptoms are the same as Curt's, only less intense. I put her to bed and spend several hours moving back and forth between the sickrooms. Darla, Thomas, Carleton, and I agree to tend to them in two-hour shifts. If we're to keep up our own immune defenses, we need to sleep.

The others end up handling the patient care and not waking me for my overnight shift. Grateful but confused when I wake up in the morning, I rush out to the dining area and find Carleton and Darla drinking coffee together. They look exhausted, but they seem to be getting along. *Interesting.*

"They're resting comfortably," Darla says. "We didn't think there was any need to bother you. In fact, Curt might be a little better today. Maybe the virus is one of those twenty-four-hour bugs."

I nod and look in on Curt. He's not as flushed as he was, but his lungs still sound congested. Not good. I'll give him more medication when he wakes up. I go into Sheila's bedroom, where Thomas is sitting with her as she sleeps. "Not much to do other than getting her to drink some water," he whispers.

I nod then ask him, "Uh, how do *you* feel?"

"Tired from getting up really early. But not sick. You?"

"Rested, thanks to you and the others." I smile. "Not sick either. But this thing seems to come on really fast. We'll need to monitor each other. I'm not sure about Curt."

I leave him to it. In the kitchen, I heat a terrible omelet in a bag and some toast, also from a bag. It isn't as bad as the eggs. *It's hard to ruin toast*, I think, and a hint of a smile turns up the corners of my mouth. In three more days, after we leave this awful place, I can eat actual food like a normal person. A real omelet, real toast, orange juice. Just thinking about it makes my mouth water.

I sit at the table. Between mouthfuls, I ask, "Anybody seen the snow level today?"

Darla nods. "It's bad. Looks like three feet or more, and it's still snowing heavily. Go up and look when you get a chance."

"Uh, what about Emily? Have you guys seen her yet?"

Carleton shakes his head. "Not a peep from her room. She must still be asleep. She hasn't been sleeping well since we've been here. That could be part of her problem."

Darla scowls but stays silent.

When I finish eating, I walk up the stairs. Looking out through the partially fogged windows, I see snow everywhere, much of it piled into drifts. There's no sign of the solar panels—unless they're under that big drift. Snow is not sliding off them and probably won't anytime soon.

There are no mountain goats and no tracks in the snow. I see only a couple of plumes of smoke coming from the town. The scene below is hauntingly beautiful, but all I can think is how hard it will be for the SUV to get through to rescue us.

I shake my head and go back downstairs. At the door to Sheila's room, I whisper, "Thomas, would you mind coming out for a moment? I'd like to talk to you."

He glances at Sheila, who's still asleep, and tiptoes from the room. "Is everything all right?"

"Have you looked outside today?"

He shakes his head.

"I can't see the solar panels at all. We won't get any new power from them until the storm's over. The thermometer says it's minus two outside, and the snow doesn't show any signs of slowing down. How long do you think the storage batteries will last?"

He rubs his chin and looks away. "I really don't know. Solar batteries provide power at night and when the sun's not shining, and so far, they've worked fine. So there appears to be good storage capacity." He pauses, thinking. "We've probably been on battery power for a while. The system must've been designed to work in these mountains, where storms like this can last for days. Even if it goes out, there's a backup generator in the shed. It should kick in when it's needed." He licks his lips. "I'd feel better if we could rake off the solar panels. Would you mind talking to Curt again and seeing if he'll allow us to do that?"

"I don't mind doing it, but Carleton should be the one confronting Curt. He's in charge of this group, not me."

"Fine. Get Carleton to do it with you."

I walk over to Carleton, where I tell him the problem.

"Sure, I'll try it."

Curt is still coughing frequently and looks exhausted. When I sit in the chair by his bed, he opens his eyes.

"Sorry, I didn't mean to wake you. But since I did, how are you feeling?" I touch his forehead. Still hot. His cheeks are flushed and his eyes glassy. He's not much better, if at all. "Do you have any other symptoms?"

He groans. "The worst headache I can ever remember. And the rest of me aches too." His voice sounds weak. "And the sore throat isn't better."

"I'm sorry, Curt. This thing came on quickly, so it might move out just as quickly."

He nods, but his dour expression says my words haven't particularly comforted him.

Carleton takes over. "While you've been sick, we've been having a blizzard. Maybe three feet of snow so far, with more to come. Much more, it looks like."

Curt shrugs.

Carleton tries again. "The snow has buried the solar panels. So far, the batteries seem to be holding out. Do you know how long they'll last with no sunshine?"

"A couple of days, I think," he says, croaking. Every word sounds like it hurts.

"That's good, but it's not long enough to last us. We need to get outside and rake off those panels so the snow load doesn't crush them. I insist that you give us the combination to the door so we can go outside and do that. I feel sure your bosses will understand this is a crisis. If the power goes off, we'll freeze to death."

"There's a generator. It's set to go on by itself when the batteries run out."

"What if it doesn't? What then?"

"It'll be fine. Now leave me alone. I need to sleep." He closes his eyes and rolls over.

Carleton and I exchange glances. We've both nursed him with not a shred of gratitude from him. I hadn't expected our plea to work, but it was worth a try. Even sick, Curt is the most stubborn man I've ever met.

We go into the dining room and sit at the table with Darla and Thomas.

Just then, the lights blink on and off. On and off. On. Off. And stay off.

My stomach lurches. *Two days, huh? Wishful thinking, that.*

After our eyes adjust to the minimal light, we share looks of disgust. If the power stays off, we might not be able to open the door at all. The others seem to have the same thought, so we push back our chairs and rush to the front door. Previously, the numbers on the keypad were brightly lit. Now they're dark, like everything else in the dome.

My head aches, and I have a hard time drawing a breath. I hope I'm not getting sick. I've never been claustrophcbic—couldn't have been an astronaut if I was—but now I feel like I'm sitting in a snow cave that has just fallen in around me.

No way out.

Carleton swears, for the first time that I've heard, and starts pushing buttons on the keypad. Nothing. No beeps. No light. He slaps at it over and over, his blows getting stronger and wilder. Doing so might help his frustration level, but it makes no difference to the keypad. The thing looks indestructible.

Finally, he stops and turns to us, an expression of despair covering his handsome face. "I *knew* I shouldn't have trusted that man. My intuition told me not to do it from the very beginning. But my... *hubris* got the better of me. I was sure I'd be famous and our group would get to go up in space. And that we'd be the first humans to contact extraterrestrials. My wishes overcame my common sense. I've let you down, and I'm really, really sorry." He plops onto a couch and sobs.

Darla goes to him and puts her arm around his shoulders.

I glance at Thomas and shake my head in frustration. *Jeez Louise. What a time to break down.* If we're going to get cut of here, we need everyone to be strong, but it isn't happening.

Thomas and I move toward the kitchen. "We won't freeze to death, will we?" I ask.

"Let me think. Three more days to get through. If the power doesn't come back on, I'm not sure of anything." He hesitates. "We could look for the combination that Curt said he put in his room somewhere. Even if we find it, the electronic lock may not work until the generator comes on. There's a dead bolt on the door, so there must be a key too. Didn't Curt say something about that when he first closed the door?"

"I think so, but I wouldn't swear to it."

"All right. You've been in his room. I think he said he left the combination in an envelope in his room. Have you seen it?"

I can't remember seeing anything like that, so I shake my head. "The room's a mess, so I might have missed it."

"Yeah, me too. Let's look now."

Curt's room is slightly larger than the others and has a small desk in the corner. We tiptoe in and start rummaging through the things on his desk: piles of papers, underwear, a small jigsaw puzzle. But no key. Our fumbling wakes him up. "What's going on?"

"We need the door key," says Thomas. "Where did you put it?"

Curt coughs for a while then whispers, "There isn't a key. Just a combination."

"There's a dead bolt. There must be a key."

"Outside."

Thomas and I stare at each other for a long moment. I don't know whether or not to believe him. I remember Suzie saying good-bye and walking out the door. "Suzie locked the dead bolt when she left. But you said there was another key."

"Outside."

"Shit, Curt, this is a crisis," Thomas says. "If the key's outside, then the combination lock is the only thing holding the door closed. Where's the combination? You said it was in an envelope on your desk."

"Get out of my room, fuckface."

Ignoring his increasingly nasty comments, we continue searching the desk until we're convinced there is nothing on or in it. Either Curt had lied or he'd moved the envelope. We close the door behind us when we leave his room.

"Okay, what now?" Thomas asks when we're settled at the table.

"We could call Suzie and have her come and get us."

He shakes his head. "I don't think she could get through the snow right now, even with four-wheel drive. We'll have to wait until the snow stops, maybe even until the road's plowed."

I try to think of other options. "Can we break out? Curt can't stop us from doing that, not in the condition he's in."

Thomas grunts. "If we did, he wouldn't be responsible. We could walk out and rake off the solar panels, and neither Curt nor his boss would know a thing."

I laugh at the vision of Curt's face as it would look when he realized we could go in and out without his approval. It's good to summon a sense of humor, even in this most difficult time. I consider the question. "What's the dome built of? Concrete, right? With adobe over it?"

"I think so." He scratches the bristly stubble he's allowed to grow since arriving at the dome. "Damn thing itches like a son of a bitch," he says, but his mind seems to be elsewhere. "Unfortunately, we don't know how thick it is or how strong." He bites his lip. "What can we use to break through?"

"Let's look."

We've searched the dome before, so we already know what's in it. There are no tools to help us break through the heavy-duty concrete. The windows on the second floor are small and high, and neither of us can figure out how to get down from them, even if we can get up there and break a window.

"Okay, let's go back to the walkie-talkie idea," I say. "We can call Suzie, and she'll call 911. They'll send someone with a big truck to get us."

"Good plan," says Thomas. "Let's just hope the—" The lights flicker on. On. Off. On. And stay on. A loud machine noise comes from the lean-to outside the kitchen. I take a deep breath and exhale hard.

"Looks like the generator has kicked in," says Thomas. We share a relieved smile.

"What the hell is that?" calls Carleton, his voice thick.

"We're saved." I explain what happened. "How shall we celebrate?"

We gather in the kitchen and use the remaining beers to toast our final three days. Nobody cares that it's still morning and we only recently ate breakfast.

As we share our relief at hearing the noisy generator, Carleton sets his bottle on the table and frowns. "Wait. Where's Emily? Nobody could sleep through this racket."

He knocks on her door. "Hey, Em, come on out. We saved a beer for you."

Nothing.

He turns back to us with a scared expression. "I'm going in." He turns the doorknob and goes inside, leaving the door open. In a short time, he yells, "Mia, will you come here for a minute?"

I make a face and set down my beer then slowly get to my feet. There has been too much emotional turmoil already on this day. I don't need another sick person on my hands. Unlike the others, Emily isn't coughing. Why not?

The young woman is lying on her side, apparently asleep. "What's up?" I ask.

"I can't wake her." He shakes her shoulder several times, harder each time. "Emily. Emily, baby, wake up."

Oh crap. That isn't good. I roll the young woman onto her back and watch for breath. *Yes!* Her chest rises and falls, slowly and not very much, but she's alive.

Looking around the room, I spot a prescription bottle that has rolled halfway under the bed. Picking it up, I read the label. Sleeping pills. *Shit.* The prescription was for fifteen pills, and now the bottle is empty. But the name on the bottle is Carleton Friend, not Emily Maxwell.

I spot another prescription bottle under the bed and dig it out. It's for a popular antidepressant. This prescription, made out to Emily, originally contained thirty pills. It's also empty. Oh my God, did the young woman combine all these pills?

"All right, let's get her up if we can." I slap her face. "Emily? Emily? Stay with us." No response. *Damn*. She's unconscious. In a situation like this, we should call 911 immediately. I have no experience with overdoses, but I think the EMTs would administer antagonists.

I'm far, far out of my depth. How can I get the young woman up and walk her around if she's unconscious? I roll Emily back onto her side and tell Carleton to stay with her while I think about what to do.

I walk out to the dining room. "We need to contact Suzie and have her call 911 immediately. Emily's overdosed. She's alive but unconscious." I glance around the room. "Anybody know where the walkie-talkie is?"

They shake their heads.

"It must be in Curt's room. Let's look. I don't care how nasty he is. This is an emergency."

"Wait," says Thomas. "He might be lying on it or something. Let's take a minute and be a little strategic here. Emily's still breathing, right?"

I nod.

We work out a plan. Whether it will succeed is anybody's guess.

Chapter 33: His Excuse for Being an A-hole

Thomas convinces Curt he'll feel better after a shower and helps him to the bathroom. While they're gone, I search Curt's room for the walkie-talkie. If I can call Suzie, she'll figure out how to deal with the emergency from there. I also want to find the envelope with the combination so we'll be ready when help arrives. I expect the combination to be a sequence of four or six numbers, but I'll be on the lookout for any set of numbers.

The shower is still set to turn off after two minutes, so I have to be quick. I hope Thomas can convince Curt to shave and brush his teeth, which will give me more time.

I riffle through the stacks of paper all over the room, searching for an envelope or any piece of paper with numbers on it. Nothing looks encouraging. Next, I search his bed and find the walkie-talkie stashed underneath it. I take it into my bedroom and return to Curt's room to continue searching. I find a box of small flashlights in a corner and carry it to my room. But that's all I find. There's nothing like a key or a paper with a series of numbers written on it.

Damn. Either Curt stashed that combination somewhere else in the dome or it's a number sequence he can easily remember. The scumbag said he wrote it down, but maybe he didn't. I want to wring his neck, but if I do, I'll never get the combination.

There must be other options, but for the moment, they elude me.

After Curt returns to his room, I give the keypad a try. Since the generator started working, the pad is glowing again. I begin with the obvious solutions: 1-2-3-4, nope. 1-1-1-1 and all the other iterations of four repeated numbers, nope. The current year, nope. I've seen Curt's driver's license and remember the year of his birth: 1963, nope. His birth month and day, nope. Okay, so the number isn't something obvious. Fortunately, the keypad lets me try as often as I want without locking or shrieking in alarm. I try every combination I can think of, with no response. Could the thing have locked itself down when the power went off or when it came back on? No. It looks the same as it always has, so it should unlock if I find the right numbers.

I move to five numbers and then to six. The combination probably isn't longer than six numbers, because otherwise, it would be difficult for the person setting it to remember. I have other things to do, so I ask the others to take over and try the numbers in some strategic fashion.

I go to my room and examine the walkie-talkie. When I pick it up, it seems lighter than I expected. I turn it on and push the button to talk, but nothing happens. Nothing at all. No light, no sound, no static. *Wait. Where are the batteries?* I open the compartment and am not surprised to find it empty. The son of a bitch removed the batteries. A few days ago, I'd thought about good and evil and how everyone was a mixture, but Curt's actions border on evil, not just stubbornness, as Emily said.

Okay, where would he have stashed the batteries? Maybe in the box with the flashlights. I open it and take out a flashlight. When I turn it on, it works. There are seven flashlights, and all of them work. Unfortunately, though, the batteries are too large for the walkie-talkie, and there are no smaller batteries in the box.

Think, Mia. You're missing something. What could it be?

My brain feels like it's packed with soft sand or oatmeal—something that impedes the neurons from firing. I rest my head in my hands and try to think rationally. Either the walkie-talkie batteries and the combination aren't in the dome, or Curt hid them someplace so obscure that I haven't been able to find them. I have no idea where else to look.

While things are quiet, I go into Sheila's room. The older woman is sitting up in bed, reading a magazine.

"How do you feel?" I ask.

"Better. I was pretty sick for a while, but I'm almost back to myself again."

I feel her forehead. No fever. I haven't heard coughing coming from the room in the past hour either. "That's great. You're doing the right thing by staying in bed for a while longer, though." I pause. "You're getting better, but Curt isn't. Do you have any idea why?"

Sheila purses her lips. "I do. He told me not to say anything, so I haven't up till now. You probably should know, though."

I nod my encouragement.

After clearing her throat, Sheila says, "He had cancer of the throat earlier in the year. I don't know how bad it was, but he had chemo and radiation on his larynx. He said he made a full recovery, but maybe his immune system is still weak. I don't know if his terrible symptoms are because of his cancer, but they might be."

"Why didn't he tell me that when he got sick? I don't know what I would have done differently, but it would have explained some things."

"He's terrified he'll lose his job, and then he'll lose his health insurance. He's on probation because he missed so much work. That's why he's acting the way he is, or at least, it's his excuse for being an asshole. He doesn't want to be known at work as the guy who failed at his job. I've tried to convince him we need to leave early, but he won't hear of it." She shakes her head and takes a breath. "I'm sorry I didn't tell you earlier. I've known for a few days now. Curt's got some good qualities, but on this topic, he's kind of... entrenched, I guess. I don't think he'll listen to reason, no matter what anyone says."

"I get that."

We sit in silence for a while. Finally, Sheila asks, "Is anybody else sick?"

"No." I don't want to tell her about Emily just yet, not when she's still sick. "I have one more question. Do you know where Curt stashed the combination for the door or the batteries for the walkie-talkie?"

Sheila rolls her eyes. "No. I asked several times, but he got cagey and wouldn't tell me. And he laughed like crazy when I asked about the walkie-talkie. Honestly, I don't think there are any batteries. I think that's the joke he played on us. He never intended to call Suzie, no matter how bad things got here."

I frown. "How in the hell did you spend so much time with this scumbag, if you don't mind my asking?"

"We played cards. I hoped to butter him up enough to tell me the combination. But it didn't work. 'Scumbag' is right. I'm going in there right now and talk to him." She pushes the covers off and gets out of bed slowly. She sways a little but seems more stable after a few seconds. After pulling on a robe, she hobbles out of her bedroom and into Curt's. I follow behind, curious how the confrontation will go.

Sheila looks at the sleeping Curt and then turns to me. "He looks much worse than yesterday," she whispers. "I don't think I have the heart for this right now."

He does look worse. Even if I wake him, I'm not sure he'll be with-it enough to tell me the combination. We go into the dining room and sit at the table while I tell her all that's happening. Emily. The snow. The need to leave early.

"Damn," she says.

"My feelings exactly."

"Look, I'll do what I can, but I don't feel up to much right now. After a nap, I'll start praying that we get some help here. And I'll see how else I can contribute." She's struggling to keep her eyes open, so she takes a step toward her room. "Hey, at least my toe is better. I can walk out of here if I need to."

I give her a fond smile as she leaves the room. Curt is awful, it's true, and Emily is in dire straits, but the crisis is bringing out the best in the rest of us, at least for the moment.

The day wears on. Carleton suggests that we try to communicate telepathically with Suzie to ask her to come and get us. We try, but my heart's not in it, and I think the others feel the same way. It'll be great if Suzie receives our message and drives up to rescue us, but I don't have a lot of hope in that direction. That part of our project seems to be over.

We straggle downstairs. Carleton sits with Emily while Darla, Thomas, and I search every inch of the structure again, trying to find the combination or the batteries. We find nothing. Nor do we find anything we can use to break through the concrete walls.

Thomas tries his luck at discovering the combination, with no success. After an hour, Darla takes over from him. And then Carleton takes a turn. None of them has any luck.

"Keep trying," I encourage them. "First, let's combine our lists. Then I want you to see how far out of the box you can think." I leave them to put together a master list.

While Darla and Carleton work on the combination, Thomas tries to figure out how to connect the walkie-talkie to the flashlight batteries. When he's done, he's able to hear some static but nothing else. He sets the contraption down on the table. "I'm afraid the storm is disrupting things. I'll keep trying from time to time, though."

We share a wan smile.

In the late afternoon, we've all given up for the moment. I check on Emily again. No change. I pat Carleton on the shoulder as he sits watch then take a break for some hot chocolate and schnapps.

In a low voice, Darla says, "I knew she was upset about being here, but enough to commit suicide?"

"None of us knew." I shake my head.

Darla clears her throat. "For what it's worth, she isn't Carleton's lover. She's his daughter."

"What? That's a surprise. When did you find out?"

"He told me last night. She's from his first marriage, and she's always been unstable. His ex-wife didn't want him around after they got divorced, so he didn't see Emily much until she grew up. He was hoping they could be closer, so he invited her here, but he asked her not to share their relationship. I don't know why he's so secretive about things. Anyway, I guess he thought his methods would cure her. But they didn't, obviously. He's been spending a lot of time with her, just lying on her bed and telling her stories or listening to her talk about her kids. He's never met them." She takes a breath. "It's so sad. I can't believe she cracked like that."

I lay my hand on her arm and give it a squeeze. "There's nothing we can do for her until she wakes up a little. And I don't know whether she will without medical attention. We've got to get her to a hospital. *Think.* How can we get out of here?"

We brainstorm for an hour but come up with nothing new.

Although she doesn't wake up, Emily continues breathing, hour after hour. Her breath even becomes a little stronger. Maybe things aren't as dire as I'd thought at first. I hope the young woman will wake up soon. The whole situation will probably come apart if she dies. I shudder at the thought. She desperately needs to be in a hospi-tal. Ideally, Sheila's prayers will work. I whisper a prayer of my own.

I go up to the second floor and look outside. Fortunately, the snow has slowed, and the sky is brighter than before. The knot in my chest loosens a little. Maybe the walkie-talkie will start working and Suzie will be able to drive up to get us.

One thing is for certain: I'm not waiting another three days to get out of here.

Something tugs at the edges of my thoughts. It's not a communication from an alien being this time but something from my own mind. I try to bring it to consciousness, but it eludes me. I sigh. Sometimes I dare to think that I've fully recovered from the brain injury. Other times—like this one—I know I haven't. My mind just doesn't work the way I want, the way it did before the accident.

In astronaut training, crews train for emergencies and discuss every potential situation so thoroughly that thinking of options becomes second nature. I did fine then and felt competent to deal with anything that might happen. But not here. Not now. I'm not technically in charge, but I feel responsible to help with my team's psychological issues, medical issues, and physical issues. The stress of it all is pushing me to the brink of my capacities. Truthfully, my brain feels like Swiss cheese. Ideas float in and out, but they aren't clear or focused, and I can't grasp them as they float by.

I want to cry, but there's no time or space for tears. I have to *do* something.

By late afternoon, Emily still hasn't awakened. Carleton allows Darla to sit with his daughter while he takes a break.

I watch him eat a package of crackers before asking, "I'm sorry to push you like this, but I need to know how many sleeping pills she likely took. They were yours, right? How many were in the bottle when you gave it to her?"

"I... I'm not completely sure. I think maybe I'd taken four or five of them. Poor Emily has struggled so much with insomnia since she's been here. I didn't offer them to her until last night after she freaked out. I thought maybe a good night's sleep would help her cope. It occurred to me to just give her one, but I thought that would look—I don't know—like I doubted her ability to make good choices. It never occurred to me she'd take all of them."

"So there were only ten pills in the bottle?"

"Maybe even less. I'm not sure."

"That's probably good news, then. Maybe she'll sleep for a while longer and then wake up enough so we can walk her around and get her functioning." I reach over to pat his arm. "Any of us might have done the same thing. Nobody thought she was so unbalanced. If we'd been able to get her out of here yesterday when she first freaked out, this wouldn't have happened."

He breathes heavily, in and out. Finally, he gives me a tight smile. "Thanks for that, Mia. You've been a godsend. But she was my responsibility, and I totally fucked up."

I want to say, "We all did, by coming here under such ridiculous rules." But there'll be time to divvy up the blame once we get out.

We're all so exhausted that we go to bed early. I hope sleep will recharge my mental batteries and that things will look better in the morning.

Lying in my bed, I consider our situation. On the negative side: Emily is comatose, Curt is getting worse, and I don't know what to do for either of them. I can't find the code and can't call out with the walkie-talkie. I don't know how we can break out if we aren't able to get through the door. And we have sixty more hours to endure until Suzie arrives to get us.

On the positive side: Emily is still breathing, Curt is still breathing, Sheila is much better, nobody else has gotten sick, and the generator is still blasting away. We have heat, and there's enough food and water to last for three more days. And in the morning, it will be only two more days that we have to stay in this horrible place.

Despite my worries, I sleep until the sound of a huge explosion wakes me abruptly. My watch reads 3:53 a.m.

Chapter 34: We've Got a Crisis Here

I sit straight up in bed, feeling like I'm jumping out of my skin. *What was that noise?* I get up in the pitch dark to check. In the living room, I run smack into someone standing in the center of the room. "What the hell?"

"Something happened." The voice is Thomas's.

"I heard it too. That's why I ran out." That voice is Darla's.

I feel for the light switch then flip it up, but nothing changes. Jiggling it a couple more times yields no results. *Shit, shit, shit.* "Check the other lights, will you?"

I hear fumbling along the other wall, and Thomas says, "No power here."

More fumbling, this time in the kitchen. "The refrigerator's out," says Darla.

I realize that it's too quiet. "Was that noise the generator blowing up?"

"Probably," says Thomas. "Let's check upstairs. I see dim light coming from up there."

We feel our way up the stairs and onto the second-floor landing. As I look up, my breath catches in my throat. The snow has stopped, and the stars are shining down like a heaven full of tiny flashlights. At last, the blizzard is over. I can't see how high the snow rises on the light pole, but what I see explains everything.

The explosion must have been a small slide. Piles of snow push up against the back of the dome, halfway to the second floor. The avalanche carried some trees and rocks with it, and from what I can tell, a medium-sized tree must have crashed through the roof of the shed and banged into the generator, knocking it out. That was probably the noise we'd heard.

"Damnation," I whisper to myself. As bad as it is, a bigger avalanche might have buried the entire dome. And trees or rocks could have punched through the windows and sucked out all our heat. I shudder, realizing we dodged a bullet. That is, assuming a larger slide isn't about to entomb us. I've heard that small slides often occur before the main event.

We need to get out of here immediately and away from the steep slope. Down the mountain to safety.

We stare at each other in the starlight. Something inside me shifts into a different, higher gear. I've felt it before, back in my astronaut training days, and I call it commander mode. I assumed that role hundreds of times in crisis simulations, and I did it well. This is no simulation, and it might be my only chance to get my crew to safety. I'll do my best to step up.

"What do we do?" asks Darla. "Try Curt again? Hang him up by his toenails until he gives us the combination?"

Nobody laughs.

"Maybe," I reply thoughtfully. "But since the power's off, the keypad probably won't work anyway." I shrug. *Focus, Mia.* "Let's get Curt out of bed. Maybe we can find the key. He said it's outside, but earlier, he said it was in an envelope with the combination. I don't know what to believe." I pause. "On second thought, get everybody up. I don't see how anybody slept through that noise. We need to gather all ideas, no matter how crazy they are."

They nod, and we go to wake the others.

Carleton is in Emily's bed, his arm around his daughter's shoulders, but he sits up when Darla and I enter the room. "What's happened?" he asks in a small voice. "I heard a terrible noise, but I couldn't face whatever it was. I'm sorry."

I'll explain after I assess Emily's health. I kneel by the motionless young woman and feel her forehead. Warm but not hot. And not cold, as in death. I shake her shoulders. "Emily. Time to get up now." Nothing. "Emily." I raise my voice. Nothing. I can't make out Carleton's face as he hovers near me. "Has there been any change?"

He sighs. "Not that I've noticed. I was hugging her to keep her warm and let her know that I'm here, but she hasn't moved, other than to breathe." He sounds dejected and hopeless, not at all like the confident man I met only two months ago.

"I'm sorry, Carleton," I say, "but we've got a crisis here. We need everybody in the living room ASAP. Put on your clothes and use lots of layers. It's going to get colder."

He doesn't answer, but I hear a rustle that must be him doing my bidding.

We wake Sheila and then go into Curt's room. He's asleep and wheezing, his lungs rattling with each breath. I fumble my way to the head of his bed and reach down to feel his forehead. Still burning hot. *Too bad*. I shake his shoulders. "Curt, wake up."

"What?" He croaks out the word. "Ow, my throat hurts."

"Get up and come out to the living room. We all need to talk. Now. Where's your robe?" I can't find it in the dark. "Doesn't matter. We'll bring you a blanket. Get up now. We'll carry you if we have to."

Sheila and I half carry him into the living room and get him settled on a couch. He's coughing again, and it sounds painful. I don't care.

When the room grows quiet, I assume everyone is here. I hand out the flashlights and warn people not to use them any more than necessary. I stand in the middle of the room and beam a flashlight up onto my face. "There was a small avalanche a few minutes ago, and a bigger one might be right behind it. That's bad, but it's not all. The avalanche knocked out the generator. With no heat, we're in danger of freezing. This is a crisis, and we need everyone to help us think of a way out of here. Curt, you're first. Where's the door key?"

He stares at me blankly. Finally, he shakes his head. "Outside," he croaks. "Suzie put it in the lockbox when she left."

"You told us you had another one."

Another shake. "No, I didn't."

The room erupts in angry shouts.

"You did too."

"Where is it, fucker?"

"Tell us."

I shine my flashlight on every face, and gradually, the room quietens. I turn the light back on Curt. "So, you lied to us about there being a key?"

Curt says nothing.

The tension in the room is like a cocked rifle. It wouldn't take much for these civilized and gentle people to turn on Curt, even physically assault him. It's tempting to allow that to happen, but it wouldn't help anything. Right now, we need to focus on getting out of here and not waste time on unhelpful solutions.

I give Curt one last opportunity to do the right thing. "Clearly, there isn't a key. We'll deal with that omission later. For now, let's talk about the combination. The keypad probably won't work because of the lack of power, but the generator might come back on again. This is life-or-death, Curt. It's no time to be coy. Now, what is the combination?" I shine the flashlight beam in his eyes.

When he tries to speak, he triggers a coughing fit that lasts at least a minute. No one gets him a glass of water. When he can finally speak, he says, "It's 2001."

"You're kidding," I say, forgetting my vow to remain calm. "Are you shitting me, Curt? Now is not the time." I turn the flashlight toward Thomas. "We tried that, didn't we?"

"Yeah, I tried it. Several times. Didn't work. He's shitting you."

I turn the light back to Curt, who holds a handkerchief to his mouth. Behind the handkerchief, he might be grinning, but I'm not sure. His eyes glitter, reminding me of Jack Nicholson in *The Shining*.

Holy crap, he's gone completely insane. I try to think of alternate reasons for his behavior, but the only one I come up with is that his high fever might be messing with his mind. Either way, talking to him is useless.

"All right," I say, "he won't tell us. Darla and Thomas, would you take him back to his room, please? And shut the door behind him." I turn the flashlight on him again. When I speak, my voice is hard. "I can't fucking believe you, Curt. Don't you get that we might die here? I don't care if you pee in your pants—you are not to come out of that room."

I consider what to do next as Darla and Thomas drag him to his room. He coughs loudly, but he's no longer my concern. These people in front of me are. When they've closed his door and sat back down, I continue, my voice clipped. "Carleton, you're next in charge. Do you want to take over?"

Shaking his head, he says, "I don't have it in me. You're doing fine, Mia."

I didn't ask for command, but somebody needs to do it, and I'm willing. A small flame of exhilaration ignites in my chest. "Everyone agree with that?" I shine the light on every face, and they all nod. The flame in my chest grows into a steady fire. All of my training has led me to this moment. I can do this.

"All right. Not that it matters who's in charge if we get buried by an avalanche or freeze to death, but let's get to it. We need ideas for how to get out of here. Even if the asshole Curt had given us the combination, it probably wouldn't have worked. He may have an override switch hidden somewhere, but I've looked and can't find it. Someone should look again, although it will be hard to find in the dark. What are your other ideas?"

Silence greets my words. Something is rattling around just outside the edges of my mind, but trying to force it isn't helping. Maybe if I invite it in, gently, it will appear. Unfortunately, I don't have time to do it gently. *Come on, come on.*

Sheila asks, her voice tinged with hysteria, "Are we going to die in here?"

Everyone speaks at once, and I stomp my foot to get their attention. "No, we are not," I say, pitching my voice low and quiet. "Get a grip, people. We need to focus."

They calm down quickly after that. Thank God, I got through to them. "Ideas, please, no matter if you think they're stupid."

Darla sounds tentative when she says, "Could we tie bedsheets together and break the windows upstairs and let someone down around the side?"

I consider. "Maybe. But with no heat and a broken window, it's going to get cold in here in a hurry. If it works, though, we'll be gone, so it won't matter. The snow is really deep, so it may actually cover up the person who goes down the side. Still, we need to think of everything. Okay, Darla, you're in charge of tying sheets together. Strip all the beds. You and Sheila work on that, all right? If you can, while you're doing it, see if you can get a mental message through to Suzie to come and get us. We'll try to think of other ideas, and let's all meet back here in an hour to report progress."

The two women hurry away to pull the sheets off the beds.

"Okay, what other ideas do you have?"

Carleton says, "I wouldn't mind beating up Curt, just to get back at him for all of this."

"Get over it," I snap. "We're not giving him any more attention." Carleton is not that kind of person, but I understand what he means. If I believed in physical violence as a solution to problems, I'd hit

Curt too. But that road leads nowhere. "Okay, I want you to look everywhere for an override switch. It might be in his room, given that it's bigger than ours. Don't harm him when you go in there. And don't respond to whatever he says unless he volunteers something useful. I'm not sure what an override switch would look like, but check out anything unusual. While you're at it, see if you can get a mental message to Suzie too. Okay?"

"Right, chief." He heads to Curt's room.

Thomas is the only one left. I pull up a chair to face him. "What does your engineering mind tell you?"

"Well," he says slowly, "the most vulnerable part of the dome is where the pipes go outside. If we had a hammer and a chisel, we might gouge out the concrete enough to allow someone small—you, maybe—to crawl out. But we don't have that. I could see what I can do with a knife and my multi-tool. It might take a long time, but it would be relatively quiet and wouldn't let much warm air out."

"Okay. Try it. Do you want help?"

"Let me see how it works. If I get anywhere, I'll call you."

"Okay. And check the walkie-talkie again, will you? Now that the storm has passed, it might work."

He hurries off.

I glance at my watch: 5:22. Two hours before daylight. The thermometer shows negative ten degrees outside and sixty degrees inside. Unless there is another slide, we have a few hours before the inside temperature meets the outside temperature.

I sit on a chair and try my best to grasp the idea that is running around the edges of my mind. Nothing, nothing, nothing. I don't believe our telepathic messages will be received, so there are two more days before Suzie shows up to take us down the mountain, assuming she can get through the snow. I hope she still has the key she used to lock the door originally. If not, she won't be able to open the door from the outside, just as we can't open it from the inside. She'll have more choices, though. For example, she can remove the outside hinges or call a cop to bash down the door.

I wonder if we can survive for another forty-eight hours without electricity. It's iffy. We can't warm up anything, which means no hot coffee or tea, but we can eat our remaining food cold. The composting toilet will still work. Everything else needs electricity. Even getting drinking water requires an electric pump.

The biggest danger is that we'll freeze to death before we're rescued. I'll keep track of how fast the temperature drops inside, and that will tell us how long we have. Emily is the most vulnerable. She should have awakened by now—or died. The young woman desperately needs medical care. The rest of us have coats, boots, and sweaters, and we can jump up and down to stay warm. That might not be enough if the temperature drops below zero. We're Southerners, not mountain people, and we'll feel the cold more than others.

If worse comes to worst, we can huddle together in a bedroom and maybe last until help arrives. Unless another slide covers the road. In that situation, it might take days for a truck to get up the mountain to rescue us.

Why didn't I get these people out of here before the power went off? I didn't try hard enough; that's for sure.

Stop. I can't kick myself or anybody else until we're rescued. I take some breaths and think about *Apollo 13*. Not only had my astronaut class analyzed what went wrong with that mission, but I'd seen the Tom Hanks movie half a dozen times with Ramón. It's our favorite movie. Those guys were in an even more dire situation, in which they would either crash-land or float out into space to be lost forever if they didn't find a solution to their problem. They coped by pulling everything they had together into a pile and looking it over while brainstorming about creative solutions.

Great idea. If our first-tier solutions don't work, that will be the second tier.

I check on how things are progressing. Upstairs, Darla and Sheila are tying bedsheets together. Letting someone down from the window would be a dangerous undertaking, especially with the snow so high under the windows that a person might smother before they made their way out. Still...

"Keep it up," I tell them. We have to consider every option, although that one won't be my first choice. Too dangerous.

Next, I check on Carleton, who's feeling along the walls for something that sticks out. He has felt all around Curt's walls and floor and even rousted the sick man from his bed so he could search between the box springs and mattress, but he hasn't found anything so far. He and Curt aren't speaking, which is a good thing. I consider whether to take Curt with us if—no, when—we break out. *Huh*. I'll deal with that at the time.

Finally, I check on Thomas. He's scraped out a few inches of concrete from around the bathroom pipes, and frigid air is entering the room. The bathroom is a better option than the kitchen, since we can close the door to keep the cold air in the room.

"This looks like the most viable option," I tell him.

He stops working and turns to look at me. "Maybe, but I'm dulling the knife as I scrape. We only have a couple of knives that'll work for this. I'm not sure I'll be able to make a big enough hole for you to climb out of with what we've got. Not soon, anyway."

"Well, keep at it. At least you're staying warm."

We chuckle. Gallows humor.

But, *wait*. Maybe we can use the exercise bikes to power the keypad. Then we can keep trying to find the combination. I've been in gyms where bikes actually generate electricity. I ask Thomas about it.

He sits back, considering. "No, unfortunately. We'd need a lot of equipment, and we don't have any. The bikes would work to help people keep warm, though." He shrugs and returns to scraping.

In a little while, everyone meets back in the living room to discuss options. The mood in the room has changed from panic to something akin to depression. People are quiet and hunched in on themselves as they settle onto the couches and chairs to give their reports.

In a nutshell, nothing has worked very well. Nobody wants to climb out a second-story window into a pile of snow and try to get through it. Carleton has given up his search for an override switch to sit beside Emily, whom he's carried to the couch, and hold her hand. The young woman doesn't seem to notice that he's moved her, and she slumbers on peacefully. Thomas can't get anything from the walkie-talkie other than a little static, and he's not sure he can get through the wall with our dull knives.

Darla tries to get a drink of water, but the faucet whines and nothing comes out. "Oh yeah, another problem with the electricity," she says. "*Brrr*. It's getting colder in here." She checks the thermostat. "Forty degrees inside. No wonder I'm cold. Crap."

Twenty degrees down in an hour. Not good. Everyone looks to me for help.

Chapter 35: Time for Tier Two

Time for tier two. "I'd like us to bring everything that has even the slightest possibility of helping us into the living room. Papers, food, medicine, clothes. Everything. We'll make a big pile and look through it to see what strikes us as useful. None of the current options are working well enough to get us out of here quickly. It's almost daylight, so let's take a few minutes to get our things together. If nothing else works, we can make a fire in the middle of the room, poke a hole in the window, and burn stuff." I'm joking, but nobody laughs. Actually, that idea has some merit. It's something to consider if all else fails.

Soon people are piling things on the living room floor. "Put papers and clothes in one pile and everything else in another," I instruct. "Better yet, put papers and clothes in a pile and spread everything else around the room. That way, we can see it all better."

I pull things out of my room. I'd brought only one small suitcase, and by this time, I'm wearing most of my clothes. I add my books, including my journal, to the pile.

After I clean out my bedroom, I go upstairs to bring down the plant boxes. My tiny seedlings have disappeared completely. No, when I look closely, I see a few brown twigs leaning onto the cold earth. I'd killed lettuce plants before by allowing them to get too hot. Now these have gotten too cold and are just as dead. But lettuce plants aren't my concern anymore. I carry down the boxes along with the useless grow lights and the fertilizer and regolith.

Someone has carried down the meditation cushions and the extra chairs. They can't get the exercise equipment or the desks down the stairs.

At last, everything that can be carried is in the living room. Someone has placed the rest of the food on the table. There isn't as much as I'd expected. We'll have a hard time getting enough sustenance if we're forced to stay here even one extra night. I sigh. When will we catch a break?

Everyone sits and looks at me. *What now?* their eyes seem to ask.

I don't know. That's the bleak, unadorned truth. But I'm in charge, so I need to think of something. I wish I felt more competent to deal with this crisis, but I won't tell them that.

While we worked, the indoor temperature continued to drop. Thirty-five inside now. Outside is minus twenty. Surely, the temperature will rise once the sun comes up. Fortunately, the living room is light enough now that we can see one another without flashlights.

"Okay, everyone, let's walk around and look at the piles. Say anything that comes to your mind." I'm as calm and as focused as my wounded brain will permit.

We study the piles. Darla says, "There's such a large pile of books and papers. We could have a bonfire. Maybe burn the place down and slip out before we roast."

Everyone laughs, and something clicks in my mind. "Does anybody have a lighter?"

"I do," says Sheila. "I stopped smoking before I came, but I brought my lucky lighter." She rummages in her pile of goods and comes up with a cheap lighter. When she flicks it, a light springs up. Everyone claps.

"I don't think the concrete will burn," says Thomas.

"Yeah, there's that." *Burn.* That word sets off sparks in my mind. It has something to do with whatever has been tugging at my mind. I sit down to think.

Nothing.

Thomas says, "Is there anything else we can scrape out the concrete with? Kitchen knives aren't doing it."

Nobody says anything. Finally, Darla mutters, "If only that clown Curt hadn't left the toolbox outside."

"Don't waste time blaming him," I tell her. "Move on." I stop in front of my plants. Is there anything in the boxes that might help? I touch everything. Yes. I'd brought a trowel, and I hand it to Thomas. "Any use for that?"

He turns it around in his hand. "I can try it. When the hole is big enough for it to fit inside, it might be useful."

I go back to the plants. Whatever is tugging at my mind has something to do with what's in front of me. It almost feels like the alien consciousness is waving again and pointing at the pile.

Dirt? What on earth good is dirt? I communicate on some level with the consciousness. When I walk on, it stops me. *Look again,* it seems to say.

I look. And then I get it. The fertilizer! It's my lab's special formula, and it contains ammonium nitrate, although I have no idea how much. It has many uses, among them the making of bombs. A small bomb, if it doesn't set off an avalanche, might blow a hole in the concrete structure.

With my heart pounding so hard I fear it might burst from my chest, I pick up the container and screw off the top. Inside is a cup or two of fertilizer. Will it be enough? I don't know. Also, I don't know how to make a bomb, but Darla has a degree in chemistry, and Thomas the engineer knows many interesting things.

I hold up the jar and try to contain my excitement as I speak in a hushed voice. "This has ammonium nitrate in it. Does anybody know how to make a bomb?"

After a moment, Darla clears her throat. "I've read about it. Farmers use it for blasting and such. And of course, there are the terrorists. But it doesn't explode by itself. It needs a fuel source and an igniter." She pauses, thinking hard. "If we use the lighter and some cloth, we might make an igniter. I'm not sure about the fuel source. It should be kerosene or fuel oil or something like that."

Seconds go by and then minutes. Finally, Thomas speaks up. "We don't need a gigantic explosion. If it's too big, it might bring down an avalanche. But a small one might be possible with what we've got."

I'm so giddy I almost giggle. A real possibility, at last! But this is no time for levity, so I take a few deep breaths to steady myself. I stare at the bathroom and purse my lips. Finally, the answer that has been niggling at the edge of my mind bursts forth.

"Guys, we could make a pipe bomb. Pull out one of these pipes and put the fertilizer inside it and then set it in the wall. That might help contain the explosion to where we want it. I don't think it'll do a lot of damage, given how little fertilizer we have, but it might loosen the concrete enough that we could pull out some bigger pieces." My voice sounds high and thin, but I think my idea might work. I look at Thomas and Darla. "Will you two work out the details? I don't want to push you too much, but it's getting colder."

"Amen to that," says Sheila.

"All right, the rest of us need to come up with other ideas in case this doesn't work."

"I don't know about you all, but I'm freezing. Getting some food in us might help," Carleton says.

I hesitate. If we finish the food, there will be nothing to eat if we have to stay inside another night. On the other hand, we need it for our own fuel. "Go ahead. Just leave enough for one more meal, in case we don't get out right away."

We dig into the food. Fortunately, everything is edible without being cooked. Score one for space rations.

Afterward, Thomas and Darla work in the bathroom while Sheila and I brainstorm other options. We need several things to try, one at a time, until something succeeds. If the bomb attempt doesn't work, the rope made of sheets will be next. Since I'm the smallest, I'm the obvious person to go over the top of the dome. I'm not looking forward to that. Getting me up to the window is the first issue. It's at least ten feet above the floor, but I can probably stand on Carleton's shoulders. Then I'll tie the rope around my waist, break the window, and clamber down the side of the dome while someone holds the other end of the rope to keep me from falling too fast. I hope the broken glass won't slice me up too badly. Then I'll wade through high snowdrifts to get to the road. Finally, I'll walk out to find help.

It's a challenge, but I can do it if I have to. Anything that gets us out of the dome is better than staying inside.

Before long, Darla calls out. "We're ready, we think."

We all gather outside the bathroom.

Darla and Thomas are wearing smug smiles.

"We can't promise this will work," she says, "but it's worth a try. There are a couple of problems. One is that we don't know how much ammonium nitrate is in the fertilizer. Also, there's not much fuel available to increase the explosion. We found some lamp oil under the kitchen sink. It was just a little, but that should work reasonably well."

She stops to take a breath. "We ripped up a few towels and tied them together to make the fuse. Then we set what we rigged up in the pipe and put it in the hole that Thomas already started. The fuse runs nearly out to the door."

Turning to me, she says, "It was your idea, so you should light it. You can run out and close the door after the fuse is lit." She grins. "What do you think?"

Everyone claps. "You two are brilliant!" Carleton exclaims.

After a pause, I say, slowly, "Okay, let's talk about what we'll do if it works. If it blows a big enough hole in the wall, somebody will need to crawl through and get outside. Then that person will stand up through the snow. I don't know how soft it is or how hard it'll be to walk out to the road. After that, they'll go for help. Maybe someone will be home at the nearest house, which is about a mile down the road. If nobody's there, it's a long walk into town." I look hard at each of them. "Who wants to volunteer?"

They glance at each other. Sheila says, "I'd do it, but, honey, you're the smallest of us. It really should be you."

The others nod, and I blink. "Yeah, that makes sense. I have to admit it sounds easier than going over the top of the dome." I think for a minute. "Do any of you want to come with me, assuming I can make it, or should I do it myself?"

More silence. Carleton says, "I'll stay here with Emily. I don't think I could carry her down a mountain."

I nod. "What about the rest of you?"

"I'm not sure I can get my foot into my boot with my broken toe," says Sheila. "As much as I want out of here, I might slow you down." She pauses. "I hate to say it, but I guess I could take care of Curt until you get back."

I turn to Thomas and Darla. "What about you two?"

"I'm in," says Thomas.

"Me too," chimes in Darla.

"All right," I say, smiling. "That's settled." I take a breath. "You said I should be the one to light the fuse. I will, if you want. But everyone else needs to be as far away from the bathroom as possible when I do it. We don't know what kind of explosion there'll be or whether it'll set off an avalanche."

Sheila hands me her lighter before going to stand near the front door. Carleton sits by Emily on the couch nearest the door. Someone yells to Curt that he might want to hide under his bed. Thomas and Darla hold hands by the door.

I open the lighter. *Click. Click.* It doesn't want to light at first. But then the flame rises high, and I touch it to the cloth fuse. I make sure it catches and is burning its way toward the pipe before I close the door and join the group at the front.

We wait.

Nothing.

Wait some more.

Still nothing.

What's taking so long? I exchange worried glances with Thomas and Darla, but we don't dare move. Not yet.

Eventually, we hear a muffled *BOOM!* It's not as loud as we'd hoped but loud enough to be dangerous if an avalanche is waiting for something to set it off. I motion for everyone to stay still, and then I hold my breath and wait.

After about thirty seconds, I exhale. We wait another two long minutes before moving. No avalanche has crashed onto the roof of the dome, at least, not yet.

I open the bathroom door. The hole has enlarged and is now maybe a foot across. Still too small but better. We look through it and see only a wall of white on the other side.

I touch the concrete around the hole and then stand. "The explosion weakened the concrete, so we can pull out chunks or at least cut through it more easily. It shouldn't take too long. Who wants to work on it? There's room enough for two."

"I do." This is Carleton's strong and confident voice, the one I remember from class. The man has seemed to shrink every day since we arrived in the dome. He has spoken little for the past few days other than to talk to or about Emily. It's nice to hear his calm voice.

Sheila and Carleton work with their knives, pushing concrete pieces into the snowbank. The others think of fresh ideas.

Thomas pulls down the stair railing that has been loose since our second day in the dome. It comes down easily. "We'll just have to be more careful when we walk up the stairs," he says.

He and Darla use the metal railing to bang on the front door, trying to knock it off its hinges. They fail.

To my surprise, I find myself praying. "Please, don't let a slide come." I don't know if God can hear me or wants to answer my prayer, but it calms me a bit as I wait.

Finally, after a couple of hours, the hole is big enough for me to fit through. I call a meeting to discuss the next options. "I'll go out and dig through the snow. It feels light and dry, and I think I can get through it. Once I'm out, I'll go around and try to open the front door. If I can't, Darla, you and Thomas will need to crawl out after me. Deal?"

The whole group cheers. I'm pretty sure I blush, but I understand their excitement. It's a heady experience to breathe the outside air after all these days and to think about actually getting out there.

I hug them all goodbye. Funny, but these people have become my best friends over the past twelve days. It's hard to imagine doing something by myself after all this time.

I push my feet through the hole. As expected, the snow is light and not heavily packed. I keep pushing until I'm able to wriggle the rest of my body through. Soon, I'm standing in the waist-deep snow.

I'm out!

Chapter 36: The Breakout

The air is so cold that pushing it in and out of my lungs hurts. Nevertheless, I can't contain my glee at finally being outside. I actually giggle when I speak. "Pass me my coat, will you?" Hands reach it through the hole. "I'll go around to the front and see if the door will open."

Walking through the drifts isn't easy. At first, I have to force my way through the waist-deep snow, a few inches at a time. I lift one foot high enough to clear the snow and bring it down as far in front of me as I can manage. Then I push down until I pack the snow enough to hold my weight before I lift the other foot and do it again.

Finally, I make it to the front door and jiggle the doorknob. Locked, of course. Looking around for a key or something to force the door, I spy a small metal box attached to the side of the building. Inside are both a key and a slip of paper with numbers written on it. They are 3-1-4-1-5. The first five numbers of pi, the ratio of the circumference of a circle to its diameter.

I exhale in disgust. I hadn't tried that. Apparently, the others hadn't either. I don't bother with the number pad but grab the key and fit it into the lock. I hear a click and have to hold back tears of relief, but it's far too cold out here to cry. After pushing the snow aside, I easily pull open the door. It's a surreal experience to just pull it open. I knock off the snow then step inside to more cheering. It's about as cold inside as out.

"Damnation," Thomas says when I show him the paper. He checks the master list. "I tried pi but only the first four numbers. I didn't go any further. Sorry, Mia. I should have thought of that."

"It's not your fault. Not anybody's except Curt. He should've told us."

Thomas and Darla don their coats and other winter clothes and are soon ready to go.

I walk into Curt's bedroom, where, between coughing fits, he asks what's going on. "I've got to go to the bathroom."

Laughter bursts out of me. "By all means, go," I say between guffaws. "There's a big hole in the wall, but it won't interfere with the toilet. Oh, FYI, we got out, in spite of you. We're leaving. You're welcome to stay or go. I really don't care."

He blanches. "You can't leave me alone. I'll freeze to death. And I can't walk down there by myself."

I take a breath. "Did you ever have batteries for the walkie-talkie?"

"No." He looks like he's about to cry.

"Does Suzie have batteries?"

"No."

Just as I'd thought—the son of a bitch was so determined to keep us inside that he didn't allow for any way to get out in an emergency. I want to slap him, but I just shake my head in disgust. "Then you've got two choices. You can get up and walk with us, or you can stay here. A few of the others are also staying. I'll send somebody for you when we get to town."

He doesn't answer, so I walk out of his room for the last time. Maybe he'll do us a favor and freeze to death.

I hug Sheila and Carleton goodbye. "We'll be back as soon as we can. Don't let Curt give you any shit."

"Stay safe, my friends," says Sheila.

The three of us walk out the door and close it behind us. A snow shovel leans against one wall, but there's far too much snow to shovel our way out. Snowshoes would be perfect for these conditions, but of course, we have none. Instead, one person will have to tamp down the snow so the others can follow in their footsteps.

We tell the others about the shovel if they want to try shoveling a path to the road. Carleton opens the door, dressed in his outdoor clothes. "I'll shovel. When you come back, there'll be a clear path for the EMTs to get to Emily."

I nod and turn my attention to getting out. I can sort of tell where the road is because of the lack of trees and how the opening winds downhill. We take turns tamping down a path to the road. The going is slow, but being outside in the fresh air and open space makes all the trouble to get here almost worth it.

An hour later, we meet a snowplow coming toward us. "You guys from the dome?" the driver asks. "I'm plowing all the way up there. Do you want to ride back?"

I glance at the others, who shake their heads. "No, we'll walk into town. But a couple of people there need medical attention immediately. If you've got a radio, please call 911 and tell them it's an emergency."

After saying goodbye to the driver, we continue down the plowed road. The walking is easier, but fatigue and cold have set in, so our pace slows. I feel like I've entered one of those dreams in which you walk and walk but get nowhere. I don't have the energy to say that to my friends, so I just put one foot in front of the other, over and over.

After a while, a car with flashing lights drives toward us. When it arrives, the police officer asks, "Are you Mia Gray?" I nod. "Your husband is flying in for you. He's not here yet, but your mom called us and said you were in trouble. She was adamant that we check it out. The snowplow driver said someone needed medical attention. Is it you?"

I nearly smile at the thought of Mom being adamant. Excellent word to describe her. "We're okay, but they need your help at the dome."

"The EMTs are on the way."

"Thanks. We'd appreciate it if you'd call someone for us." I give him Suzie's cell number, and he continues on up the hill.

I glance at Thomas and Darla, who are staring at me, open-mouthed.

"How in the hell could your mom have possibly known?" asks Darla.

"I don't know." I flash back to the urgent message I'd sent tele-pathically to my mom and Ramón. That must have connected, at least to one of them. Gratitude settles into my soul.

We continue our trek toward the town. In a few moments, the Jeep rolls up.

"Hey, what happened?" asks Suzie. "I never heard from Curt, so I thought everything was okay."

We get into the car, which is blissfully, wonderfully warm. "Uh, did you receive any telepathic distress signals from us in the past few days?"

She shrugs. "Not sure. Everything I received recently was gar-bled. I didn't know what to make of it." She carefully turns the car around and heads toward town. "What happened?"

"That's a long story." We all start talking at once.

Soon, everyone except Curt, Emily, and Carleton is sitting before the fire at the retreat center. The medical staff airlifted Curt and Emily to the nearest hospital, and Carleton went with them.

I sip hot chocolate while waiting for Ramón's plane to land. He'd texted me before he left that he was borrowing a plane from the base and would land in Alamosa. He wasn't sure what had happened, but my mom had called him and insisted something was wrong. It would take a few hours for him to get to me, but he was coming.

When I can stop crying, I call my mom.

"Oh my God, Mia. I've been waiting by the phone all day. Are you okay?"

"Yeah, but how did you know there was a problem?"

"I thought I heard you calling my name a few days ago and asking for help. I wasn't sure, though, so I waited a while. But I kept feeling like there was an emergency, so today, I called Ramón and told him. We decided he could get there faster than I could, so he's on his way."

I tell her the short version of our escape. I'm about to go into more detail, but a police officer steps into the retreat center and gestures that he needs to speak with me.

"Got to go, Mom. I'll call you later."

I'm in the middle of giving a statement to him when Ramón rushes in the door. When he sees me, he says, "I got your message. I'm here."

I run to him and jump into his arms.

We stay in the retreat center that night. After making the sweetest love I've ever known, I tell him about our time in the dome. "It wasn't horrible at first, but things got worse and worse." I hesitate. "Have you ever had to deal with anything like that?"

"Being in command of the space station was always like that, with things going wrong every day and having to fix them. But there was nothing malevolent about the problems or the people." He hugs me tightly for a few seconds. "I never understood why you felt you had to go there. Will you explain?"

"Yeah. Certainly." I need to be completely honest with him, and that requires digging deeply into my motivations. "I was utterly lost after Jeb grounded me. I thought if I could find a way to get into space—any way—I wouldn't feel so lost. It sounds ridiculous, given what happened, but I was willing to take a long, long shot at getting my heart's desire."

"But, *cara,* why would you risk your life to do it? That's the part I don't understand."

I sigh. "At first, I didn't realize I was risking my life. That came later. But I agree it was a stupid thing to do, given how little I knew about what I was getting into. I had lots of time to think while I was there—at least the first week, before it all went to shit—and I realized what a great life we have together, you and I. Yes, we have our problems, but I shouldn't have run away from them. That was wrong, and I'm sorry."

We lie in silence for a few moments. "Uh, I sent you a telepathic message of love from the dome and asked you to meet me here in Crestone. Is that why you came?"

He does that squinty thing when he's thinking that I love. "I'm not sure. I thought about you a lot, and I sort of felt that things might get better when you left that place. But I didn't get a specific message, no. Your mom did, though, and she asked me to come. So I came."

It was that simple for him. He got a call, so he dropped everything and came. What an amazing guy. "I made it out by myself, but I've never been so happy to see anyone in my life. Thank you, thank you, thank you, thank you."

He smiles and kisses me again.

"I learned something else when I was in the dome," I say, softly. "I've finally accepted that I won't be an astronaut again. I won't get to space. You and Jeb were right. I'm really not up to it." I pause. "Will you mind having a wife who's not an astronaut?"

He stares at me, mouth agape. "You're kidding, right? I only encouraged you to apply because you wanted it so much. Now I won't have to worry about you all the time. You can do whatever you want, and I'll support you."

I lie back, my smile so big it threatens to split my face in two.

After a moment, he continues. "I've had time to think, too, and I realize I was too controlling. It's what I do when I'm confronted with a problem to solve. You're far more to me than a problem to solve, so I guess I did it even more. I'm sorry about that." He pauses. "But I felt pretty locked out when you just up and left me without even talking about it."

"I'm sorry." I've said those words a dozen times since he walked in the door. I'll repeat them as often as needed until he forgives me.

"I know." He pauses to get the words right. "Things look hopeful today, but I'm not so sure about tomorrow. Can you promise you'll try to work things out between us? We can go to counseling or whatever you want. But no more walking out the door without notice. Will you promise me?"

"I promise." The tears start again. "And I promise I'll talk to you about it the next time you get too controlling. I'll insist that you stop if you don't get it the first time. I don't need to be mother-henned by you. I appreciate all you did for me, but you can stop now."

He laughs. "Clearly. I'll work on it."

Chapter 37: Ever the Hero

Carleton arrives at the retreat center in the morning, completely spent. He sobs as he tells us that Emily died last night in the hospital. We all cry, too, and then we surround him with hugs and positive energy. Maybe it helps a little, but of course, nothing will ease his pain.

He checked on Curt before leaving the hospital, and he seemed to be okay. Carleton knows nothing more than that.

I can't help but reflect on the injustice of Emily dying and Curt living. I wish I could fix it so there would be a different outcome. But I can't. And that thought makes me almost unbearably sad.

Everyone else leaves the next day, but Ramón and I remain at the retreat center for a couple of days. I give statements to the police and the FBI but refuse to speak with any of the reporters who approach me. Eventually, we're cleared to leave, and we fly home to Houston.

For days, our story is major news. I'm proclaimed a hero for saving everyone, but I know I'm no hero. A hero would have gotten everyone out as soon as Emily freaked out. Maybe even before, when we first realized how unbalanced Curt was. After speaking with Karin about my reactions, I've come to accept on a deep level that my brain doesn't process information as quickly as it did before the accident. My reactions aren't the same either. Oh, I'll probably be fine in normal circumstances, but I'd rather not push it by being in high-stress situations again.

I lie in bed for days, grieving Emily's death and eating every bit of fresh food I can find. Eventually, the reporters find another story and leave me alone.

I read on the news that Curt had contracted pneumonia because of the virus and was hospitalized for a few days. His cancer hadn't returned. After his release, he was arrested and charged with false imprisonment and a bunch of other things. He posted bail and is recuperating at home. That's all I ever want to know about that scumbag.

Emily's funeral will be tomorrow in Orlando. Ramón and I will fly in to attend it and then stay with my mom for a few days before driving my Tesla back to Houston.

I've been too exhausted to talk with anyone from the dome, but we've shared a few texts. When the phone rings after lunch, though, I answer. "Hi, Darla. How are you?"

"Up and down." She sounds as exhausted as I am. "I'm glad I don't have to go back to work until after New Year's. You?"

"I'm so, so sad. But I'm slowly improving."

There is silence on the line. Too much has happened for us to engage in light chatter, but it's hard to talk about the real things, either, such as the ongoing nightmares of being stuck in a locked building with a crazy man. I sigh, and I hear an answering sigh from Darla.

"Are you coming for Emily's funeral?"

"Yeah. We're flying out this afternoon. You? Are you still with Carleton?"

"I'll be at the funeral but not with him. We broke up. We both agree it's for the best. We've kept in touch, though. He found out that Emily has had postpartum depression since the birth of her second child. This was actually her third suicide attempt. None of that matters to Carleton. She was his only child, and he holds himself responsible."

Darla clears her throat. "After the funeral, he's taking some time off to find his father's people in the Navajo Nation. He says he needs to regroup. I guess we all need to."

I shiver. "I keep thinking about Curt and how horrible he was. And how stupid I was to get into such an outrageous situation to begin with. I received my check from Space Tours. Plus, they'll pay me another forty thousand if I agree not to sue them. I'm still thinking about it."

"Same here, but I signed their form. I just want this whole thing behind me." After a pause, Darla asks, "Do you think Curt was really crazy, or mean, or sick? I can't figure it out myself."

"I don't know. He was mean even before he got sick, so I'd guess that was it. But he definitely had a crazy side. Plus, he was willing to risk everything to get what he wanted." I don't add that, for a while, I was almost as single-minded as Curt about getting what I wanted, though I don't think I would have endangered people's lives to get to space. Still, I don't sympathize with Curt. If he'd acted the way he should have, Emily would still be alive.

"Space Tours wasn't responsible for Curt's actions," Darla says, pulling me out of my reverie. "They knew about the dome, of course, but they would never have made us stay there if we didn't want to. They didn't know about the contract Curt made us sign or how he locked us in. He was a loose cannon, and they have fired him. Did you know that?"

"Yeah, I saw it on the news." I take a breath. "Enough about Curt. Have you spoken with any of the others?"

"Thomas and I stay in touch. He's doing okay. I haven't heard from Sheila, other than that her toe is fine, and she's going to Jamaica for a couple of weeks. She won't be at the funeral."

More silence.

Finally, Darla asks, "How do you feel about being called a hero?"

"Terrible. Our escape was a team effort, and to give me all the credit is just wrong. One day, I'll talk to a reporter and set the record straight, but I haven't had the energy to do that yet."

We agree to have dinner after the funeral. After we hang up, I feel marginally better. During the ordeal, I had thought those people would be my best friends for life, but now I dread seeing everyone but Darla, who really might be my best friend for life.

At the Orlando airport, Ava and I hug for a long time. "I'm so glad you're back. And I'm happy to see you again," she says as she hugs Ramón. "I've missed you."

He smiles. "I've missed you too."

Driving to Mom's house, Ava reports about the sale of the nursery. "The closing will be in a couple of months. Imagine, an orchid nursery! Mom's beside herself with joy. The new owners will even hire her to work part-time for the first year to help with the transition. And they'll keep the existing staff, plus add more."

"That's so great. Mom seems happy."

"Now she is. While you were in the dome, she was so worried she could barely function. After the first week, she started telling me that things weren't going well. She just knew, she said. She'd talk with Ramón every couple of days and then call me to ask what she ought to do. She was ready to come out and check on you herself, but I told her not to."

I laugh. "The Gray mom to the rescue? Seeing her snowshoeing up that road would have been a sight."

Mom rushes out of the house as soon as we turn in to the driveway. She hugs me, hard and long, when I get out of the car.

"I was so worried."

"How did you know I was in trouble?" I've asked her that before, but I still can't get over the miracle that it happened.

She lets me go and steps back. "I just felt it. One night, I heard you calling for me." She smiles. "I don't know why you're surprised. After all, we're connected. Always have been." Her smile morphs into a fierce look. "You should have listened to me to begin with."

"You're right. I shouldn't have gone." For the past week, those words have been uppermost in my mind. The whole thing was a weird, questionable enterprise from the start. But I learned lessons about myself that I might not have learned otherwise. Karin is helping me sort them out. In our last session, she told me that my journey through the stages of loss is nearly complete. I've finally reached the acceptance stage. I'm not sure about that, but I'm grateful for her support—and everyone's.

Mom lets me go and stares into my eyes. "That's true. But you helped everyone escape. Besides, you're different now. I could sense it as soon as I talked to you on the phone. Something happened out there to help you heal yourself."

I sigh. "One thing is that I finally let go of the guilt for not saving Ben."

She grabs both of my hands. "Honey, what happened wasn't your fault. If I'd known you felt guilty all these years, I would have reassured you about that. Sometimes, bad things just happen. You grieve for them then do your best to move on." She shakes her head. "I'm not saying it's easy. I still wonder what Ben would be like as an adult. But I don't dwell on it. I'm sorry we haven't talked about this before."

We hug again, tears streaming down both of our cheeks.

The funeral is excruciating, as expected. Listening to Emily's friends and family talk about how much they'll miss her is almost too much to bear. To get through it, I focus on Ramón's arm around my shoulder. Afterward, the four of us—Darla, Thomas, Ramón, and I—go to our sports bar for burgers and beer. It'll probably be our last time together for a while. I don't know how I feel about that. Actually, I'm having a hard time summoning any feelings at all after having them wrung out of me at that funeral.

We chat about our plans for Christmas. We're all still in recovery mode, so eating, resting, and being grateful for life is the extent of them.

"What about the Peace Corps?" I ask Thomas.

He looks thoughtful. "I'm not making any decisions for a while." He glances at Darla. "Depending on how things go with this lady, it'll be a joint decision. She might want to go with me." He blushes and takes her hand. Her smile is the happiest I've seen in a long time.

Gosh, how could I not have seen that coming? "Congratulations, you two. I hope it works out for you." I grab both of their hands and give them a squeeze. Something good came out of our time in the dome, after all.

"What about you, Mia?" asks Thomas. "Did you put together your life plan?"

I chuckle and glance fondly at Ramón. "I don't trust myself to put together a long-term plan just yet. I'm extremely grateful this guy took me back. We'll talk about it and come up with something."

"Hey, what about going to work for Space Tours?" asks Darla.

"No way. I withdrew my application. I couldn't work for that company after all that happened, even if they weren't to blame." I grin. "Fortunately, NASA didn't press charges for my stealing the plants and the fertilizer, so I still have access to my lab in Houston." We laugh.

We talk a while longer, but the conversation eventually runs dry. Finally, Darla asks, "Do you think you'll use the skills Carleton taught us?"

I nod. "The telepathy thing brought Ramón back to me. I'm extremely grateful for that. And I do the meditation exercises every day.

But as far as trying to reach out to extraterrestrials, no, I won't do that. How about you two?"

"Nah," says Thomas. "I'm done. I'm convinced I hypnotized myself into thinking I'd made contact."

"Me too," Darla says. "It's not one of my greatest memories. I think we were all hypnotized to think we'd heard from life on other planets. I remember the music from the rainbow, though. It's the best thing that happened for me, besides getting to know Thomas." She throws him a smile.

We leave shortly after that, vowing to stay in touch.

Ramón and I spend Christmas Day on the road. We stop for lunch at a barbecue restaurant and eat a giant meal of pulled pork, baked beans, and slaw. I appreciate the simplicity of the meal. It doesn't feel like a time to be celebrating.

Later, when Ramón is driving, my phone rings. The number seems familiar, but I can't place it. "Hello."

"Mia. This is Jeb. I just want to wish you a merry Christmas. Am I interrupting your celebration?"

He's never called before to wish me a merry Christmas. I don't know what to think. My pulse races, but there's nothing more he can do to me. "No, not at all. We're driving home from Florida. Merry Christmas to you."

He clears his throat. "I won't take much of your time. I want to congratulate you for what you did in rescuing those people. It's something a seasoned astronaut would do, and I'm proud of you. In fact, we're ready to do another medical assessment of your fitness for duty. I suspect the doctors will agree that you've completely healed."

I'm too shocked to respond right away. Just when I've come to terms with not being an astronaut, I have the opportunity for a do-over. Thoughts tumble over each other: what my life will look like if I make one decision versus the other. After a long moment, I say, "Uh, thanks, Jeb. I appreciate the offer, but I don't think so. I'm looking forward to doing something less stressful. But it means the world to me that you offered."

"Sure, sure. Any time. Merry Christmas, again." And he's gone.

When I repeat the conversation for Ramón, he chuckles. "That's the wildest Christmas present I've ever heard of."

"Did you know about this?"

"No, darlin', I didn't. But if he'd asked me, I'd have said you're ready to come back."

I reach over and kiss his cheek. "That's an even bigger gift. Why don't we stop for the night? I see a sign for a motel up ahead."

Back at home, there's one more thing I have to do before I can enter the next phase of my life. The next morning, I ask Ramón if he'll go with me to the scene of the accident. He's surprised by my request, but he agrees. I have the accident report, so I know the spot where it took place.

The school is deserted because of the Christmas holiday, so there are few cars around. I slide into a space, and we walk together to the intersection where Ashley hit me. I know now it was an accident, and I've forgiven her, but I'd still like to know why I walked into that street in front of a car.

My heart beats faster as we approach the intersection. I see the crosswalk. Any skid marks are long gone. No cars are coming, so I walk out a few steps. Ramón is beside me, holding my hand.

Suddenly, I'm back in the moment.

Cars are all around, coming and going, so I wait at the corner. And then I hear a flock of geese overhead, honking as they head north.

I glance up to see them and get lost in my thoughts about the trip to space that's coming up so soon. Without checking for cars, I walk out into the intersection.

I let go of Ramón's hand and wipe tears from my eyes. "It was the damn geese that distracted me," I tell him. "Geese. What do you think of that?"

He shakes his head. "I'm sorry that it happened, but at least you know. Can you let it go now?"

"Yes. Definitely."

Chapter 38: A New Direction

The next July

Ramón and I are moving to Cape Canaveral next week, but I take a few days from my packing to return to Crestone. After a great deal of soul-searching and discussion, we both decided we've had enough of risking our lives, even for such a laudable goal as exploring space. It's time to leave that to others. We're ready to slow down and live normal lives, maybe even consider becoming parents. That part is still an open question.

I've thought a lot about Jeb's offer. Even though my original reason for wanting to go to space was because of Ben, I developed my own passion for it over the years. Whenever I watch the ISS cross the night sky, I think of the poem "High Flight," and it brings a pang to my heart—and sometimes a tear. I'll probably always regret at some level that my life got turned in a different direction, but I know I made the right decision to not try to regain my old life. Not everybody who has such a terrible accident has the opportunity to make a new life for themselves. I'm grateful for the healing.

I've taken a job at Kennedy Space Center, where I'll direct the effort to grow plants for space journeys. I'll have more responsibility and more autonomy than I had at Johnson. And Ramón will create training programs for the public so they can understand the astronaut experience. Whatever the future brings, we'll face it together.

Before we move across the country, though, I need to see the place where my life changed so dramatically. Working with Karin has taught me that closure isn't just a word. It's a real thing, a closing off of memories in a fresh way.

I fly to Denver, rent a car, and retrace our trip from last December. I even stay at the same retreat center, although in a different room.

When I wake the next morning, I realize I'm a little tired from the trip but not too bad. The big surprise, though, is how content I feel at a deep level. Whatever happens today, I'll get through it and return to the life I've chosen, where I'm not afraid all the time.

After breakfast, I explore the town. Giant blood-sucking mosquitoes are out in force, as are tourists who swarm into all the spiritual centers. The trees have leafed out, desert flowers are blooming, and the town is bustling. It isn't the same quiet place I remember from half a year ago.

I'm eager to see the dome. A spiritual organization has bought it to use for meetings and retreats. A team will come in a week to clean it out, and the new owners gave me permission to look around. My heart is light as I hike the four miles up the dusty road. My leg has completely healed, and I don't even wonder if I can do it. Of course I can, especially with no snow.

As I walk, I think about all that has happened in the past year and a half. I remember the vow I made to take my plants to space or die trying. It almost happened—but not in the way I'd intended. Gosh, I was so intense back then. I'm glad to have lightened up some.

Two hours later, I round a curve and see the dome. Truly, it's in a beautiful location. The place looks peaceful, like nothing bad ever happened there. Someone has cleared away the avalanche debris and built a heavy snow fence partway up the mountain. The new owners won't need to worry about avalanches.

The power is on, and the keypad combination is the same, so I enter the number that has been seared into my brain—31415—and the green light turns on. I open the door and go inside.

The inside looks much the same as it did when we left it, and I wander from room to room. Crews shipped our possessions back to us and cleaned and stripped the beds, but the stair railing is still in a pile near the door. Someone patched the hole in the bathroom wall so animals can't get in. I stand in the bathroom and stare at that patch, wondering how I wriggled through such a tiny hole. Desperation allows people to do many things they wouldn't have done otherwise.

Upstairs, the room seems to echo with the group's efforts to contact other consciousnesses. The projector is gone, but Carleton's notebooks are still stacked on a desk. I slip them into my backpack. Carleton has dropped out of sight and is presumably sitting in a hogan somewhere with his Navajo relatives. I'll send his calculations to SETI sometime, but there's no rush. Even if beings elsewhere in the universe know we exist, it will take many centuries before they arrive for a visit.

I walk back down the stairs and through the dome, remembering the struggles that took place in each room. I sense no reverberations of desperation or madness. Curt pled guilty and was sentenced to three years in prison for his crimes. Justice has been served, as far as I'm concerned.

The dome needs some work to put it to rights, but otherwise, it's a pleasant place in the mountains. Spiritual seekers will enjoy it, and maybe they'll find what they're looking for here.

I wander outside to the shed. Inside, sitting on a shelf and protected by a plastic cover, is the random-number generator. Someone turned it off after we left. A long piece of paper sticks out the bottom, and I pull it up to examine it. Random numbers have been printed for many inches. Then there is a section in which the numbers are sequential: one through four thousand. *What the...?* I blink and shake my head then look again. I find several instances where random numbers have been replaced by sequential numbers.

So, I think, chuckling to myself, our efforts succeeded, at least for the random numbers. I remove the thumb drive and tear off the sheet of paper. I'll give all this data to Carleton when I find him. I hope he'll be pleased with what he accomplished.

I go around to the front and close the door. The green light appears on the keypad. The new owners will probably replace the electronics or at least change the combination. I won't know, for I will not return to this place.

There are many ways to fly and many ways to touch the face of God. Going to space is just one of them. I'm ready for the next part of my journey.

Author Note

In *Mia's Journey*, I wanted to tell a story about recovering from a traumatic brain injury—my story, but not exactly. I was never an astronaut, never hit by a car, never fired from my job. But there are certain truths that are beyond the personal, and I've attempted to convey them in this novel. Everyone's experience of brain injury is different, but the instant when everyday life is irrevocably changed is common to them all.

You've read Mia's story, so here's mine. One day, when I was on sabbatical from my tenured faculty position at the University of Denver, I tripped while running backward to hit a ball in a racquetball game. Off-balance, I couldn't keep my head from slamming into the concrete wall behind me with tremendous force. The sound was like a ripe melon hitting the ground after falling from a second-story window. I was sure I was going to die, but instead, I was completely incapacitated for more than a year. It was my fifth lifetime concussion, and the effects are cumulative.

Although my boss was very nice about it and gave me as much time as I needed to recover, I never did heal enough to return to my position. I found myself adrift, unable to function as I had before, with no income and no identity. I would need to create a new persona that didn't include the stresses of college teaching.

Like Mia, I was unable to return to the field I loved and for which I had extensively trained. Many of the situations Mia found herself in after the accident were based on my own. I left my romantic relationship, bought a house where I could be alone to process how my life had changed, found a therapist, and because Western medicine had little to offer, I dove into the world of alternative healing. My version of Carleton was someone else, and there was no Curt, no dome, and no avalanche. Eventually, like Mia, I discovered a part of myself that had always been present but hadn't been fully developed: I wanted to write fiction. It was my second chance at finding an identity that worked for me. I went back to school and trained for this new role and found that working at home, alone, suits me better than lecturing before a group of students. Both Mia and I struggled as we traversed the stages of loss: denial, anger, bargaining, depression, and finally, acceptance. Years later, I regard the accident as an unwanted gift, but a gift just the same.

As I prepared to write this novel, I knew I wanted the main character to have a career that was glitzier than that of a mere college professor. What could be worse than an astronaut who is forced to give up her dream of going to space? So I had my character. I read every book I could find about female astronauts, and then all astronauts. I watched Chris Hadfield's MasterClass on space exploration, participated in the Astronaut Training Experience at Kennedy Space Center, watched innumerable NASA videos, and consulted with everyone I could find who knew about astronaut training.

Next, I delved into the power of intention, as well as various psychic phenomena. Part of my own recovery led me to learn about energy healing, and I actually became certified as a chi kung energy healer. The classes Mia attended were based on my own experiences in this field.

Although we are completely different people with different healing trajectories, Mia and I are both doing well now, although neither of us will ever be the people we were before our injuries.

If you're interested in learning more about healing from brain injury, one place to start is the Brain Injury Association of America (https://www.biausa.org). You may also want to find a psychotherapist, a speech therapist, or a neurologist who specializes in treating traumatic brain injury survivors.

The book focuses mostly on the edge of science as it is known today, but everything that I wrote about has been reasonably well-documented. Well, except for the contact with extraterrestrials. I made that up.

Numerous space simulations have been undertaken in the past decade. Many have failed, for similar reasons as the one in this book. You might be interested in the documentary *Red Heaven* (2020), about a Mars simulation in Hawaii. Oh, by the way, NASA is recruiting for a yearlong simulated Mars mission, if you're interested.

Here are a few of the sources that were especially helpful to me.

Almost Heaven: The Story of Women in Space. Bettyann Holtzmann Kevles, 2006, MIT Press.

"How Do Plants Grow in Space?" Marina Koren, The Atlantic. January 30, 2019. (And others of her articles, which were all extremely helpful.)

Successfully Surviving a Brain Injury: A Family Guidebook, from the Emergency Room to Selecting a Rehabilitation Facility. Garry Prowe, 2010, Brain Injury Success Books.

The Power of Eight: Harnessing the Miraculous Energies of a Small Group to Heal Others, Your Life and the World. Lynne McTaggart, 2017, Hay House UK.

The Way of the Explorer. Dr. Edgar Mitchell with Dwight Williams, 1996, G.P. Putnam's Sons.

Wisdom Chi Kung: Practices for Enlivening the Brain with Chi Energy. Mantak Chia, 2008, Destiny Books.

Acknowledgments

Writing this book was a huge stretch for me, and many people helped along the way. First and foremost, The Tall Pines Fiction Writing Group helped enormously, reading several drafts and offering wonderful feedback on all of them. A huge thank-you goes to Josh Pollock, Heather Starsong, Jenn Perez, and Lily Larson for all of your support over the years. And thanks to my ever-supportive critique partner, Judy Wise, for all the time you took reading and talking about the book with me. Thank you, Damaris Jarboux, for the years of training in chi kung healing and for reading the draft and offering some great suggestions.

A lot of people weren't aware they were helping me, but their work helped enormously. Thank you to Marina Koren, who writes about space for *The Atlantic* magazine; Chris Hadfield, who gave a class on being an astronaut for *MasterClass*; Lynne McTaggart, who writes books about the edges of science, several nursery owners who walked me through the ins and outs of running a nursery; and Spafford Ackerly and Kathy Ballek, who let me stay in their Delightful Dome in Crestone for a few nights as I did research for the book.

Special thanks go to Joel Blum and Domenica Blum, who sat around with me for several long afternoons, brainstorming ways for the book to end. It took a while, but we finally nailed it. I couldn't have done it without your scientific expertise. And thanks to Rich Andrews, farmer extraordinaire, who explained fertilizers to me.

A number of people read drafts of the book, among them Flora Quinby, Suanne Schafer, Kathy Dolan, and Rachel Dacus. Thank you so much for that and for offering your feedback. If I forgot someone, please forgive me. This book has been in the works for several years, and my memory isn't what it used to be.

Many thanks to Lynn McNamee of Red Adept Publishing for taking *Mia's Journey* under her wing. Thanks to Virge Buck for patiently proofreading every episode for its Kindle Vella incarnation.

Finally, many thanks to my first reader and husband, Daniel Booth, who patiently talked through the storyline with me, over and over, and read several drafts without once complaining about the time it took.

About the Author

Diane Byington has been a tenured college professor, yoga teacher, psychotherapist, and executive coach. Also, she raised goats for fiber and once took a job cooking hot dogs for a NASCAR event. She still enjoys spinning and weaving, but she hasn't eaten a hot dog or watched a car race since.

Besides reading and writing, Diane loves to hike, kayak, and photograph sunsets. She and her husband divide their time between Boulder, Colorado, and the small Central Florida town they discovered while doing research for her novel.

Read more at www.dianebyington.com.

About the Publisher

Dear Reader,

We hope you enjoyed this book. Please consider leaving a review on your favorite book site.

Visit https://RedAdeptPublishing.com to see our entire catalogue.

Check out our app for short stories, articles, and interviews. You'll also be notified of future releases and special sales.